SILKEN SERVITUDE

I feel her small soft perfectly formed hands press against my breasts and I cannot resist allowing my own hands to fall onto her hosed thighs. I feel warm firm skin through the erotic film of sheer nylon, and my hands inch gently beneath a sea of lacy frou-frou petticoating.

'Feel me, Shelly. Feel the core of me, my pretty sissy petal.'

Yet when my hands finally reach the top of her thighs and move toward her nyloned sex, I encounter Mistress Anne's wicked, so sensual ecstasy belt. I press against a nylon-sheathed, hard rubber panel and Myriam squeals with pleasure. I know that fitted to this panel is a large ribbed vibrator and that it is now locked deep inside her, and as I push against the panel, it digs deeper into her long-tormented sexual heart.

'Take it off and fuck me. Please . . . please!'

SILKEN SERVITUDE

Christina Shelly

This book is a work of fiction.
In real life, make sure you practise safe, sane and
consensual sex.

First published in 2005 by
Nexus
Thames Wharf Studios
Rainville Rd
London W6 9HA

www.nexus-books.co.uk

Typeset by TW Typesetting, Plymouth, Devon
Printed and bound by Clays Ltd, St Ives PLC

ISBN 0 352 34004 5

Contents

You'll notice that we have introduced a set of symbols onto our book jackets, so that you can tell at a glance what fetishes each of our brand new novels contains. Here's the key – enjoy!

cp (traditional)

cp (modern)

spanking

restraint/bondage

rope bondage/hojojutsu

latex/rubber/leather/enclosure

fem dom

willing captivity

medical

period setting

uniforms

sex rituals

Part One: Induction

1

Trainee Housemaids

A month has passed since our release from the Nursery. It is four weeks today since Pansy and I were freed from exquisite baby bondage and allowed to take up our new roles as trainee housemaids in the Sissy Maids Company. Under the watchful eyes of our mistresses, we have been expertly transformed into she-male slaves, our only purpose to serve and bring pleasure to womankind. We are willing slaves: this elaborate regime of female domination is one we accept with a pure fierce enthusiasm. Thanks to the careful preparations of my beautiful Aunt Jane, the glorious woman who originally feminised us and then agreed our imprisonment in this strange kinky castle of submission, we were already well versed in the perverse joys of sissy servitude.

Today is Friday, and on Friday afternoons, for a few wondrous hours, we are freed from the usual elaborate restraints that are our near constant companions and allowed to be together in a most intimate and exciting way, to be together as the sissy lovers our mistresses are so very determined we become. We are enveloped in each other's arms on the large double bed that dominates the circular room we have shared since our release from the Nursery. I stare hungrily at Pansy's large unrestrained sex and contemplate wrapping my cherry-red lips around the purple stem of this beautiful sex flower. I run my hands over the semi-transparent pink silk of her sexy baby doll night-dress and she moans with a dark angry pleasure. I remember the first time we experienced the joys of each other's helplessly petite bodies when we were both still male, locked in a school storeroom, astonished by a homo-erotic need whose true expression was to be found in a regime of strict feminisation overseen by my gorgeous Aunt and Pansy's cruel beautiful guardian, Ms Hartley. A vision of Ms Hartley's tall prim form ignites in my tormented mind and my sex, already rock hard, seeks a place beyond rigidity, an explosive release whose final expression is something like death. I kiss Pansy's soft moist lips and taste her own powerful need; I stare with an addict's desperate longing into her pretty wide blue eyes and remember those incredible days leading up to our entry into the Sissy Maids Company.

Brought up by my 'Aunt', actually a close friend of my long-dead mother and father, I had been a pampered and isolated young man. Handsome maybe, intelligent certainly, I lived in a world dominated by my Aunt, an ex-model in her late forties who had remained stunningly beautiful. It was she who had discovered my secret longing for all aspects of the feminine and the powerful transvestite desire this inspired. And it was she who had guided me on the road from her 'nephew' Michael to her sissy niece, Michele, or, as I came to be known, Shelly. And it was she, as I have noted, who encouraged my strange friendship with Dominic and, with Ms Hartley's help, his rapid transformation into Pansy. And it was she who had introduced me to the amazing Lady Emily Ashcroft and the startling conspiracy of beautiful dominant women that was the Bigger Picture.

4

I run my hands over Pansy's shapely pink nylon-stockinged thighs and she moans with a kitten's sensual animal pleasure. My hands move beyond the stocking tops to her soft silky-smooth upper thighs. She gasps and her soft submissive smile widens and the glaze of desire covering her lovely eyes thickens: the smooth utterly hairless skin of her body is ultra-sensitive thanks to the potent medical treatments of the last four weeks. Her cock twitches. My hands work towards her fat bulging testicles and the small silver ring that has been attached to the flap of skin at the base of her scrotum by her gorgeous training mistress, the fierce redheaded dominatrix Anne, one of the founders of the Sissy Maids Company. Her nipples are also ringed, and diamond studs have been fitted to her left nostril and into her unbearably cute navel. I share this elaborately kinky body decoration, thanks to the perverse creativity of my own mentor, Ms Amelia Blakemore, the School's beautiful and endlessly imaginative matron.

I stroke Pansy's balls and she squeals with pleasure. I think of the first time I met the amazing Emily Ashcroft and became aware of the startling project of the Bigger Picture: the complete feminisation of the male sex and the establishment of a new world order of female domination. In many ways an absurd and bizarre project that had left many powerful and foolish men laughing contemptuously. But Lady Ashcroft, a former Tory peer, was quite serious. She had left the House of Lords and sought out like-minded women across the world. And there were very many of them. Thanks to a chance encounter, she met Helen Blaine, a beautiful determined woman, who had, with the assistance of two close friends (and lovers) already started the erotic transformation of a weak but helplessly pretty male into a sissy sex slave.

Indeed, Helen's great genius had been to see, quite independently of the Bigger Picture, that there was a real commercial opportunity in the sissification of the male. In a world of violent, angry and power-hungry men, women wanted love and respect; they also wanted liberation through control. Helen had founded the Sissy Maids Company for these women. Initially, it was little more than a local neighbourhood entertainment for her friends. Using just two transvestite slaves, SMC provided domestic and personal services for a handful of enlightened females. Yet the demand grew very quickly, and soon they were offering the services of a growing team of mainly male (but also female) slaves to women over a much broader geographical area. Thanks to the Internet and the patronage of Lady Ashcroft and her supporters, the Sissy Maids Company became a national enterprise within a year, and a crucial part of the global ambitions of the Bigger Picture. Lady Ashcroft's spectacular country mansion became the SMC training academy, and it is in the underground chambers of this glorious house that I am now teasing my sissy love, Pansy, towards a bout of prolonged sexual adventure.

I take her large boiling hard cock in my left hand. I feel a pounding pulse. She widens her long feminine legs and raises her pert girlish bottom. I smile at her and slowly lick the blood-red-nailed index finger of my left hand. Then I slip it beneath her balls and seek out her very well-stretched and eager arsehole. Normally, our sexes would be tightly restrained with a tight pink rubber sheath and three cruel cock rings, and our arses would be firmly plugged with fat, long and very hard vibrators. But this afternoon, we are free of all restraint. Access is open and total. My finger slips into her anus and she screams with delight.

'Oh please, Shelly . . . *please!*'

In the past few weeks, I have come to realise the true nature and size of the Bigger Picture project. At first, I took it to be a small political party with a very narrow focus, but now I understand it to be a global political movement with many powerful female members. A movement with the finances to establish sophisticated networks of enforced feminisation in every major industrial nation; a movement with access deep into established political infrastructures; a movement able to fund a research and development programme that has produced new techniques of 'stealth feminisation', the most striking and effective of which is Senso.

Senso is the key to it all: a fabric whose chemical make-up has been purposefully designed to impact on the hormonal balance of the male and produce feelings that associate submissiveness and feminine behaviour with sexual excitation. Senso: the fabric that will lead the Bigger Picture to eventual global domination. Senso: the fabric that is already being sold through a micro site of the SMC website – 'Christina's Silken Slavery' – in the form of elaborate and beautiful fetish wear for transvestites and other slaves. A fabric that is also, thanks to Lady Ashscroft's connections in the world of fashion and design, being secretly incorporated into a vast variety of everyday male clothing and thus establishing the psychological foundation for a truly global women's movement. Not one based on outdated notions of equality and justice, concepts that have been blown away by the realities of modern history, but on firm concepts rooted in the control of destructive male urges and the exercise of female power through the dictatorship of the feminine. Concepts embodied in the principles of the Femocracy.

'You know I love these moments,' Pansy whispers, her voice hoarse with dark desire, her eyes tightly closed. 'To be free of bondage.'

I smile and push my finger deeper. 'But you love your bondage as well . . . surely.'

She gasps and returns my smile. 'Oh yes. So very much, my love.'

Most nights, our mistresses ensure that we sleep together in this bed, but hardly ever free from restraint. No: most nights Pansy and I are secured in slender pink Senso body stockings, our cocks tightly restrained, vibrators buzzing furiously in our tender sissy arses. There a number of types of Senso, and the body stockings are cut from the type that most resembles sheer nylon. This thin delicate material torments our ultra-sensitive and utterly hairless bodies, which are much more susceptible to the chemical impact of Senso than the average male body. Even after nearly thirty nights of its special embrace, we squeal with a fundamental pleasure as the soft material is drawn up our feminised forms. Over the stockings go rubber sleep-sacks, skintight from toe to neck, imprisoning and immobilising our deliciously tormented sissy forms. In our sissy mouths are stuffed the soiled panties of our many mistresses, fat pungent gags that are held in place with thick strips of pink adhesive tape. Over our heads are pulled sheer pink Senso stockings, plunging us into a fetish wear netherworld of fierce and bottomless desire. Then, utterly helpless, driven mad by kinky she-male desire, with the vibrators buzzing at full power in our ultra-sensitised arses, we are left side by side on the bed – so close but so far – to contemplate the day's events and the joy of our absolute and inescapable submission to womankind and the philosophy of the Bigger Picture.

8

I revel in the pleasure I am giving her and in my own expertly crafted femininity. Like her, I am wearing a semi-transparent baby doll. Mine is a shimmering white, as are my panties (which, unlike Pansy's, have not been removed), and my stockings. All my sexy attire is, of course, cut from various varieties of Senso, and my silky sissy form burns with submissive feminine desire as I pleasure the gorgeous, helpless she-male beauty. Her powerful musky perfume washes over my own heavily scented form and I place another soft delicate kiss on her beautiful lips. Our tongues touch and our mouths widen. She screams with pleasure as my finger goes even deeper into her back passage, and her cock presses into my other teasing hand.

My eyes fall on the small but very apparent orbs that are her nascent breasts. A daily cocktail of hormones and other very special chemicals have seen our skin soften, our breasts grow and our hips broaden. Very soon, we will both be subject to complex surgical procedures that will leave us both with large ultra-sensitive breasts, a thought that drives me wild with sexual anticipation, and which I know Pansy is looking forward to with an equal enthusiasm.

'I can't wait until I can kiss your new breasts,' I whisper, 'until I can suckle you.'

She moans her deep inescapable need and I plant a kiss on her left rosebud through the erotic Senso material of the baby doll.

'And I'm sure Taylor will be thrilled when he sees you fully feminised.'

She nods and smiles, her eyes wide with sex need, her mind filled with thoughts of her training master.

Under the terms of our training regime, the first four weeks have been spent as trainee housemaids.

We will soon undergo a period of physical alteration – the Operation – before being entered on the full-blown maid placement scheme, and, if we perform well on our placements, we achieve full graduation. Then, it is planned that Pansy and I will be returned to Aunt Jane's house. Here, we will help to establish a West Country branch of the Sissy Maids Company, aided by Ms Hartley and the headmistress of my ex-School, Ms Henrietta Blunt, together with Ms Blunt's two beautiful daughters, Juliette and Justine.

As I continue to cover Pansy in sweet sissy kisses, I think of Justine. My sex twitches and stretches and a gasp of terrible need slips from my mouth. Beautiful regal mysterious Justine, a young woman of my own age, a woman who made it clear she intends to become my true and final mistress. The woman who, I know, I most love, and by whom, I know, I will eventually be totally possessed.

But then Pansy squirms in my arms and my thoughts return to this strange academy and our mistresses and masters. During the four-week trainee housemaid period, our education has been governed by three individuals: the training mistress, the training master and the sissy mentor. I have been honoured to have Mistress Helen, the Chief Executive of SMC, as my training mistress. Under her firm and deeply erotic guidance, I have learnt the true meaning of absolute submission to the glorious dominant female. A gorgeous plump brunette, with startling honey-brown eyes and a taste for intricate and bizarre bondage, Helen has summoned me to her chambers at least three evenings a week for the past month. Here I have learnt my role of slave object in a most ruthless and exciting way. It has been made clear to me that, as a sissy maid, I will never be allowed sexual union with a member of the female sex. Indeed, my only role is to provide various oral pleasures, and to act as a humbled and humiliated, yet profoundly willing maid servant. Dressed in my trainee house-maid's uniform of a pink Senso silk dress (a gorgeous rose-patterned sissy masterpiece with long puffed sleeves and a very short petticoat-smothered skirt), a white silk pinafore, ultra sheer and seamed white Senso nylon tights and pink patent leather five-inch stiletto-heeled court shoes, my long blonde hair tied in a pretty ponytail with a sweet pink silk ribbon, my hands sealed in white glacé gloves, my ankles hobbled with a six-inch silver chain to ensure the daintiest of steps and the sexiest of wiggles, I have, on numerous occasions, minced with an increasingly instinctive femininity before this splendid beautiful woman and done her kinky bidding without even a whimper of opposition. Often tightly gagged with her panties or a fat long rubber penis gag, I have never bothered to hide the fact that I am utterly smitten by her imperial beauty and absolute incredibly elegant authority.

Helen, being a woman of the Bigger Picture, is always careful to represent her power in sexually arousing dress. There are no simplistic feministic notions of the oppression of fashion here: the mis-tresses glory in their sexual allure, and use it as a key weapon in their control of the weak sex-obsessed male. Thus she wears the gorgeous uniform of a subtle dominatrix: simple grey or black skirts that fall just above the knee, very tight nylon sweaters that accentuate her large shapely breasts, long perfectly formed legs sheathed in the sheerest black or grey nylon tights, three-inch-heeled black patent leather court shoes. Her thick long black hair is always bound in a tight stern bun with an elegant diamond clasp. Her full generous lips are always painted an almost shocking blood red, as are her long razor-sharp fingernails.

My greatest honour is to curtsey sweetly before her, making sure to reveal my lace-trimmed Senso silk panties, and then kneel to kiss her gleaming leather shoes, before slipping my head beneath her stylish skirt to worship her with my now expert tongue. As moans of pleasure fill her pristine chambers, I feel an overwhelming sense of love. As I taste her sweet cunt, and as her sex juices leak over my painted faced, I am lost in a state of truly selfless bliss. As she binds and gags me in strange, painful and deeply humiliating positions, leaving me exposed to the whip, her kinky hands and various wicked implements of sexual torture, I squeal my endless submissive love into my inescapable gag and feel the bottomless bliss of absolute surrender.

Each sissy trained in the SMC academy is also allocated a training master. Although a sissy's ultimate aim is to serve her mistress in any way she sees fit, she must also have the skills to pleasure men. This is in order to ensure a true sense of servitude and to reinforce the focus of sissy pleasure on the arse and the cock.

Within the Bigger Picture, the emphasis is on the power and authority of the woman, but it is recognised that the core philosophy is one of power and control built around the rituals and practices of sadomasochism. Thus there will always be a place for the submissive female and the dominant male. Subsequently, the academy has two highly gifted training masters: Bentley and Taylor. I have been allocated to Bentley, and Pansy has been allocated to Taylor.

Bentley is a strikingly handsome Afro-Caribbean. Nearly six feet four inches tall, with a broad muscular body frame, he has been a lover of Lady Ashcroft and a professional dominant for many years. He desires and admires transvestites and is openly bi-sexual. Within SMC, he is the acknowledged male expert on the training of sissies, and I have had the deep and endlessly erotic pleasure of being under his strict instruction for the past thirty days.

At first, the idea of being trained by a man was the most challenging of all the requirements of my sissification within the SMC academy. My masochistic bi-sexuality had been well established by Aunt Jane and my relationship with Dominic/Pansy. But Dominic's feminine beauty and manner and his subsequently very successful sissification put him in the highly erotic and deeply ambivalent category of she-male. There was and is nothing feminine about Bentley. His masculinity is pure and aggressively obvious. His control over me is very similar to the control of a man over a female slave. The pleasures he seeks from me are the pleasures a man would demand from a woman, pleasures I give with a helpless willingness. This was not the case at first. He is strong and stern. Like Mistress Helen, he revels in dressing me in the most dainty and outrageously sissified costumes, in exaggerating my ultra-femininity through dress, gesture, movement and perverse discipline. Attired in pretty, amazingly intricate little girl frocks of Senso satin, sheer white tights and pink Mary Janes, my hair tied in a pretty pink silk ribbon, my mouth stopped by a phallic shaped dummy gag, my head imprisoned in a gorgeous Victorian bonnet, I find myself on my hosed knees before him, my silk-gloved hands bound tightly behind my back, my nylon-sheathed ankles also tightly tethered. I face his open legs, my bottom stinging from the hard merci-less spanking he has just so expertly inflicted, and I watch with wide helplessly girlish eyes as he unzips his leather trousers and slips out his huge rock-hard cock. I squeal with pleasurable anticipation into my dummy gag and wiggle my tightly plugged bottom helplessly. I know tonight I will suck this fearsome sex weapon dry and then teasingly revive it so that I can be fucked senseless.

As I torment Pansy's sex, I remember my times with Master Bentley and feel a quiver of deep dark excitement flow through my delicately sissified body.

'I can't wait for Taylor to see me with pretty bouncing titties,' she whispers, pulling herself a little further onto the bed.

I smile gently and find myself thinking of her training master. Despite Bentley's physical strength and his absolute authority over me, I have always felt a strange gentleness in him, even when I am bound and gagged and held firmly over his powerful thighs, my panties down around my knees, my pert wobbling backside receiving a sound and merciless spanking. With Taylor, however, I have seen nothing but the cool sadistic exercise of power. In Taylor's ice-blue eyes there is the sheer pleasure of unquestioned control. An ex-American army captain, Taylor is tall, spectacularly muscular and frighteningly hard. On the face of it, he is merely the second training master, but over the last four weeks it has become clear that he plays a much wider role in the Bigger Picture. It is well known that his original association was with no less a personage than Eleanor Groves, the ex-wife of an ex-U.S. president, and one of the most famous women in the world. Through Ms Groves's friendship with Lady Ashcroft, Taylor, who had been her personal bodyguard, came to work for SMC. His attraction to sissies is very clear. Yet, unlike Bentley, Taylor is also a servant of women. It is obvious that he acts as Mistress Helen's personal bodyguard and

14

almost as her butler. It has also become clear that he services the heterosexual mistresses, particularly Lady Ashcroft and the occasionally bi-sexual Mistress Anne. It is therefore perhaps surprising that he is far harsher on the sissies, and that poor Pansy certainly suffers at his hands.

As our lips meet again, I notice a thin red line running across Pansy's left thigh, and I know this is a fading memory of the ivory-handled riding crop Taylor uses to punish and 'inspire' Pansy. I also know there are a lot more of these wicked lines crossing her perfectly formed bottom. I both pity and envy her. When I am in Bentley's powerful arms, I am always aware of his absolute control, but I also know that he is essentially a professional dominant. To him, the rituals of punishment are associated endlessly with the giving and taking of pleasure. With Taylor, this has never been the case. His commitment to domination is therefore deeply political, driven by a belief in his power and the power of the Bigger Picture. It is detached from emotion, and therefore far more dangerous. And it is this danger that arouses me, and which very clearly arouses lovely Pansy, for her feelings for Taylor are obviously deep and intensely positive. And, despite his cruel demeanour and authoritarian manner, Taylor appears to recipro- cate these feelings; for it has been made very clear to all the mistresses and housemaids that Pansy is very much the sole property of Taylor. She is not be taken by anyone, except him and, perhaps strangely, me. For some reason, it seems to amuse Taylor to know that his sissy slave has a pretty, eager sissy girlfriend, a role I fulfil with a helpless enthusiasm.

As I contemplate Pansy's sensual welts and her blissful suffering, I can't help thinking how unlucky (and thus how very lucky) she has been with her

15

masters and mistresses. First there was Ms Hartley, the powerful, wicked and cruel guardian who took such a dreadfully dark pleasure in her role as the co-creator of the lovely helplessly sexy ultra-feminine Pansy. Then there is cruel sadistic Taylor. And, on top of this, we have Mistress Anne.

Mistress Anne, the co-founder of SMC, a gorgeous statuesque redhead who I have never seen in a dress or a skirt, yet, despite this, an intensely feminine and very beautiful woman. A little younger than Mistress Helen, with cool emerald-green eyes, she is a figure that inspires genuine fear in all the housemaids, male and female. Often dressed in beautiful light-coloured expensive silk trouser suits and very high-heeled leather boots, her naturally long orange-red hair tied in a tight bun, she has a well justified reputation for sadistically inventive punishments, a fiery lesbian temper and a considerable sexual appetite. Poor Pansy always returns from her regular 'training sessions' with Mistress Anne utterly exhausted, her poor sex inevitably battered by some dark penile torture, her arse spread wide by sinister intruders, her buttocks cherry-red from harsh prolonged spankings, her lips and tongue worn to sandpaper by her mistress's insistence on constant oral pleasuring. Yes . . . poor Pansy is so lucky.

Then, of course, there are our sissy mentors. Here I am, without doubt, the luckiest sissy in the world. For my mentor is the stunning Christina, the very first sissy trained by Mistress Helen. I have been her helpless admirer since Aunt Jane allowed Pansy and me access to the SMC website and the Silken Slavery micro site. It is Christina who has been the gorgeous icon of SMC, who has so wondrously featured in all their teasing ultra-erotic web-based marketing, who is the star attraction of so many of

16

their very high class video productions – elegant erotic films streamed on the web and also available to buy on video/DVD. It is she who has teased me so expertly to a full realisation of my true deeply masochistic sissy personality. Over the last four weeks, we have made gentle sissy love at least twelve times, and each time it has left me in a state of soul-washed bliss.

Gorgeous perfect Christina. The senior housemaid, the sissy wife of Mistress Donna (the third of the original founder members of SMC), a tall incredibly curvaceous brunette with dark-brown eyes and the body of an ultra sex-bomb. A spectacular fantasy figure made startling reality by the techniques of the SMC. Her long perfectly formed legs always tightly sealed in the sheerest sexiest hose, her 42-inch bust, so deliberately designed by SMC, a promise of my own future transformation – ultra-sensitive pale rose orbs of sissy perfection that I have kissed and suckled with privileged lips. Her own full ruby-red lips have slipped so softly and expertly around my own para-doxical manhood and teased me to a screaming, profoundly joyous orgasm on many occasions and I have sobbed my helpless gratitude into a multitude of inescapable and relentlessly kinky gags. To be like her is all I ask.

I think of being taken by Christina and I think of bondage. Every time she has taken me, she has ensured that I have been very tightly bound and gagged. Her visits are normally announced by the arrival of Annette, Mistress Anne's personal maid, and Christina's long-term sissy love. She is Pansy's sissy mentor and, perhaps unsurprisingly given her mistress, a cruel redhead with an aloof superior manner. When Christina is about to visit, Annette arrives to remove Pansy to some dark and mutually arousing entertainment while I am so very willingly ravished. I am always 'specially prepared'. I am already dressed in a suitably alluring sissy outfit, and it is only a matter of laying me out on the bed and then securing my arms and legs, inserting a pair of soiled panties deep inside my mouth and then taping them tightly in place. Then I am left wiggling and moaning, my cock always released from its cruel and deeply erotic restraint, ready for Christina's kinky attentions. Then she arrives, in her splendid senior housemaid's costume: a black Senso silk dress covered in an erotically elaborate design of sparkling black roses, whose subtle outlines are only clearly visible at one particular angle under the powerful light of our room. This dress appears painted to her fabulous body, its tight unforgiving journey over her incredible chest marked by a terribly erotic and real tension between discomfort and erotic embrace. Over the dress is secured a gorgeous white Senso silk lace-edged pinafore, with her name printed in elegant red letters across its chest. The pinafore is tied tightly in place with a huge sissy bow at the base of her spine. Beneath the very short dress is an ocean of layered frou-frou petticoating, through which a pair of lace be-frilled satin panties are clearly visible. Her legs are wrapped tightly in sheer black Senso nylon tights with narrow perfectly straight seams that trace an erotic pathway leading straight to her gloriously plump but also exquisitely shaped bottom. Her small girlish feet are elegantly imprisoned in sparkling black patent leather court shoes with striking five-inch heels. On the pointed toe of each elegant shoe is a small diamond rose. Her long thick jet-black hair is bound in a very tight perfectly formed bun held in place by a diamond clasp that is made up of letters that spell the word 'Chrissie'. Fitted carefully to the top of this wondrous hair sculpture is a small lace-trimmed maid's gap with two silk ribbon tails that run down the back of her head. Her lips are, as always, painted a deep cherry red and coated in a sparkling gloss that turns every smile into a sensual promise of forbidden pleasure. Around her perfect swan neck is tied a black velvet choker, with a blood red ruby centrepiece that exactly matches her shimmering teasing lips.

She looks down upon me with sex-fired honey-brown eyes, her envelopment in Senso ensuring that her gorgeous she-male body is trapped in a tight film of merciless sexual need. I moan helplessly into the fat panty gag filling my own sissy mouth, the taste of what I know by sweet experience is Mistress Helen's cunt adding to this moment of pure erotic bliss. She smiles slightly and moves towards me with the elegant grace of an expertly trained sissy maid. I know that beneath the lovely dress is a further array of spectacularly restrictive femininity: a tight red and black whale-boned corset that holds her slender sissy waist within a cruel but incredibly exciting embrace, a delightful Senso silk brassiere that torments her ultra-sensitive and very large breasts, leaving her feeling as if her boobs are being teased by a hundred pairs of sissy lips every second of every hour of the day. And over all this, a short black silk petticoat, a teasing Christmas present from her own true love, Mistress Donna, the absolute empress of her body and soul.

I meet her stunning soul-melting gaze and squeal with a terrible girlish desperation into the gag. Her beautiful smile widens and she carefully sits down beside my tethered form on the bed, her short skirts rising as she does so to reveal a detailed glimpse of her gorgeous Senso silk panties, with the outline of her large tightly restrained cock clearly visible. During previous visits, it has been obvious the restrainer has been removed by Mistress Helen (the only person other than Mistress Donna allowed to do so), and that, as a consequence, I should expect to be fucked hard and long, a pleasure Christina has showed me is both explosively immediate and, given the right lover, darkly subtle. But today – the day that replays in my dreams – she has come to milk me, to indulge a passion for oral sex that is drilled into each sissy maid from the very first day free from the inducting pleasures of the Nursery. So, I am to be given a terrible profound pleasure and also give pleasure to one of my numerous sissy lovers. I moan with a feverish anticipation into the panty gag and await my glorious fate.

And now, as I prepare to slip my own carefully painted lips over Pansy's hard hungry tool of love, I feel my own tethered sissified sex stretch angrily in its merciless rubber restrainer, held so tightly in place by the cruel cock rings, each marked with the black rose logo of the SMC, and know that I have reached the very edge of my true self; that I have taken a long strange journey from being the spoilt feminine 'nephew' of a beautiful, loving and very dominant Aunt to being a very pretty, soon be utterly convincing she-male slave bound and tightly gagged to a vast conspiracy of gorgeous, dominant and very powerful women. This journey has reached its final section. In the last four weeks, I have learnt to consolidate and develop the skills I began to learn under the watchful and expert eye of my Aunt. Possessed of a natural feminine grace, I have passed every deportment test with flying colours. As I wiggle-mince around the training chambers and private rooms of the SMC academy, my hosed knees and ankles never more than a few inches apart, my pert, shapely and very tightly pantied bottom wiggling helplessly beneath the sea of frou-frou petticoating, the eyes of my mistresses and the other maids are helplessly drawn to my perfect deeply erotic grace. As I walk in the highest of heels, my white nylon-sheathed thighs rubbing together, I wish so very very much I had breasts, and I so desperately look forward to the day when I will have them. I remember when Christina first revealed her perfect ample bosom to me and whispered her joy at their beauty and teasing sensitivity, then gasped with a pleasure I so very much wanted to be my own as I pressed my lips to each long hard nipple and sucked hungrily on her feminine perfection. Yes, breasts will be the final finishing touch to my intricate physical transformation. They will also provide me with the perfect counterpoint to the helplessly erotic gyrations of my bottom. Then, I will truly be able to walk like a woman.

Yet it is not just movement that has been learnt and perfected. The domestic skills taught under my Aunt's exciting guidance have been very finely honed, and I am now an expert ironer, cleaner and washer. My deep transvestite fetishism has been a major learning tool in my significant expertise in feminine fashion. Always interested in the trappings of femininity – an interest expertly manipulated and developed by my Aunt – I now find myself in sole charge of Mistress Helen's wardrobe, a wondrous privilege rather than a job, and Pansy and I, when not tightly gagged, spend much of our free time talking obsessively about the treasures contained in our mistresses' wardrobes. We even have highly erotic conversations about the various types of panty gags we are forced to wear. Indeed, it was one such highly charged hoarsely whispered conversation that inspired our current bout of slow-burning furious lovemaking.

21

As I finally wrap my lips around Pansy's hot hard twitching cock and taste her salty sweaty flesh, I know that I am almost deliriously happy, that, in my mistresses' hands, I have become my true inescapable self. I think of the skills I have learnt, the skills of movement and servitude, and the sexual skills. Yes, these are all so much at the heart of the new personality that is Shelly. But they are only the parts of a greater whole, the work of sissy art that is the personality and body that I am becoming. And it is as I think of this work of art, that I think of Ms Blakemore, the School's beautifully plump and gifted Matron, and the woman who, after my glorious, much-missed Aunt, I have come to most admire and who has, undoubtedly, had the biggest influence on me. As Pansy squeals with a volcanic wordless pleasure as I feel her cock expand to breaking point, I think of Ms Blakemore with the most affection and, without doubt, the most desire. For it is she who has taught me about the amazing entirety of my she-male self, the happiness of absolute submission to the Bigger Picture and thus the ecstasy of surrender to all womankind.

2

Ms Blakemore

As Pansy's cum explodes into my mouth, as I taste the salty nectar of her darkest desire and swallow it with a now very familiar enthusiasm, I remember my days with Ms Blakemore. As poor Pansy squeals with uncontrollable and savage pleasure, the gorgeous ample form of Ms Blakemore fills my helplessly sissy mind, emerging from this whirlpool of memories like a black angel from a sea of sex.

She is probably no more than 35. Born on the island of Grenada, but brought up in the United States, she is a stunning Afro-Caribbean beauty, with milk-chocolate skin, large fiercely intelligent and very dark brown eyes, and full perfectly formed lips (always painted the darkest and bloodiest of reds). Her naturally straight hair is a shimmering jet, thick and long, but often tied in a tight bun. She is nearly six feet tall, and this helps balance what is undoubtedly a very plump physique. But in her ample frame are very apt proportions: broad strong hips, long surprisingly shapely legs, splendidly large but firm breasts and a beautiful if helplessly chubby face. A frame that is at its most striking in the erotic uniform of SMC Matron: a tight knee-length white dress with a button-up front, very sheer white nylon tights, and matching white patent leather court shoes with cruel and terribly exciting six-inch heels. A figure of startling maternal power, we were first introduced to her during the bizarre and delightfully kinky induction undertaken in the School's wickedly erotic Nursery. Strangely, she had played only a slight part in our induction, the majority of the supervision having been undertaken by Christina and Annette. Yet as soon as I was out of Nursery and undergoing the early stages of my sissy maid training, I was summoned to her office, which was directly next door to the Nursery.

I had been working in the laundry room when Annette entered the large warm sweet-smelling room filled with washing machines, dryers and great piles of our mistresses' clothing (which we care for with a helpless deeply fetishistic fascination) and told me that I was to report to Ms Blakemore immediately. As trained, I curtsied deeply before the gorgeous cruel-eyed redhead, who was already forming a very strong and sado-erotic bond with Pansy. I then followed her from the room and down the long hallway off which were the main underground sissy training facilities of the SMC academy, including the movement studio (where I had been taught further refinements to my sissy deportment by the very pretty, gentle-hearted Mistress Donna), the dressing and make-up training rooms (where Mistress Anne and Annette had been far less understanding), the classrooms (where we received lectures and instruction on the philosophy of the Bigger Picture and our role in the greater scheme of things), the kitchen and domestic training suite (where we were so ably instructed by Christina), the trainee maid quarters and the Nursery, the domain of the gorgeous Ms Blakemore.

As I tottered behind the beautiful deceptively petite Annette, my eyes were drawn to her impressive form. She was wearing the uniform of the senior housemaid: a black Senso silk dress, black seamed tights, a white silk and elegantly named pinafore, very high-heeled court shoes, glacé gloves and a dainty maid's gap resting on a carefully sculptured bun of spectacular red hair. Thanks to Senso and the relentless torments of my sissy desire, I was finding myself constantly attracted to every inmate and employee of the SMC academy. Annette was the second maid trained by the stunning trio of mistresses who had founded the company, and like Christina she moved with a grace that was both erotically formal and surprisingly relaxed. As my eyes fed on her great she-male beauty, I found myself fantasising about her life with the cruel gorgeous Mistress Anne and, as usual, my tightly restrained cock fought for release from its unyielding rubber and steel prison.

As a trainee housemaid, I was, as usual, dressed in a pink Senso silk dress, a white Senso pinafore (unnamed), very sheer Senso nylon tights (also seamed), plus pink, five-inch high-heeled ankle boots with butterfly buckles and pink silk ribbon lacing. A dainty pink maid's cap rested on my carefully styled hair, which Mistress Helen prefers that I wear in a ponytail bound with another pink silk ribbon. White glacé gloves covered my small girlish hands. Beneath my dress I wore a tight white Senso rubber waist-cincher corset, white Senso rubber panties beneath my tights and a pair of heavily be-frilled white Senso silk panties over them.

I minced down the corridor with the tiniest and daintiest of steps, my bottom wiggling furiously, my heart filled with excited sissy anticipation. My previous encounters with Ms Blakemore had been brief but terribly impressive, her powerful ample presence filling me with a natural sissy submissiveness. Yet it was not this alone that drew me to her: in her eyes there had always been a dark irony, almost a mocking approach to our intricate feminisation. She had the subtle indifference of the intellectual, rather than the fiery passion of the zealot that was so common amongst the other mistresses.

Annette had brought me to the Matron's office door next to the Nursery. She knocked lightly and stepped back. A simple 'come' was her response. Annette smiled gently and gestured me forward. I opened the door nervously and tottered as sweetly as possible into the office.

Before me I found the gorgeous form of Ms Blakemore, in her striking Matron's uniform. She was sitting at a glass-topped desk working at a computer. As I minced into the middle of the room, my sissy heart pounding, she seemed to ignore me totally. Unsure what to do, I performed the required deep curtsey, raising my skirt and petticoats to reveal proudly my nylon sheathed-thighs and panties.

As I rose, I found myself looking straight into her large dark eyes and my heart skipped a beat. She smiled gently.

'You really are lovely, Shelly. Perhaps our most striking catch so far.'

I bob-curtsied my appreciation of this compliment, knowing never to talk before a mistress instructed to do so.

Ms Blakemore then rose slowly from her black leather office chair and came over to examine me in more detail. The sweet smell of her sandalwood perfume washed over me and I tried my very hardest not to stare with a helpless obsessive admiration at her large tightly restrained bosom.

Her eyes caressed my body and I quivered with a terribly exciting mixture of fear and desire, a potent potion of ambivalence that is the standard emotional response to this army of beautiful and very determined women.

'You look so very lovely in your pretty maid's out-fit. Do you like it?'

I nodded and then performed an affirmative bob-curtsey.

'You may talk, Shelly.'

'Yes, mistress; I like it very much.'

'Of course you do. Thanks to Senso.'

I hesitated and then responded. 'I liked it before Senso. Senso just makes it . . . better.'

She smiled and stepped back from me, her eyes filled with an amused appraisal.

'Yes, your Aunt has told me all about your eagerness for panties and hose. You were a very lucky sissy to find such an imaginative mistress so early on in your transformation.'

I tried not to show my surprise at this new information: Ms Blakemore either knew or had been talking to my Aunt.

'Yes,' this gorgeous woman continued, her sensual shimmering eyes reading my sexed-up sissy thoughts, 'I've got to know your Aunt very well over the last few weeks. She is a very impressive woman. And she has told me a great deal about you, babikins. A great deal.'

I swallowed and tried to stifle a moan of helpless sissy pleasure. But I failed miserably and my eyes fell once again on her splendid chest.

'You really are rather agitated. I think we should do something about that.'

She turned and walked back towards the table. My eyes instinctively settled on her large round arse, its outline stretched taught against the white fabric of the Matron's dress. From the table she took a familiar oblong metal box. My eyes widened and my moans increased. In the centre of the box was a small pink dial. She turned it with a cruel smile and I felt the vibrator that was permanently lodged in my back passage begin to buzz at a much higher level. I squealed with pleasure. She laughed and put the control box down on the table. Then she took up a larger velvet-covered box, removed the lid and revealed a dummy gag. I had not worn a dummy gag since my release from the Nursery, and the look of disappointment that filled my eyes brought a mock tut of despair.

'Oh dear, little babikins doesn't want her dummy.'

I looked at this stunning vision of imperial female beauty and fought another moan of helpless pleasure. She laughed again and then quickly fitted the gag, its clear rubber ribbed phallic-shaped teat filling my mouth in a very complete way. She tied it in place with the two pink silk ribbons that were attached to its heart-shaped pink plastic base, leaving a fat pink bow at the base of my neck beneath the sissy tail of my pretty ponytail.

'There . . . much better.'

My eyes wide with desire, the vibrator boring into me, this gorgeous wicked woman towering so amply over me – once again, I was in sissy heaven.

'Now,' Ms Blakemore continued. 'About your sexy Aunt.'

She then proceeded to tell me that she had met Aunt Jane on at least three occasions outside of the Academy, and that they had discussed me in detail. It was clear that Ms Blakemore had been sexually attracted to Aunt Jane. My Aunt's lesbianism had been very clearly revealed to me over the last six months, and it was something I accepted without question or judgement. She had been sexually involved with Ms Hartley and, if anything, her sexuality made her even more attractive to me. Lesbianism, it seemed, was very common among female dominants – a rather obvious, and of course deeply erotic fact.

These two splendid powerful women had amused themselves with tales of my willing feminisation (a fact that aroused me terribly). Yet as well as the dark pleasures of transforming me into an utterly convincing and obedient she-male slave, they had also discussed, it seemed, another talent.

'My Aunt told me that you can draw, Shelly.'

I nodded, confused by this sudden change of direction.

'She says that you draw very well – that you used to draw her.'

I nodded again, the vibrator now beginning to make concentration very difficult.

Ms Blakemore smiled. 'In that case, we have something in common.'

My eyes widened with a non-sexual interest that managed to cut through the sinister intruder pleasuring my widened helpless back passage.

'I attended art college for two years before I decided to transfer into medicine. Perhaps I had some promise; who can tell. But my skills have come in handy here. Indeed, I've played a major part in helping to design the brand image of SMC, including its website. I've also designed quite a lot of the fetish wear that we sell via mail order.'

I listened as well as I could, trying not to wiggle or moan, trying to keep my eyes away from Ms Blakemore's startling bosom.

'Anyway, to cut to the chase: your Aunt has shown me quite a few of your drawings. Of women, of clothes. Your little fetish masterpieces. And very impressive they are too. Your pictures are filled with an obsession, a helpless inescapable fixation. And that makes you the perfect person to help us market Senso.'

My eyes widened further with surprise.

'All the ladies agree that you and Pansy are the most impressive sissies to arrive at SMC since Christina and Annette. I think Pansy's role will be a little less profound than yours, especially given the little passion that seems to be developing between her and Taylor. However, you, my dainty darling, really do have an important role to play in our plans for . . . well, world domination, I suppose.'

Of course, the grand vision of the Bigger Picture had already been explained to me. I knew that SMC was essentially a weapon to create the basis for a new social order dominated by an elite group of women. I knew that the Bigger Picture had very powerful advocates in a number of countries, including the previous First Lady, Eleanor Groves. I also knew that the expansion of the SMC training academy model was taking place both regionally in the UK and in a number of other western and eastern countries. But how advanced the actual plans were . . . well, I really had no idea of the true magnitude of this great erotic conspiracy.

'I need you to unleash that kinky sissy imagination of yours,' Ms Blakemore continued, leading me over to a large white leather sofa positioned opposite the desk.

'You know Senso is a major breakthrough for our ambitions. The chemical properties are truly astonishing, and the impact on the male hormonal system – well, I don't have to tell you about that. As a weapon of control, there is nothing stronger in our arsenal than the overwhelming and uncontrollable nature of male desire itself. You are being led by your cock to total servitude, Shelly; and your sex will surely follow, if we manage this opportunity properly.'

She sat down on the sofa and ordered me to place my hands behind my back.

I moaned into the gag as the vibrator continued to torment me. Then, to my astonishment, Ms Blakemore slowly unbuttoned the first three buttons of the Matron's dress, quite deliberately revealing the creamy brown edges of her splendid tightly restrained breasts. This truly astonishing and incredibly erotic spectacle inspired a particularly load moan of frustration and her cruel beautiful smile widened.

'See how easy it is to control you,' she mocked, a coolness entering her powerful gaze. 'Resistance isn't futile, Shelly – it's impossible. And Senso will provide the tool to allow all men to be reduced to your level of helpless sissy submission. But the big question for us is: distribution – getting it into the market place, getting men who have no interest in panties and hose exposed to its effects and then to take control of them. Well, that's actually not so hard. We begin with stealth: we introduce this endlessly pliable fabric, which can so easily imitate so many other fabrics, into mainstream male fashion. We design stylish, contemporary male clothing and sell it through a front company. On the face of it, a new male fashion house; in reality, a sub-company of SMC. And each item of clothing sold is cut from or mixed with Senso. This, my sweetness, is how we begin the process. Indeed, this is the way we are beginning the process as I speak. The front company is up and running and using the distribution networks established by SMC for its fetish wear and audio-visual entertainments across Europe and the United States. We already have a number of key SMC satellite units in the major western countries, and we have very significantly expanded the recruitment and education of female dominants over the last twelve months. These units are the vanguard for a much more loose-knit group of dominant cells scattered over virtually the whole of North America and a large number of European countries. It is they who will help their male partners, nephews, sons, brothers buy the Senso-infected clothing, and they who will then begin the process of subtle transformation of these males into sissy slaves. And that, dear heart, is where you come in.'

I listened, amazed as always by the breadth and depth of the Bigger Picture conspiracy, tormented by my own desire, the desire which assured my endless and helpless need to be trapped in this intricate maze of sissification.

'The costumes we have designed over the last twelve months have been very much in the classic sadomasochistic fetish wear mode. They are certainly popular, but with a rather restricted market. If we are to expand our feminisation project, we need a subtler range of sissy attire, something that perhaps reflects a more intimate view of the sissy rather than the maid or the schoolgirl or any other number of ridiculous fantasy stereotypes. We need a genuine sissy range, Shelly; original and distinct clothes for sissies, rather than uniforms. Obviously here, in this training academy, the uniform is a vital part of the educational experience. But for the future sissies . . . well, they need something different, my pet; they need a brand identity.'

She sat forward and crossed her long firm legs. The skirt of her white dress rode up her broad muscular nylon-sheathed thighs and my eyes widened with a fierce submissive need. This woman was utterly gorgeous. She was my ideal in every way: ample, powerful, intelligent. An imperial beauty. I was helplessly devoted to her already.

'So, you and I are going to start thinking about exactly what this brand is. We get the men into Senso menswear, then we brand them as Bigger Picture sissies.'

I nodded my half-understanding and she laughed.

'I think you've had enough of me talking, babikins. Now get down on your knees.'

I spent the rest of that morning pleasuring Ms Blakemore. Like all the SMC mistresses, she was a deeply sexual woman and made sure that I demonstrated my already infamous oral skills to the full before having me returned to my quarters.

Over the last four weeks, I have found myself spending a surprisingly significant amount of time with the glorious Ms Blakemore. At least three evenings each week have been spent in her elegant chambers on the top floor of the SMC mansion. Here, I have discovered the true power of her intellect and the spectacularly perverse nature of her desire. I have become her willing sex toy and her eager pupil; the helplessly feminine and submissive object of her most bizarre and wicked attentions.

The first time, after our initial meeting, that I was summoned to her private chambers was relatively late on a Monday evening. After a particularly hard day of instruction and servitude, that included my first and very taxing video session with Master Bentley and Mistress Helen, I was relieved to be put to bed by Christina. By the time I was brought down from the studio, flushed, violently aroused, yet also exhausted, the lovely Pansy had already been secured in her tight Senso satin sleep-sack. She had also been panty-gagged and hooded with a pink nylon stocking. She moaned her angry and relentless need into the gag (held in place by strips of pink duct tape) and received a slap from Christina for her disruptive silliness. Within a few minutes, I was cocooned helplessly in my own pretty pink sack and moaning angrily into my own fat panty gag while Christina, as punishment for Pansy's outburst, placed our arse vibrators on full for the entire night. Yet no sooner was I falling into the sweet delirium of my latest bondage ordeal than the door opened and Kathy, the tall very beautiful female slave of Mistress Helen, entered the room. Without any explanation, she freed me from my lovely torment (although not the tasty panty gag) and marched me from the room, much to Pansy's annoyance, as we had both begun to snuggle up together to enjoy the kinky night ahead.

Within a few minutes, dressed in my Senso silk pink baby doll and panties, matching Senso nylon stockings and a pair of open-toed pink feather-covered, three-inch high-heeled mules Kathy had pulled from the bedroom wardrobe, my hands tied behind my back with a white nylon stocking, my sissy lips still taped tightly shut, I was standing before Ms Blakemore's door, my heart once again pounding with girlish anticipation.

The door opened and I found myself facing Mistress Helen. Dressed in a tight elegant black velvet skirt, a high-necked white silk Victorian blouse and black leather ankle boots with striking five-inch heels, she was, without a shadow of doubt, the perfect representation of the dominatrix. I looked up at her with worshipful eyes and she smiled her slight thoughtful smile.

'You look lovely, as always, Shelly. Enjoy your evening with Ms Blakemore.'

She then floated past, leaving me enveloped in a mist of sensual rose perfume. Kathy curtsied deeply, her eyes filled with desire and love, and tottered after her beautiful all-powerful mistress.

'Come in, Shelly.'

I followed Ms Blakemore's cool ironic voice into the chamber, wildly expectant, furiously aroused.

Like most of the mistress rooms on the upper floors of the mansion house, Ms Blakemore's chambers began with a relatively small semi-circular anteroom off of which were four rooms – two to the right and two to the left. In the middle of the room was a large red leather sofa and a coffee table. Resting on the coffee table were a number of books and a pile of vaguely familiar drawings.

I wiggle-minced up to the table. As I was in my relatively scanty night wear, my angry sexual stiffness was embarrassingly apparent through the slender material of the Senso silk panties, which were themselves fully exposed thanks to the shortness of the dreadfully sexy baby doll.

Despite having my hands tightly lashed behind my back, I performed the deepest curtsey possible and beheld the amazing image of Ms Amelia Blakemore. That night she was dressed in a black silk dress that reached just beyond her knees. With black silk tights and three-inch-heeled court shoes of black patent leather, her hair worn loose, her lips painted blood red, she looked overwhelming beautiful, her plump physique both a testimony to ample beauty and the inescapable erotic power of the truly dominant woman.

She looked me over with amused, yet also aroused eyes and I fought a moan of helpless need.

'You look quite lovely, as usual.'

I bob-curtseyed my appreciation of this teasing

comment and felt my sex fight that little bit harder against its tight rubber and steel prison.

'I want to spend some time with you, babikins. Over the next few weeks, you and I need to do some serious thinking about setting our little silken trap. I want us to think about all your wild fashion fantasies, and I want you to learn the truth of your absolute slavery to all women through your submission to me. I have spoken to Mistress Helen, and, given your unusual talents, she has agreed that we can get to know each other in a way I would not normally countenance for a trainee housemaid.'

With this, she rose to her elegantly high-heeled feet and ordered me to follow her to one of the rooms leading from the anteroom.

Soon, I found myself in a large study, its walls lined with book-laden shelves and pictures. I found myself looking at the pictures with a sex addict's helpless fascination, for here were the most extraordinary erotic visions: pictures of startling warrior women subduing both men and women, pictures of stunning she-male beauties with the bodies of glamour models, yet also with huge male sexes locked in a dark variety of painful restraints. Pictures of the other mistresses: of Helen, Anne and Donna. Then, to my amazement, pictures of Christina – pictures of her tied and gagged, pictures of her at the feet of her various mistresses, pictures of her making mad sissy love to Annette – all in the same beautifully detailed precise style, all almost photographic in their reality and impact. The work of a very skilled artist.

'You like my little doodles?' Ms Blakemore whispered, inspiring an enthusiastic nod.

Yes, these were more than doodles, and I am sure she knew it. They were the work of a very accomplished artist, and my admiration increased dramatically as I studied the perfect erotic detail of her provocative renditions.

In the centre of the study was a large circular table covered in drawings, some of which I immediately recognised as my own work.

'We free ourselves in art,' she whispered, and sat down at the table, pondering my pictures of Aunt Jane, of various fictitious and very glamorous women, women I had so desperately wanted to be. 'You were obviously already trying desperately to express your true self in these drawings. To proclaim your true sissy identity. The pictures of the other women, particularly. They even look like you. You were creating Shelly. Perhaps it was even these pictures that inspired your Aunt. A fascinating thought. Yes, we should most certainly see you as a work of art, Shelly. A little sissy masterpiece in the making.'

I stared down at the pictures and saw immediately the striking resemblance between these early visions of classic female beauty and my own feminised self. Ms Blakemore's observation provided a stunning insight into the process of my creation. These pictures had been seen by my Aunt and in some way influenced the design of me, the image of sissy ultra-femininity she had constructed in such a loving and erotic manner that had been christened Shelly.

For the next hour or so she encouraged me to draw, to open up the vast whirlpool of dark desire that was my imagination and let its choppy swirling waters fill page after page of white paper. Using a pencil, I quickly found that what was initially a trying task soon became relatively easy: once the flood gates were open, it was just a matter of bringing the torrent of fantastic erotic images under control fast enough to produce coherent images.

I don't really remember that much about this first 'design session' with Ms Blakemore, mainly because what followed was so unforgettable. But in these initial images of strange sissy attire, there was the germ of an idea: clothing for the third sex, a unique design for those who stood so helplessly between male and female and craved absolute submission to the fire-eyed goddess of a deeply masochistic sexual need. Not slave uniforms, but clothing that represented a more subtle subjugation; a style that emphasised the extremity of the ultra-feminine.

The drawings were teased from me by Ms Blakemore with encouraging comments and advice. Her perfume tormented me as I worked, my hands free, but the panty gag still tied in place. This continuing bondage in such an odd environment only inspired me more, and by the time she put down my pencil and led me from the room, I was tormented by a wild fierce arousal and a corresponding need to obey her in any way she would now see fit.

As my eyes drank up her superbly full form, she led me by the hand to her bedroom, a large oval chamber covered in red wallpaper shot through with vein-like tendrils of glossy black. Here there were no drawings, but there was a large oval bed, a built-in wardrobe that covered one half of the curving blood-coloured wall and, in the centre of the room, a white chair.

'Sit,' she ordered.

I obeyed. She glided over to the wardrobe and opened one of a series of white wooden doors. From inside she took a striking white silk robe. She returned to the middle of the room and placed the robe on the bed, her smile elusive and disturbing. Now I knew I was in for a long testing night.

I watched with startled sex-filled eyes as Ms Blakemore proceeded to remove the long black silk dress, her eyes pinned to my writhing sissy form, in particular my very apparent and angry sex, struggling so pointlessly in its layers of cruel restraint.

'After art, there should always be relaxation.'

The dress fell to the floor and I gasped with astonished admiration into the mouth-filling panty gag. I was in the presence of the divine.

Ms Blakemore stood before me in a striking black silk body shaper, the black tights and the gorgeous shimmering court shoes. A vision of plump promise, of ample perfection. My need at this point was beyond any simple description. I was wrapped tightly in a totally unyielding cocoon of sexual frustration. My cock, perhaps more than at any point since my arrival at the SMC academy, was begging for release from its wicked layers of erotic imprisonment. I squealed with a terrible black hunger into the panty gag and a look of genuine concern crossed the black beauty's lovely face.

'Dear me, babikins, you're overheating. We'll have to do something about that . . . eventually.'

Then, to my surprise, she knelt before me and very slowly slipped the baby doll's pink Senso silk panties down to my knees. My rubber- and steel-sheathed cock popped desperately upward and her wicked ironic smile widened.

Then she took its boiling sleek length in her right hand and I felt myself fall into a grim black hole of never-ending sexual torture.

'What a pretty little cock you've got, Shelly. Even in this terrible rubber prison, its beauty is obvious. And that, for me, is a terrible temptation. Because I just love to paint beautiful things.'

What happened next inspired the highest pitched and most desperate of sissy squeals; for Ms Blakemore proceeded very gently to unclip the steel cock rings and allow my long-tormented sex to expand to near full erection within the awful rubber restrainer. As she freed me, she laughed in a way that I found strangely comforting.

'Of course, you all think this is our greatest cruelty; this terrible cock restraint. Keeping you poor sex-crazed sissies in penis bondage day in day out. But, as I'm pretty sure you realise, Shelly, this is the essence of the Bigger Picture. When all is said and done, the total control of the cock is the key to the door to paradise.'

Then she slipped the rubber restrainer off my sex, taking up the rim of ultra-thin rubber at the base of my bulging testicles. As she began this dreadfully testing and teasing process, she looked up at me with a harder darker countenance.

'Keep still, Shelly. One wrong move and I may have to operate sooner than anticipated.'

This enigmatic remark inspired an instant fear-induced stillness. I felt a stream of sweat cross my marble-painted forehead and hang threateningly over my left eye. My sissy heart pounded with fear and desire.

And that is how I sat: utterly terrified, so terribly excited, biting down hard on my fat panty gag, trying to think of anything but this awful beautiful moment. Yet the only thoughts that would come were thoughts of my other amazing adventures in this spectacular sissy training academy, thoughts of my other gorgeous wickedly imaginative mistresses, thoughts of pretty, ultra-feminine Pansy, thoughts of the wonderful sissy exemplar, Christina. A brief image of Kathy's so long black nylon-sheathed legs in the corridor, perfect objects of true female physical existence, their exactly straight seams rigid confessions of the discipline of body and mind at the heart of our robust training regime.

Then, with one stern tug, I was free of the restrainer for the first time since Christina had so expertly teased me to sissy explosion on the last night of my delightful imprisonment in the Nursery. A well-gagged gasp of relief fought its way past the panties and Ms Blakemore's beautiful smile widened considerably.

'There,' she whispered, her honey-brown eyes glistening with a harsh cruel desire, 'all done.'

I stared down at my freed diamond-hard sex with true astonishment, then my eyes wandered helplessly over to the wondrous form of Ms Blakemore imprisoned so erotically in the tight black silk body shaper. Her very large chocolate breasts, almost exploding out of the bra section, were rising and falling rapidly. I moaned and felt my cock press with an aching black need into the base of my stomach. Her wide firm thighs, sealed so erotically in sheer black silk, also tormented my wide sissy eyes.

Then she carefully rose to her high-heeled feet and returned to the bed. Much to my disappointment, she slipped her fabulous generous form into the black robe and went over to the wardrobe, returning a few minutes later with what appeared to be a metal paint pot and a long thin artist's brush.

'I think a little bit of body decoration is in order before we go any further.'

Moaning with sissy fear and unrelenting sexual need into the panty gag, I watched with horror and excitement as Ms Blakemore knelt before me once again. She then carefully unscrewed the top of the tin and placed it by my stockinged feet. Inside the can was a thick dark pink-coloured paint. She dipped the brush into the paint and looked up at me, her beautiful dark eyes filled with erotic mischief.

41

'It seems a shame to leave this beautiful cock unadorned, Shelly. It also needs sissification. Now, don't move an inch.'

I squealed with shock and masochistic delight as she then proceeded to paint my swollen, long-tormented and furious sex a dainty shade of dark pink. As the soft damp brush ran across my boiling tortured skin, it was if I were being teased by the silken eyelashes of an angel. I moaned and squealed, but I knew that to move was to invite both punishment and, possibly, a more accidental physical pain. So I remained once again stilled by a deep arousing terror.

A look of total concentration had enveloped Ms Blakemore's face. She was very careful, and a slight girlish smile shaped her beautifully full cherry-red lips. She covered my aching sex totally. The paint was particularly thick and easily took to the hot slick surface of my agitated sex. Indeed, within a few minutes, my sex and my fat almost bursting balls were a deeply humiliating dark pink.

'The paint is quick dry and fixed with a dye agent. It won't wash off, and it will take at least six weeks even to begin to wear off.'

I looked down at my decorated sex in amazement. What greater and more appropriate symbol of my feminisation and the philosophy of the Bigger Picture was there than this sissification of my absurdly paradoxical manhood?

Ms Blakemore rose to her elegantly attired feet and I looked up at her with the wide eyes of a cult devotee. In her presence I was indeed mindless, or rather, mentally crushed. I was a child and an angry utterly submissive desiring engine.

'Now, last time, you proved a particularly apt eater of my big pussy. This evening I think I'll take Helen's advice and test out your suckling technique. Then, if you're a really good little sissy, I'll put you in my little pleasure machine and let you drain out some of the spunk tormenting those pretty balls.'

And so this beautiful elegant buxom woman led me to her bed and a new realm of incredible sissy pleasure.

As she slipped off the shimmering black silk night robe and reacquainted me with the perfection of her ample form sheathed in the highly erotic body shaper and ultra sheer black silk tights, I uttered a gasp of angelic surrender. What was to follow, while not unexpected or beyond the realms of my already considerable sissy experience, was a particularly powerful manifestation of submissive pleasuring. As Ms Blakemore teasingly slipped the narrow black silk straps of the body shaper over her perfect shoulders, her honey-brown eyes burning like red-hot pokers into my own, I felt I had moved onto a new level of sexual being. The light in the room seemed suddenly to burn whiter, brighter, as if I were about to witness some great annunciation. Behold, the august and cosmic truth of the divine goddess!

And this divinity was quickly and spectacularly revealed as she gently glided the bra cups of the body shaper over her vast tits and exposed their great beauty to my sex-stretched cock and desire-widened eyes. I cried out in shock and awe and her teasing always ironic smile grew into a radiant confession of her tortuous intent: not only was I to give pleasure, but I was to be devoured by the overwhelming natural force of her very physical being. I was to be swallowed whole and refashioned.

Once her splendid fulsome light-brown orbs were fully exposed, Ms Blakemore sat back on the bed, resting her plump form against cream silk pillows and spreading her long muscular legs wide.

'Come closer, Shelly.'

I obeyed without a millisecond's hesitation. 'Kneel before me, Shelly. Kneel and worship.'

She laughed as I bob-curtsied and then struggled up onto the bed. As I knelt before her, she quickly removed the tape and panty gag. I gasped with relief and a paradoxical desperation.

'Drink your fill.'

And of course, I obeyed, lowering my quivering carefully decorated lips to her left breast and slipping them apprehensively over its long hard dark nipple.

For the next twenty minutes I pleasured her, my own unrestrained sex harder than ever and only a few inches from her thighs. I knew that the moment my cock brushed against the ultra-erotic silk material of her hose, I would explode all over the bed and my mistress, and I knew this would lead to some dreadful punishment rather than the vague hope of release she had promised. So I fought myself desperately and tried to concentrate on giving her pleasure.

My success in this endeavour was eventually confirmed when she began to moan deeply, even angrily, and her hands fell upon my head and pushed my face into the eternal maternal warmth of her generous bosom.

'Oh yes, Shelly, that's it – you're definitely getting there.'

As her pleasure increased, so did her movement. Soon I found myself shaken by her hands and bounced like a sissy rag doll on her considerable knees. Her physical reaction, like her body in general, was generous. She released a series of increasingly primal and loud moans and then the cursing began.

'Fuck, yes. That's it, you fucking perverted little prick. That's . . . harder. Harder, fucker!'

At first, I wondered what an earth she wanted of me. Then, as she bounced me on the bed, I accidentally bit her nipple and she unleashed a bizarre squeal that was a perfect fusion of pain and pleasure.

'Yes, you cock sucking sissy bastard – that's it. That's IT!'

And so I bit her again and she screamed primal joy into the void of an eternal desire, a huge deafening scream that seemed to come from the very edge of human pre-history. This was her orgasm. And as she exploded, I was pushed violently aside. As we jump into the abyss of sex and death, the final sound is the cry of orgasmic shock.

I lay on the bed and felt the room spin around me. I was on a sex Catherine wheel, a vast circular firework ignited by Ms Blakemore's volcanic passion. And as the room slowed, as the gyration of coming passed, the sound of her desperately heavy breathing faded in – slight at first, then louder, then very loud.

'Fuck,' she kept muttering between hoarse breaths. 'Fuck.'

Then, very suddenly, she pulled herself up.

I looked up from my prone position at this startling vision. A topless wild-eyed Ms Blakemore covered in a layer of thick sex sweat. She shook her head and then returned my gaze. It was as if she were emerging from a trance. The look of animal possession faded and the light of ironic intelligence returned to those gorgeous honey-brown orbs.

'My, my, Shelly – you have a rare talent. And for that, I think you deserve a reward.'

She climbed off the bed and told me to do the same. She then ordered me to strip off the baby doll and stockings. Soon, I stood naked before her, my sex an aching totem of unbearable frustration, my eyes filled with painful need.

She pulled the body shaper back into place and took me by the hand, leading me towards the wardrobe.

'I designed this little toy a few months back and have tried it out on a few select sissies. Annette particularly enjoys it.'

I listened, perplexed, as Ms Blakemore halted before a separate wooden panel at the end of the wardrobe. She slid it back to reveal a dark chamber. She leant inside and flicked on a light. I found myself looking at a truly bizarre and disturbing sight. Built into the far wall of the chamber were a series of thick white leather straps, four in all, which ran down the length of the wall. Below the second strap, to my astonishment, was what appeared to be a large very long pink dildo, rising out of the wall in an obscene, provocative and very frightening manner, its edges cruelly ribbed, its pointed tip glistening in a very threatening way. Hanging from a hook in the ceiling was a clear rubber tube. Attached to one end of the tube was what appeared to be a pink rubber sheath that was bisected by a series of very thin wires. At the other end of the tube was a strange mask-like device as the centre of which was set a large pink rubber ball gag. And hanging from a hook on the left side of the chamber was a pink rubber body suit and matching hood.

Ms Blakemore proceeded to remove the body suit and hood. I moaned my fear and she smiled reassuringly.

'Don't worry, Shelly – this isn't a punishment. This little toy is designed to bring pleasure and calm to the sex-addled sissy mind. It's essentially a milking device, to help you relax and prepare for the forthcoming rigours of your training.'

I looked up at her with helplessly trusting eyes and her gorgeous teasing smile widened.

She then made me pull the body suit up my silken sissy form. Almost immediately, I realised this was

Senso rubber and I squirmed with delight as it caressed my body.

It soon became apparent that the suit was a particularly odd and cunning creation. For a start, whereas initially it looked very much like there were two legs, there was in fact only one leg which enveloped and squeezed together my own legs as I pulled it upwards. What appeared to be the second leg was in fact a single arm glove positioned at the rear of the suit. As I pulled the suit up over my torso, Ms Blakemore stepped forward and helped me stretch my arms behind my back so that they could be slipped into the glove, thus squeezing them tightly and rather painfully together. Unseen at the time was a small hook at the tip of the arm glove which was then attached to an eyelet fixed to the lower back section of the suit. This ensured that my arms were stretched tight and totally immobilised.

It was only as the suit was secured in this way that I noticed the strange lace-lined holes positioned over the crotch section and the area directly over the cleft between my pert girlish buttocks. To my astonishment, Ms Blakemore then proceeded to slip a long elegant hand into the hole over my sex and gently extract my hard, tortured and still unrestrained sex. I squealed with delight and terror and she laughed teasingly.

'There, the jack is well and truly out of the box.'

So there I was: cocooned in electrifying Senso rubber, my sex exposed and furious, facing a very strange and ultra-kinky chamber of erotic torment.

Then she lifted me up. Taking me easily in her broad powerful arms, she lifted me from the soft bedroom floor and into the sinister chamber, carefully positioning me so that my back was resting against the strapping fixed to the wall and I was facing directly outwards towards her divine form.

Then she took up the sinister eyeless hood and I fought a deep moan of very genuine fear.

She stepped inside the chamber and pulled open the hood. I looked at her with absolute terror and she smiled reassuringly.

'You'll be blind, deaf and dumb, my little beauty, but the heightened pleasure will soon overwhelm any brief fear you may experience.'

I nodded, helpless, frightened, my cock as hard as diamond-reinforced steel.

She then stretched the Senso rubber hood over the top of my head and slowly pulled it down my face. The last image I saw that evening was of her shadow-covered and very beautiful face, her red lips curved into a gentle loving smile and her honey-brown eyes filled with cruel amusement. Then I was plunged into utter blackness as the hood was pulled down the rest of my face and secured carefully around my neck. To my surprise, my mouth was exposed: there appeared to be a circular hole in the hood to allow the mouth to remain uncovered. There also appeared to be tiny air holes positioned around my nostrils, as I could breathe freely.

I moaned into the darkness and then felt Ms Blakemore begin to secure me to the wall using the thick leather straps. As the straps that ran across my chest and stomach were secured, I felt the exposed space between my buttocks push hard against the long ribbed vibrator. The well-stretched space between my buttocks opened easily and soon the long ribbed intruder was working its way into my widening anus. My moans increased as I was so intimately and erotically impaled. Eventually, all the strapping was tightly secured and I was held firm both by the straps and by the sensual embrace of the vibrator.

As I squirmed helplessly on the virbrator, I felt a looser elasticated strapping being pulled over my rubber hooded head. This I knew was the strange mask, removed from its hook on the wall and now being lowered into position over my briefly exposed mouth. I felt soft rubber being pressed against my mouth and opened it instinctively. The ball gag section of the mask was then pushed deep inside and the mask covered my stopped mouth.

A few seconds later I felt Ms Blakemore's hands once again manipulating my long-tormented sex. I screamed helplessly into the gag mask and then felt the sheath, connected to the gag mask by the clear tubing, slide carefully over my aching desperate cock.

I was utterly and beautifully unable to resist. I squealed and tossed my head. I bit deep into the soft rubber of the fat gag. This was unbearable torment, and I loved every second of it. But this was only the beginning.

Once the sheath had been slid over my cock and balls, I found myself standing in utter darkness and a deep harsh silence punctuated only by the rapid beating of my sissy heart. Then it began: a slow light vibration in my backside. The vibrator had been activated. I squealed with pleasure as the vibrations increased in intensity. Then, to my added astonishment, something quite wonderful occurred: a strange massaging throb began to pass through the sheath tightly imprisoning my cock. What was even more wonderful was that the sheath was in no way a restrainer. Therefore, in a few beautiful seconds I was sure to ejaculate uncontrollably.

Yet even this incredible pleasure was not the end, for at the same time as the sheath, via the strange vein-like wires I had noticed, began to gently masturbate me, a set of lovely electrical tickles were passing across my already highly sensitive nipples. The body glove was making love to me.

I squealed and wiggled and awaited the inevitable with a terrible aching need. Then I felt the edge of the orgasm, like the top of a huge wave, begin to break open into an explosion of unbearably bright stars, a painful and at the same time utterly pleasurable eruption of white hot light that left me screaming into the strange, very soft, but utterly effective gag.

The cum exploded out of my cock like champagne from a suddenly unstopped bottle. It flooded into the tube that ran up the suit and directly into the gag. And as my cock emptied, I felt a strange, very light rumbling within my mouth. Something had activated within the gag. And within seconds, I found out what and why. Yes, very quickly, something wet, sticky and salty began to seep through hidden pores in the gag and into my mouth, a liquid whose taste I now knew very well: semen! Yet not just semen – my own semen!

The initial response to this awful realisation was one of utter horror. I struggled uselessly, I cried, I screamed out for release. Yet even as I was doing this, my deflating sex was being re-energised by the renewed vibrations of the sheath and the increasingly powerful ministrations of the wicked vibrator. And within less than a minute, I was stiffened and facing the truly kinky and sinister nature of this dark chamber and Ms Blakemore's 'desiring machine'. Here I was to be milked and then fed on my own milk. Here I was to be drained and filled. Here, the helplessly physical addiction to submission and bondage that had been so expertly created by an army of gorgeous determined and very powerful women, was to be tested to a truly explosive limit.

And for how long? At the time, I had no idea. I had no idea that for the next twelve hours or so I was to be subjected to the most extreme and bizarre test of my forced and welcomed feminisation; a test that would leave me utterly shattered, unsure of my own identity, brain- and body-washed. A test so severe, that I would be allowed to sleep in Ms Blakemore's quarters for a whole day to recover. A test that would destroy any final vestiges of resistance or doubt and ensure my true and utter commitment to my permanent sissy slavery and the ambitious aims of the Bigger Picture.

I stroke Pansy's sex back to life and remember the physical challenge of that long night. I pull myself up onto the bed and she carefully positions me so that my pert sissy bottom is facing her body. She pulls my pretty pink panties down my delicately stockinged legs and I whispers words of helpless undying love. I feel her renewed sex press against my buttocks and I welcome her, widening my legs, exposing myself, giving myself. As she slips into me, I remember the wondrous testing of that night and the tests that lie ahead and a smile of absolute acceptance covers my pretty, sissy face.

3

A Philosophy of Desire

Images of Ms Blakemore and her beautiful tortures continue to fill my mind as Pansy penetrates me. I gasp and feel a familiar physical splitting. Pansy's cock stretches me to the limit and the sensation of rupture deep within my sensitised form is the ultimate feeling of a helpless submission to my glorious sissy fate. As she builds a suitably arousing pumping rhythm, I press my backside against her and beg her to push harder and faster. She cries her own wild pleasure and I push my face deep into the silken sheets of our chaotic shared bed.

Since the incredible adventure of the desiring machine, Ms Blakemore has continued to train me in the arts of total submission and in the erotic ways of the Bigger Picture. Seeing me as her latest work of sissy art, I have been subjected to further exciting moments of body decoration: my nipples have been pierced and fitted with small silver rings, a diamond stud has been attached to a further piercing in my left nostril, a slightly larger pink ruby stud has been fitted in my navel, and, most bizarrely, and erotically, a large heavier golden ring has been fitted to a piercing made to the strip of tender flesh at the base of my scrotum.

Then there has been the further body painting. Strange tendril-like tattoos of hot pink have been added to my ankles, and two roses, one red and one pink, have been printed onto my buttocks. Now, I wear long pointed pink false fingernails and my toenails are painted in exactly the same shade of this particularly sissy colour. A black beauty spot adorns my left lower cheek.

Yes, I am Ms Blakemore's pretty work of sissy art.

At the same time, I have continued to work up various ideas for new sissy attire in her chambers, a tense deeply interesting prelude to sexual submission and an evening losing myself entirely in the dark joys of the desiring machine. And then there have been the wonderful Sunday sessions in the Nursery.

On Sundays, I see little if anything of Pansy. This is because on Sundays Pansy entertains Master Taylor and Mistress Anne. What happens during these all-day servicings remains deeply secret. Pansy appears both highly excited and deeply disturbed by them. She always returns in a state of physical exhaustion, her eyes wide with something approaching shock. Yet, despite this evidence of trauma, there is always the terrible proof of her own helpless and deeply masochistic arousal: her savage erection and the moans of a heightened sexual torment as we are sealed in the sexy sleep-sacks and she wiggles desperately towards my own tormented tethered form during the night.

While poor Pansy is led off by Annette to her Sunday testing, I find myself returned to the kinky delights of the Nursery with my darling mistress, Ms Amelia Blakemore. And this is, without a doubt, the highlight of my sissy week.

As Pansy torments me so wonderfully, I remember last Sunday and a dark deeply satisfied yet also slightly troubled smile ripples across my glistening pink lips.

I am brought to this marvellous chamber of delights very early. The sense of time in the SMC academy is always only an estimate: there are no clocks in the underground training quarters, and the only real indication of time is provided when we are allowed into the main house, where there are windows that indicate approximate light and dark. Yet, we are always hauled from our bound sissy slumber by clearly very tired maids, and our own sense of physical being is cut through with a strange feeling of insufficiency. Normally, I expect to sleep at least seven hours. We are in bed by a time I assume to be just before midnight and up by an hour close to 7.00 a.m. On Sundays, however, I would say it is at least an hour earlier.

We are dressed in two very different but equally splendid outfits. Normally Annette and Kate are our guides in this erotic and very deliberate dressing. Interestingly, we are dressed separately, one at a time, one viewing the preparation of the other. For some reason, Pansy is always dressed first, and I am left on the bed tightly secured in my teasing sleep-sack, the highly aroused tightly bound and gagged witness to a strange preparation.

Pansy looks forward to her Sunday sessions with a dreadful trepidation. During the night, I can feel her pretty sissy form quake through the tight deceptively slender material of the sleep-sack, a trembling whose vibrations run at the very similar frequencies of fear and desire. She whimpers into her fat panty gag (which, on Saturday nights, is always certain to belong to Mistress Anne) and presses her body into mine. Virtually immobilised by my own tight night restraints, I can only moan sympathetically and seek the relief of a sex-tormented sleep.

And as I watch her preparation for the tests invented by Mistress Anne and the handsome cruel

Taylor, I begin to get a sense of the causes of her trepidation. She is stripped completely naked and her restrainer and phallic plug are removed. There is much moaning and struggling as these teasing wicked companions are extracted from her beautiful silken body. Then she is naked, strikingly exposed, with the carefully toned but intensely feminised body of a sissy athlete. I look at her appallingly hard sex, so strange and yet so familiar in its denuded glory, the cock of a man on the body of a slender silky-smooth sissy.

Her beautiful sex-streaked eyes behold her preparation with a painful arousal. Next Kathy removes a new and very special restrainer from a pocket in her silk pinafore and Pansy's gorgeous eyes widen with the helpless terror of a beautiful damsel in distress. For this restrainer is made from a harder blood-red rubber and lined with hundreds of very tiny pins. As the beautiful female maid, her own eyes filled with a sadistic, even vengeful pleasure, stretches this terrible tormenting device over Pansy's sex, the poor she-male moans and whimpers.

'No, please. Don't. Ohhhh . . .'

But even as this fiendish restrainer is being stretched over hot hard sex meat, the dainty sexy sissy's pleas for mercy are transmutating into gasps of deep dark masochistic pleasure. The blue of her perfect eyes seems to be surrounded by a ring of sex flame, and her body quivers with the indescribable bliss that floats between pain and pleasure.

Any further erotic outbursts are silenced by the introduction of a very large, also blood-red rubber ball gag attached to two thick white leather straps. Poor Pansy's soft pink-painted lips are forced apart with cruel indifference by Kathy and then the ball is forced deep into her mouth by Annette. The gag is so big, the poor sissy's jaw appears stretched to breaking point and her cheeks bulge furiously. Yet even as she is struggling with this terrible torment, the two wickedly imaginative maids are considering the next tortuous development in the ultra-kinky Sunday morning dressing.

After the gag comes a pair of Senso red rubber panties. Very thin and terribly tight, they are pulled up Pansy's long shapely legs and then literally snapped into place over her tormented painfully imprisoned sex. She squeals as the whip crack of the material striking her tender sex flesh fills the room and tears of pain, humiliation and a terrible inescapable hunger pour from her eyes, the outline of her tormented deeply agitated cock clearly visible through the bulging film of arousing Senso.

After the panties come matching Senso rubber stockings, very long and very beautiful, that soon cover each leg from her pretty painted toes up to the very edge of the panties. A black Senso rubber corset is then pulled around her slender sissy waist and pulled very very tight. Her eyes bulge as this wicked pressure is applied to her girlish frame, and a darker shade of red covers her taughtly stretched cheeks.

Over the corset goes a tight red rubber mini dress, a creation of pure fetishistic brilliance, with a very high white lace-lined neck and long tight sleeves, whose cuffs are also lace trimmed. In the middle of the front of the dress is a black rose, the symbol of the Bigger Picture, an emblem also associated with the double rose logo of SMC (one black and one pink). But it is the single black rose that I have now come to understand as the secret mark of this secret and very serious society of dominant powerful women. The skirt of the dress barely reaches Pansy's perfectly formed ballerina thighs. It is also very tight, and this new layer of restrictive rubber Senso adds further distress to my sissy lover's gorgeous eyes.

Once the dress is pulled down tightly in position, Kathy takes Pansy's amazing Sunday footwear from the wardrobe, a birthday gift from Master Taylor. Pansy faces the thigh-high leather boots with a look of renewed excitement and terror. She moans into the mouth-widening gag and awaits her terrible deeply erotic fate.

The boots are jet black. They have astonishing seven-inch heels that turn the instep into a cliff-like drop towards the floor. The soles of the boots are thick black platforms as long as the heels, and the front of each boot dips strangely, to ensure that poor Pansy's feet are bent into a very uncomfortable forward arch. These, I have learnt, are hobble boots, and they ensure that their wearer is only ever able to manage the most careful and limited totter.

A network of black silk laces run from the base of the boots up to the thigh area. Kathy and Annette spend at least ten teasing minutes slowly and very carefully securing the laces as tightly as possible, so that each boot is virtually welded onto each rubber-sheathed leg, leaving poor Pansy even more restricted in the movement of her legs.

Yet even now the beautiful wide-eyed sissy is not free of torment; for as soon as the boots have been bound to Pansy's legs, the maids turn their kinky attentions to her rubber-wrapped arms. A matching red Senso leather arm glove is extracted from the wardrobe and within a few minutes, the lovely whimpering she-male beauty has had her arms pulled painfully behind her back and forced into the wicked glove, leaving her with one leather-fused arm, her shoulders pulled painfully together, causing her chest to jut forward uncontrollably and her balance to be made even more precarious. And after the glove comes the hood: of the same blood red as the rest of this kinky costume, made from the slender Senso rubber. Eyeless and mouthless, but with a speckle of breathing holes around the nose area. Poor Pansy squeals with genuine fear as this is quickly slipped over her head by Kathy and then pulled cruelly into place.

Thus, my gorgeous ultra-sissified friend and lover, Pansy, is enveloped in Senso rubber, bound, gagged and hobbled. In this woeful and outrageously eroticised state, she can only stand helplessly still as Kathy attaches a thick leather collar around her rubber-sheathed neck and then a long silver chain leash to the collar. Then, with a single violent tug, the female maid leads poor Pansy from the room. The sissy, whimpering helplessly, totters forward, blind, deaf and dumb, her cock on fire, her body bound tightly and without mercy. And as soon as she has minced off to her mysterious Sunday fate, Annette trains her eyes on my own tightly tethered and helpless form.

Within thirty minutes, I am ready for my regular Sunday trip to the Nursery. I wear a beautiful white silk dress with a very short and wide skirt that rests on a sea of sissy frou-frou petticoating. The dress, like Pansy's, has a very high neck edged with lace that tickles my dimpled girlish chin. It is held tightly against my body by white pearl buttons that run from the neck all the way down to just above the explosive skirt.

A pattern of silk embroidered roses has been sewn into the expensive silk fabric of the dress, and over it is tied a cream silk pinafore, across the middle of which, in an elegant pink handwritten style, is written my name.

Beneath the sea of gorgeous petticoating is a fat very soft wool and cloth nappy bound tightly around my waist and between my legs. Over this was been very carefully positioned a pair of pink semi-transparent plastic panties. Beneath the nappy, my long-tormented sex is tightly sealed in an ultra-sheer white nylon cock glove held in place by a dainty pink silk ribbon tied around my scrotum in a pretty and very fat bow. My legs are sealed in very fine white Senso silk stockings covered in glittering silver stars. The lovely teasing stockings are held in place with wide pink elastic garters covered in layers of pink and white lace. My feet are bound tightly inside dainty white silk booties, also tied in place with pretty pink silk ribbons in fat sissy bows.

Beneath the lovely intricate dress, I am held firmly in the grip of a pink satin panelled corset, reinforced with stern plastic rods, and small circular metal weights have been added to my constantly teasing nipple rings.

My hands are held captive by fat fingerless mittens made from rubber-lined white silk, and a beautifully ornate white and pink silk bonnet has been slipped over my head and tied tightly in place at my chin with more thick pink silk ribbons in another glorious fat and elegant bow.

All this and the dummy. Its teat is actually a fat orb of pink rubber rather than a teat, a kinky variation on the theme of the ball gag, which rests on a large oval plate of pink plastic. Attached to either side of the plate are strips of outward facing adhesive tape, and once the dummy has been pushed deep into my mouth, it is the adhesive strips that hold it firmly in place.

As soon as Annette has forced the dummy home, I experience a most familiar and delightful taste: Ms

Blakemore's spicy sex. I know she has slipped this kinky pacifier between her cunt lips the evening before and that this sweet reminder of her most intimate delights will stay with me for the rest of the day.

And if this wasn't enough, there is the new vibrator: at least an inch longer than anything I have worn before, also much wider. Made of hard pink plastic, its long tip slightly curved, its surface covered in hundreds of tiny wicked bumps, it buzzes at a low but still utterly infuriating frequency as Annette loads me onto the special 'baby trolley' – essentially a porter's upright trolley painted hot pink. As I am strapped into position, her hands gently caress my stockinged thighs and she whispers her desire.

'This is when I want you the most, Shelly,' she says, her fingers teasing the edge of my plastic panties.

I look at her in amazement and moan my own need into the fat dummy gag. I have never been with the beautiful emerald-eyed Annette. She is very much Christina's property, but there is no restriction on her in the way there is upon Pansy. In her eyes I see a familiar and disturbing cruelty. When she says she wants me, I know she wants me in a special dark way; that she seeks to control and torment me. She is very much a creature of her supremely wicked and gorgeous mistress. Yet even as I realise the perverse suffering she would inflict upon me, I cannot help but be deeply aroused by the prospect.

She removes her hand and I am wheeled off down the corridor, my eyes forced wide by the buzzing of the vibrator and my impending adventure with the beautiful all-powerful Ms Blakemore.

By the time we reach the Nursery, I am in a state of some considerable sexual torment. I squeal with a dreadful angry delight as I am wheeled into the large circular room and discover Ms Blakemore waiting for me by the playpen.

Dressed in a tight white sweater, a knee-length black shirt, white tights and black patent leather court shoes with wicked five-inch heels, she is a striking image of plump maternal authority. She smiles at my obvious agitation.

'You look delightful, as usual, babikins.'

I am wheeled over to the playpen and then released from the trolley. Ms Blakemore takes a mittened hand and gently guides me into the playpen. I taste her sex and my tormented eyes feed on her huge tightly restrained breasts. The powerful musk odour of her perfume washes over my babified form and I know I am in sissy heaven.

I am made to kneel down in the playpen. Ms Blakemore then takes numerous lengths of pink silk ribbon from a pocket in her wide black skirt and uses them to tie my mittened hands behind my back and then secure my bootied ankles tightly together. Then she quickly binds my knees and, as a finishing touch, uses the final ribbon to tie my elbows very tightly and painfully together.

'There,' she whispers, 'snug as a bug in a big fat nappy.'

I squeal with a massive masochistic need and she laughs mockingly.

'Poor little thing.'

My buttocks press against my tethered ankles and I feel the huge vibrator push deeper inside me. A memory of being penetrated by Master Bentley explodes from the whirlpool of sex-maddened thoughts possessing my poor sissy mind.

'It'll soon be breakfast time, my pretty baby,' Ms Blakemore whispers, 'but I thought we'd start with a little foot worship.'

I watch helpless and ultra-horny as she proceeds to bring a white chair from the centre of the Nursery and place it in the large playpen directly before me. She then lowers herself gracefully and carefully into the chair. Her skirt rides up her legs, to reveal more of her splendid wide thighs sheathed in the soft white nylon. I gasp with pleasure into the dummy gag and she widens her legs slightly to give me a view of the dark delights that await my attentions a little later in this long holy day of twisted desire. She kicks off the left shoe and I behold her long perfectly formed left foot wrapped in the sheath of erotic nylon fabric. Through its fine semi-opaque film I can see that my gorgeous mistress has painted her toenails a dark bloody red.

She arches her instep and points her toes towards my stopped mouth. I squirm and feel the vibrator burn with even greater force inside my tormented arse. She leans forward and, with one sharp tug, pulls the dummy gag free. She then pushes the warm stockinged bottoms of her toes against my upper lip. I moan and then the foot is in my mouth.

For the next ten minutes I suck and kiss her feet, a gesture of absolute and profound submission that sends high Richter-scale seismic shudders through my babified form. And Ms Blakemore is also deeply moved by the experience, her eyes closed, her mouth open, regular ripples of pleasure passing through her ample gorgeous body and down into my hard-working mouth.

Eventually, I am relieved of this deeply pleasant task and the dummy is popped firmly back in place. The taste of her fills me with a powerful dark adoration and, as I look up at her, my eyes are glazed by a terrible sex-love that brings a nearly awkward smile to her full perfect lips.

'Today I have planned some special variations on our usual Sunday treat,' Ms Blakemore says, slipping her somewhat damp feet back into her lovely sexy shoes. 'We will have two special visitors a little later on, and there will be a more educational aspect to the diversions.'

The next hour is spent very much in the tradition of previous Sundays. I am left trussed in the pen for twenty minutes with the vibrator buzzing angrily in my tenderised arse. My aching unrestrained cock burns furiously in the soft ultra-teasing nylon stocking and I fight the impact of its endless beautiful caress. I know that if I come, Ms Blakemore will punish me in some dark terrible way and also refuse any further 'diversions'. This, plus the endless caress of the Senso baby clothing, drives me to low tormented moans of need. I am possessed by a scorching desire for my utter and eternal submission to this plump all-powerful dominatrix.

During this period of incarceration in the pen, Ms Blakemore prepares the large adult-sized high chair that dominates the centre of the Nursery. I watch through a film of masochistic sexual surrender as my gorgeous buxom mistress elegantly and carefully prepares a large baby's bottle full of sugared full-cream milk, warmed and laced with hormones that will further the gradual feminisation of my physical form and prepare me for the surgical interventions known as 'the Operation'.

This is my breakfast and, as I am tightly strapped into the chair and the plastic detachable table is snapped into place over my helplessly exploding petticoats, my stomach rumbles helplessly.

Ms Blakemore smiles softly, removes the sex-soaked dummy gag once again and gently slips the fat teat of the bottle into my mouth. I suck willingly and desperately, emptying its creamy contents in a few minutes, my eyes wide and pinned irresistibly to Ms Blakemore's large tightly imprisoned and unbearably exciting breasts.

'There's a good girl,' the black beauty whispers. 'That's it . . . every last drop.'

And when the bottle is finished, I am faced with a bowl of pink mush – powdered eggs, more full-cream milk and food colouring. I am fed this via a large plastic spoon, and my utter splendid humiliation is complete.

Once the food has been delivered, the dummy gag is replaced and I am helped from the chair. It is at this point that the door to the Nursery opens and I gasp with surprise into my tasty gag for standing in the doorway is Lady Emily Ashcroft, founder of the Bigger Picture, most important patron of the Sissy Maids Company, and one of the most influential women in the country.

A striking honey-blonde in her early fifties, a woman who genuinely appears ten years younger than her actual age, Lady Emily Ashcroft had been a key Tory voice in the House of Lords until her controversial expulsion for her increasingly extreme and articulate views on the establishment of a new order of radical feminisation. She was the very public face of the Bigger Picture. A close friend of Eleanor Groves, the equally controversial and now ex-wife of the last Democratic American president, Lady Ashcroft personified the complex ethos of the Bigger Picture: a feminine radicalism, a power politics rooted in sadomasochism and the control of male desire. Not the suppression of male need, but its redirection as a tool of female power.

Lady Ashcroft is dressed in a startling white silk suit, with a matching high-necked silk blouse. She is wearing five-inch-high spike-heeled ankle boots of white silk-lined leather. Her hair is bound in its usual tight bun, and her heart-stopping ice-blue eyes behold my intricately babified form with a mixture of amusement and cruel arousal.

'Still as lovely as ever, I see,' she says, her crisp aristocratic voice filled with the authority of the natural dominant.

'Are you talking to Shelly or me?' Ms Blakemore responds, stepping forward into Lady Ashcroft's tight and passionate embrace.

The two women exchange a long and very erotic kiss. Lady Ashcroft's hands rest gently on Ms Blakemore's impressive bosom. This terribly erotic moment leaves me whimpering with an awful frustration into the tight mouth-filling dummy gag.

Then they part and face me.

'She really is a stunner,' Lady Ashcroft whispers, her voice hoarse with desire.

'One of the best,' Ms Blakemore replies. 'She'll be irresistible after the Operation.'

'And talented, too. The pictures you sent were superb. Clothes impregnated with a sissy's helpless desire. I met with Celine yesterday and she agreed we should start manufacture as quickly as possible. She is already taking huge pre-orders of the male attire across the U.S. She assures me that the male line will be available across most of Europe by the end of the month. Eleanor and Sophie between them have already recruited over 500 trainee mistresses, most of whom have suitable male hosts. By the end of the year . . . well, we're predicting there will be as least as many trainee sissies across the globe. This number will increase exponentially over the next five years.'

I listen in amazement. Of course, the true purpose of the Bigger Picture has never been in doubt, but here is the Plan, here is the awful real truth of their impressive ambition: the subjugation of all men, and the creation of a global Femocracy. The Plan is now very much becoming reality.

Ms Blakemore looks down at me with a gentle thoughtful smile on her beautiful lips.

'And pretty Shelly will have a vital role to play.'

'Jane is pressing on with the South West regional training facility. We will trial Shelly's designs via Christina's Silken Slavery and a number of other fetish and cross-dressing sites. After graduation, Shelly will join her Aunt and assist in the operation of our first regional academy.'

The mention of my gorgeous Aunt's name inspires a moan of frustration. Lady Ashcroft's smile widens.

'Yes, she misses you too, my pretty sissy petal. But you'll be together again soon . . . don't worry.'

I moan with helpless pleasure at this thought and Lady Ashcroft's eyes widen with cruel contemplation.

'Helen tells me you've been taking a very special interest in this one. And not just because of her artistic talents.'

Ms Blakemore nods carefully, her eyes pinned to mine.

'Mainly for professional reasons, of course. As we discussed. But yes, also for my own amusement. She has a number of other talents . . .'

Lady Ashcroft laughs and envelopes me in her imperial gaze. 'I know.'

Yes, she knows. I remember my erotic adventures with this stunning woman; I remember the taste of her sex and the physical perfection of her mature, yet still very beautiful form. I remember the squeals of animal pleasure as she came, the sounds a teenage girl would make. I consider how odd this all is: that they should have such absolute power over me and the paradox of my knowing their most intimate and helpless moment, the irresistible moment of absolute surrender that is the orgasm.

Ms Blakemore smiles knowingly and lets her eyes travel hungrily over Lady Ashcroft's splendid form.

'Helen tells me you've just returned from Sados.'

'On Friday evening. These are early days, Amelia, but the site is already very significantly developed. By the end of the year, the first training facilities will be up and running.'

A word that hangs like a flashing neon question mark in my tormented sissy mind: 'Sados'. The invocation of the vision of the Bigger Picture. What is this place called Sados?

Lady Ashcroft turns her striking blue eyes towards my babified form and I feel a shiver of utter submissive terror wash over me, a feeling of incredible and utterly erotic helplessness. These women are goddesses and I am nothing but their willing believer slave.

'Jane has already agreed to allow Shelly to visit once we are open for business.'

Ms Blakemore also turns to face me.

'The regional centres are just the beginning, Shelly. A worldwide network of local training facilities, most smaller than this, will be the feeders for a central training hub. Here, trained and physically perfected sissies will become she-male soldiers in the coming battle of wills. And they in turn will be sent out into this sad bitter angry world to bring a new message of hope based on power, submission and absolute female control of brutal male urges. Sados is the hub, my pretty little sissy baby, the centre of all our secret dreams. It is here we will take those inducted into the sissy life and turn them into converts to our Philosophy of Desire.'

A Philosophy of Desire. During the past weeks, there have been numerous 'academic sessions' in the classroom facility of the underground training chambers. Most have been led by Mistress Helen. It is here that Pansy and I have been carefully instructed in the basic ideas and principles of the Bigger Picture, ideas and principles encapsulated in the core notion of the Philosophy of Desire.

The most powerful tool in this philosophy is the core notion of 'sublimation', the re-channelling of male aggression and desire into a relentless craving for femininity and submission to womankind, the creation of a deeply masochistic personality constantly plagued by a furious sexual need whose result is the pretty, helplessly dainty and ultra-feminine sissy maid.

In some – perhaps many – men, this desire is already present. In many others, however, it is something that needs to be created and then carefully teased into an explosive force of control.

This is, without doubt, a form of feminism; for its aim is the liberation of the female from the bonds of male control. Yet this is no equalitarian or socialist vision of a society of equals. The Bigger Picture is a picture of power, a picture that recognises that inequality is at the heart of all human desire and endeavour. Women will dominate men by controlling their own desire for control, by turning their fierce will to power upon itself, by using this savage pool of fundamental energy as a tool for their own domination. Thus, the male will not be imprisoned and restrained against his will. No: he will crave his subjugation, he will desire it as he now desires to control others, to control things, to dominate and destroy the world and its other inhabitants.

'In a way,' Mistress Helen had said during one lesson, as we sat in our special 'school uniforms' of

Senso black nylon tights, black patent leather Mary Janes, Senso grey rubber gymslips marked with the black rose, Senso white silk blouses and red Senso satin ties (also marked with the black rose), 'this is the ultimate expression of Marxism, Freudianism and even the writings of Nietzsche via the Marquis de Sade. We have taken the ideas of the greatest minds of patriarchy and transformed them into a genuinely feminist project. Power and aggression, the subconscious, the mutation of desire into a weapon of control, the progression of history through a complex battle of opposing and developing forces. Ultimately, this is all about dialectics, ladies: the urge to destroy and dominate as the motor of history that leads to its own transcendence.'

I had listened to this learned interpretation of our fate while my anal plug buzzed and my cock struggled angrily with its tight cruel restrainer. I listened to this as my eyes worshipped the startling form of Mistress Helen, dressed in a black silk blouse, an ankle-length black skirt and six-inch-high stiletto-heeled court shoes. An image of pure unquestionable power, a force of power and history bound together in an irresistible force of change.

And in the Nursery I see this same power and history in the steely gazes and divine bodies of Ms Blakemore and Lady Ashcroft.

Ms Blakemore leads me back to the playpen. I am told to kneel and then I am tightly rebound. My body vibrates with a fierce need for this sissy bondage, and as I am made so utterly and wonderfully helpless my wide sissy eyes, filled with adoration and thanks, encounter the dark irony of Ms Blakemore's.

'There we are,' she whispers. 'Nice and snug.'

I moan with pleasure and she returns to the imperial beauty that is Lady Emily Ashcroft.

As I moan into the sex-stained dummy gag, as I remember the pleasures given to and taken from these beautiful women, Ms Blakemore presses a small pink button built into the far wall by the door and an electric humming fills the room. I watch in utter astonishment as a large rectangular section of the wall slides upward and a long white leather sofa glides mysteriously forward from within the dark recess revealed. The women take a seat on the sofa and the door to the Nursery opens.

Kathy enters in her splendid housemaid's attire. She is carrying a silver tray on which rests a bottle of expensive French wine, its elegant phallic form covered in icy condensation, and two tall wine glasses. She curtsies deeply before the two mistresses, revealing thick yet light frou-frou petticoating, heavily befrilled white silk panties and beautifully shaped thighs sealed in sheer erotic black nylon. The mistresses behold her with a desiring interest, eyes appraising her long legs, her firm tight bosom, her soft cherry-red lips, her tightly bound jet-black hair, her gleaming green eyes. She too has met these women and served them in every way. She is Helen's personal female slave, but in the Company of Slaves, we are all (Pansy excepted) a shared and well used resource.

At the front of the sofa is positioned a small cleverly attached table. This has dropped into position as the sofa has moved forward. Kathy bends down and places the tray on the table. As she bends forward, her befrilled tightly pantied bottom is fully exposed to my helplessly aroused view. I gasp with pleasure into the dummy gag.

'Is Annette ready?' Lady Ashcroft asks.

'Yes, mistress. At your command.'

Kathy's voice is deep, sensual and clear. She was once the senior manager in the same company that employed Christina and Helen. Now she is subordinate to both and truly happy. Looking at this beauty reminds me of another subtle element of the Philosophy of Desire: although at heart this is a philosophy of control through feminisation, it does not mean there will not be female slaves and, in some cases, male dominants. All have a role to play in the wider politics of power and domination.

'Bring her in,' Lady Ashcroft continues.

Kathy curtsies again and turns to leave.

'And tell Bentley to begin the projection at 2.00 p.m. precisely.'

A few minutes later, after Lady Ashcroft has poured drinks for herself and Ms Blakemore, and they have chatted more about her visit to this mysterious place called 'Sados' (a conversation that reveals it to be a private island in the middle of the Pacific Ocean), Kathy returns with Annette. But this is Annette as I have never seen her before, Annette in a state of complete and very severe babification.

The colour is pink: startling, befrilled hot pink. First of all the dress – an amazing concoction of pink Senso satin and white lace-frilled hoops that run from the high neck down to the very short skirt. Even the long puffed sleeves are hooped with white lace. Over this grand astonishment is tied a white Senso silk pinafore, tied in a very fat sissy bow at the base of her spine. Across the chest of the pinafore is her name, printed in elegant pink handwriting, and directly beneath it is a pink rose. Her hands are tightly bound in pink Senso satin fingerless mittens, which are tied firmly in place with pink silk ribbons. The skirt of the dress is smothered in a lake of multi-layered frou-frou petticoating, through which can be seen large pink plastic panties covered in a very delicate rose petal design. The panties are pulled tightly over a huge nappy. Her legs are wrapped in sheer pink Senso nylon stockings held in place with lovely lace-edged elasticated garters. The stockings are decorated with beautiful diamond-shaped raindrops that sparkle in the powerful electric light of the Nursery.

Her feet are imprisoned in beautiful hot-pink satin booties that have a much higher ankle wrap than my own; indeed, these booties are almost knee length.

Over her beautiful red hair, which has now been curled into a sea of sissy ringlets, is positioned a truly spectacular pink Senso silk bonnet, complete with thick front flaps that have been pulled tight over her lower face and above which only her pretty emerald eyes are visible, eyes tormented by the equal forces of deep humiliation and dark relentless desire.

She shuffles forward, moaning slightly into an unseen gag, a moan that is clear evidence of a buzzing anal intruder very similar to my own.

'How wonderful!' Lady Ashcroft cries, putting down her glass and rising to her high-heeled feet. 'A pretty little companion for baby Shelly. I do believe this is Annette.'

Annette looks up at Lady Ashcroft with even wider eyes before performing a deep desperate curtsey.

'Put her in the pen and then get Christina to help with the suspension sacks.'

Kathy curtsies and leads a terribly tormented Annette over to the pen. I look up at her with sex-wild eyes. The buzzing in my own long-teased arse has suddenly increased very significantly, and I suspect a sinister hand with a remote control.

Annette is put into the pen, forced to kneel so that she is directly facing me, then she is tightly bound in exactly the same manner as myself. We are then pushed very closely together, so that our delicately hosed knees are touching.

Annette's back is now directly towards the two mistresses, and her wonderful sexy visage blocks out any proper view of the women. I stare into Annette's gorgeous helplessly expressive eyes and feel a terrible sense of masochistic excitement. Today is very obviously to be a day of imaginative torment at the hands of these wicked stunning female dominants, and both of us are clearly in a state of wild anticipation.

Within a few more minutes, the lovely senior housemaid, Christina, has entered the room. Easily the most gifted and enthusiastic of my sissy lovers. I see teasing partial glimpses of her and note a change in Annette's demeanour. There is a sudden look of intense jealously in her pretty eyes. And behind the jealously there is the dark anger and aggression that I have seen on more than one occasion previously, at the core of which is a delight in cruelty, domination and control, a most paradoxical emotion for such a delicately babified sissy.

I blush and try to avoid showing my desire, thus confessing my past with this stunning sissy. There is clearly a very strong love between Annette and Christina.

I hear doors open, panels slide apart. There is much strange preparation beyond us, and Annette appears as baffled as I am to its meaning or purpose.

After a few minutes, Christina's long black nylon-sheathed legs enter my restricted view. She is standing a few inches from the playpen. Next to one perfectly shaped leg I can see a long silver pole balancing on a wheeled tripod. I moan inquisitively into the dummy gag and hear a high-pitched sissy titter. She is obviously amused by the no doubt deeply perverse fate that awaits us.

Seconds later, more black-stockinged legs are in my frame of vision. These, I know, belong to Kathy,

Mistress Helen's personal maid and Christina's charge. Then another pole. Then the door to the playpen is being opened and the beautiful merciless Ms Blakemore is standing over us.

She gently turns both Annette and myself so that we are positioned side by side and staring out of the playpen towards the sofa. The maids then position the poles so that they stand at either side of the playpen. I look over towards the pole nearest to me and see hanging from the curved top a large clear plastic bag filled with a thick white liquid. Running from the bag is a clear rubber tube. At the end of the tube is what appears to be a phallic-shaped screw gag. I notice that Annette's pole has exactly the some attachments.

Suddenly, Ms Blakemore is on her knees before us. Her skirt rides up her long beautifully shaped and muscled thighs and we moan a chorus of worshipful desire. I stare at the marvellous spectacle of her gently rising and falling breasts and then gaze helplessly into her large golden-brown eyes. She smiles with a genuine love and I feel my sissy heart soar with adoration.

She leans forward and, with expert elegant hands, unscrews a circular front piece covering the centre of my dummy's heart-shaped plastic plate. Christina then bends over the railing of the playpen and takes the front piece before handing my gorgeous mistress the phallic end of the rubber tube. Then, to my utter astonishment (and not insignificant concern), Ms Blakemore carefully inserts the phallic end inside the dummy. Indeed, it is soon very clear that the ridged cock-shaped end of the tube is specifically designed to 'dock' with or screw into the dummy gag. Thus, I am soon attached directly to the tube that runs up into the sinister plastic bag.

As I contemplate this bizarre development, Ms Blakemore attaches poor moaning Annette to the tube running from her pole, unbuttoning the thick front panels of her pink Senso satin bonnet to reveal a large hot-pink heart-shaped dummy gag.

Once we have both been secured, the gorgeous dusky and very ample dominatrix gets to her feet and orders Christina to 'turn them on'. The beautiful senior housemaid performs a deep panty-revealing curtsey of understanding and utter obedience and turns a tiny plastic tap positioned between the bag and the tube. I watch in astonished terror as the thick white liquid begins to pour down the tube towards my dummy gag.

'Two litres of sugared milk laced with a rather powerful hormonal stimulant and mixed with a cup of sissy spunk,' Ms Blakemore explains.

I moan with a mixture of horror and helpless masochistic excitement as the liquid reaches the gag and soon soaks through tiny perforations in the fat dummy teat and seeps into my mouth. For the next thirty minutes, Annette and I drink helplessly, swallowing in order not to choke. For the next thirty minutes we writhe in our intricate babification, the strange, almost savoury taste of the mixture a terrible accompaniment to the on-going and highly peculiar preparations we witness with wide sex-teased eyes.

As Ms Blakemore and Lady Ashcroft return to the sofa to discuss our sissy fates, Christina and Kathy mince about the Nursery desperately, their legs so close together, their high-heeled steps tiny and delightfully dainty, the sound of their nylon-sheathed thighs rubbing together so very erotically tormenting our girlish ears.

'The Operation will take place next week,' Ms Blakemore says, her beautiful eyes pinned to Christina's superbly buxom form as the lovely she-male pulls from a cupboard in the Nursery what looks like a giant pink plastic cock fixed to a metal tripod.

'Recovery will take three to four days, but I am confident that the end result will be flawlessly apparent inside a week. The new techniques I've been working on with the lab people are truly revolutionary leaps forward in cosmetic surgery. Christina and Annette were worthy prototypes, but their transformation took many months. With the new techniques, we will be able to guarantee at least fifty fully transformed sissies a week at the production facility on Sados.'

Lady Ashcroft smiles and nods, sipping carefully from the glistening glass, her free hand idly stroking Ms Blakemore's finely hosed left knee.

'Splendid. The camp is designed to be a production line of sissification, and your technology will ensure design becomes reality. The training rooms and factory areas are already under construction. The medical facilities will be finished within the year. Once the regional feeder centres are fully established, then we can provide the island with at least ten sissies a week. Within five years, this number will rise to fifty. Within another five, it will have grown tenfold. Then the Femocracy can be fully established.'

The plan is simple and brilliant: use Senso and a growing band of female disciples to ensnare a suitable group of male submissives, prepare them in the way that Aunt Jane prepared me, then send them to a regional training centre for their induction into the Bigger Picture. Then, they are shipped to Sados where further, more detailed training and the Operation completes their transformation into perfect sissy slaves; sissy slaves who can be returned to their

76

home countries and regions to assist in the further feminisation of even more males – a sinister, exponential process that would create the startling Femocracy of the Bigger Picture within ten years; a transformation of the world on a scale not seen since the Roman Empire.

As this latest revelatory discussion takes place, Annette and I are consuming the milk and feeling a new level of physical excitation. The already increased buzzing of the vibrator has added a new level of ecstatic torture to the marked additional sensitivity imparted by the kinky drug that laces the milk/semen mixture. Soon, we are both writhing helplessly in our intricate delicate baby bondage and our moans provide a bizarre background for the sinister discussions.

At the same time as our gorgeous suffering grows, Christina and Kathy set up two of the disturbing giant plastic cocks before the far blank wall of the Nursery. Each one is at least four feet tall, with a long curved and delicately ribbed head. And as soon as they are positioned side by side, the two maids return to the Nursery wardrobe and begin to extract more sissy attire. Yet what might at first seem clothing is soon revealed to be something very different and far more bizarre.

The maids step forward and lay the peculiar materials extracted from the wardrobe on the floor. Rather than clothing, the materials are revealed to be two small pink quadrangular Senso satin mats, with a long thin length of ribbon running from each edge. Two more familiar items are then removed from the wardrobe: pink nylon body stockings of the kind that Ms Blakemore imprisoned me in during the long night locked in the dreadful beautiful desiring machine.

A body stocking is placed in the centre of each mat.

Then, a new and frightening development: Kathy minces over to the far wall of the Nursery. She presses a button near what I take to be a light switch. There is more electronic buzzing. Then a panel in the ceiling opens and, to my sissified astonishment, two thick pink plastic-coated chains descend, each with a gleaming large silver hook fused to its end.

By the time the maids have positioned the chains directly over the two mats, Annette and I have consumed the milk mixture and our stomachs are heavy with the thick perverse liquid.

Lady Ashcroft then rises from the sofa and strolls over to the pen.

'I suppose the question you will be asking, and will continue to ask as the afternoon progresses, is how does this torment teach us anything we didn't know already? Well, that is, without doubt, a good question to ask. And my response is, you are not here just to learn. You are also here to serve, and part of your servitude is to bring pleasure, my sweets: to give us, your mistresses, pleasure. You undoubtedly do that in a physical sense; but there are some of us who enjoy something a little more elaborate, a little more . . . involved. I suppose the basic truth is that we are sadists, and that to torment you amuses us. And in that case, there is no real need for any further attempt at explanation.'

As she returns to the sofa, Christina enters the pen and begins to untie us. In a few minutes, we have been untied, detached from the milk bag and wobbled on our bootied virtually numb feet to the centre of the mats, our eyes wide with fear, helpless fascination and a furious sexual arousal.

Interestingly, each mat has an oval hole cut into the centre and, as the two maids begin to undress us, I wonder what kinky use this might serve.

78

We are soon stripped down to our restrainers. Then, to our further surprise, the restrainers are also removed, as are the large buzzing vibrators. We squeal with helpless angry pleasure as these most intimate symbols of our sissy status and subjugation are removed. Yet no sooner are we facing the rigid purple truths of our kinky desire than we are being helped into the single-legged and armed body stockings and our naked sexes are being pulled through the flower-shaped hole positioned over the crotch section, a hole whose kinky sister is positioned over the dark space between each pert tormented sissy buttock. Then a very familiar device is produced – the ultra-kinky rubber sheath and attached rubber tubing, the device that had so fiendishly fed me my own come in the absolute darkness of Ms Blakemore's wicked desiring machine.

This time, there is no mask-like gag. The sheaths are slid over our steely cocks and pulled gently into place. The tubes are fitted with the same ringed phallic ends as those running from the milk bags. They will be fitted to the corresponding slot in the dummy gags. Yet here is the terrible truth of this new arrangement: as we stand in the centre of the strange mats, the tubes leading from our sheathed sexes are attached not to the individual sissy's dummy gag, but to the other's.

Before we can truly comprehend the purpose of this latest humiliation, we are made to sit in the centre of the mat, so that our exposed bottoms are positioned over the hole. Then, our arms are forced behind our backs and bound tightly together at the wrists and elbows with white nylon stockings. We are then forced to pull our knees up towards our chests. Our ankles and knees are then also secured tightly with more stockings. Then, in this strange position, we must watch helplessly as the satin mats are drawn up around us, creating a sack that engulfs our squashed tethered forms completely, consuming and very tightly constricting our sissified forms into two satin balls.

The ribbon edges sown into the four corners are brought together and bound tightly by the two maids, creating a strange four-legged handle which is then slipped over each hook. Christina then returns to the far wall and once again presses the small plastic button and suddenly we are being pulled into the air. We squeal into our dummy gags, each of which is now attached to the tube leading to the other's tightly sheathed sex. As we move slowly upward, it becomes painfully apparent that the space between our buttocks is fully exposed and open to kinky manipulation. The true nature of this manipulation does not become apparent until we are at least five feet in the air. Then the chain stops moving upward and we hover helplessly, moans of genuine fear fighting their way past the fat dummy gags.

The maids then set about arranging the giant plastic cocks so that they are directly beneath our swaying forms.

And it is at this point that Ms Blakemore rises from the sofa.

'We thought you'd like to see a little film Pansy has been spending her weekends working on with Christina, Helen and the masters,' she whispers, her voice thick with alcohol and desire. 'I think it is, by a long way, our finest work. Clips are already being uploaded onto the website, and the DVD will be available from the beginning of next month. Of course, it doesn't seem fair to make you watch them having all the sissy fun, so we've arranged a very special viewing experience to enable full empathy and maximum arousal.'

To our horror, we are then lowered very slowly towards the cocks, which almost immediately start buzzing and vibrating furiously. We squeal helplessly into the gags. The women clap and laugh as we wiggle uselessly in the fiendish sacks, our bottoms performing a helpless ballet of terror. The pressure on our backsides is considerable and forces the cheeks wide apart, thus presenting an exposed and deeply vulnerable orifice ripe for the kinky attentions of the cocks.

I feel the damp tip of the large, long and intricately ribbed plastic cock press against my arse and squeal angrily into the fat dummy gag. The women's laughter increases in wicked volume and the cock begins to slip inevitably between my pert sissy buttocks. Beside me, poor Annette is subjected to the same dark, awful and deeply erotic suffering.

Within a few minutes, we are effectively impaled on the cocks. The heads and general widths are much thicker than anything we have previously experienced. It is the pressure of our body weight that ensures that the cocks work their way deep inside us, bringing tears of exquisite agony to our pretty, so very carefully made-up sissy faces.

Yet this is only the beginning of the afternoon of torments, for as we wiggle on the end of the cocks, the two litres of sweet thick milk begin to work their way through our intestines.

As the Nursery darkens, a hidden camera beam cuts through the darkness to strike the far wall of the Nursery. As the first seconds of the latest SMC masterpiece are projected before our helpless sex-tormented wide sissy eyes, I become aware of the urge to urinate, an urge to which I am made far more susceptible by the torments of the vibrator. Also, this same vibrator is driving me quite mad with arousal and, given that my sex is unrestrained, I am now facing the urge both to come and to piss. Thanks to the darkness, I am unable to see what is happening to poor Annette, but I can well imagine, and soon, very soon, I know she will flood the tube running from her sex to my mouth, just as I will do exactly the same into the tube connected to her fat inescapable dummy gag.

As I feel my bladder finally give way, my eyes are drawn to the film flashing before my tortured eyes. I surrender with a moan of utter despair and accept the inevitable. And as I relax, three words, in large white letters, flash onto the wall before my tormented tightly packaged body: *Visions of the Future*.

4

Visions of the Future

Petal was happy to be home. It had been very sad to say goodbye to Mistress Dee at the station, but they would be apart for only a week, and it had been agreed that Daphne would stay with her to help around the house and make sure she didn't get too lonely. Yes, the thought of gorgeous sexy Daphne was foremost in her sissy mind as she gave the taxi driver a credit token and climbed the steps of the elegant London town house that was now Mistress Dee's home.

As she wiggle-minced up the steps, the taxi driver, a stern-faced mistress from the Eastern sector, un-leashed a loud teasing vixen whistle and the pretty sissy blushed with pride and embarrassment. Her black rubber Senso micro-mini, a classic Shelly design from SMC (of course), barely covered her hips, never mind her Senso black nylon-sheathed thighs and, as she carefully tottered up the steps on five-inch high-heeled, black leather court shoes, her heavily befrilled panties were open to the eyes of all women as her shapely backside wiggled helplessly. Last year she had won the British regional final of the Western Sector Sissy Beauty Pageant and, as a consequence, was a local celebrity. And just to take one look at this beautiful example of first generation sissification was to see why.

Petal was just over five feet ten inches tall, a strikingly tall blonde with unsettling ice-blue eyes, designed in the large helplessly wide look now so very fashionable with the cosmetic centres. Her heart-shaped face, perfectly proportioned by nature – with a little help from Mistress Doctor Felicity (Mistress Dee's personal cosmetician) – was a striking justification of the mass sissification programme undertaken by the Femocracy in its first year of office. Petal had only been sixteen then, two years past the minimum age for changing, and her mother had been only too happy to have her packed off to one of the new training academies run by SMC Corp. And thanks to her then son's collection of Senso male undies, so was he.

Due to her very early conditioning, Petal's transformation had been a relatively simple process. There had been no late night visit from a Fempol squad; no removal to a Trans Camp tightly gagged with mummy's panties and sealed in an immobilisation suit. No, Petal, already overcome by the hormonal stimulations of Senso, was happy to be enrolled in the regional SMC academy. Indeed, she qualified as a full housemaid within three months, top of her class, and was returned to her mother's home to spend twelve wonderful months in a specially organised domestic placement. At the end of this delightful introduction to the joys of submissive femininity, she was placed on the register of Sissy Maids and quickly snapped up by Mistress Dee at one of the regional auctions, fetching the highest price of her cohort and ensuring that her mother was provided with a regular income for the rest of her life.

Mistress Dee, a beautiful brunette in her late forties, had been involved in the Bigger Picture since the very beginning. Now a senior member of the Western Sector governing council, she was a close friend of a number of members of the Global Assembly and knew the Grand Mistress personally. To be the property of such a distinguished mistress was truly a great honour, and Petal thanked the Goddess each day for her good fortune.

Mistress Dee had been summoned to Sados with less than forty-eight hours notice. Of course Petal was bitterly disappointed that she would not be able to serve her mistress for a whole week, but the thought of being with Daphne was more than enough to raise her spirits and her tightly restrained and constantly stiff sex.

As she turned the key in the front door to Mistress Dee's luxurious town house, Petal turned towards the taxi and waved a black silk-gloved hand sweetly. The driver looked at her with a fierce cruel desire and she felt a quiver of helplessly masochistic excitement rush across her gorgeous sissy form.

She knew she was beautiful, she knew she was very special. She was wearing a short black velvet jacket with lace-befrilled and puffed sleeves and the expensive intricately patterned black silk gloves that Mistress Dee had bought as a goodbye treat. The black rubber mini skirt was a teasing confection whose soul purpose was to reveal her long perfectly formed legs, which were sheathed in the sheerest black Senso nylon (tights by Shelly, SMC). As were her shoes: elegant, erotic, black patent leather court shoes, with tapered razor-sharp heels leading to the tiniest of diamond-plated tips.

Around her slender pale neck she wore a choker of white pearls, a tight lavish necklace that covered the polo neck of her ultra-tight second-skin black nylon sweater, whose sole function was to display her stunning, forty-inch chest to maximum effect, an effect somewhat dampened by the lovely black pearl-buttoned jacket. But with her tiny tightly corseted waist, the jacket could not hide the erotic perfection of her figure, a fact the driver's whistle acknowledged in a raw, sexually explicit manner.

Yes, with her hair in a tight bun secured by a diamond clasp formed in the shape of the black rose, her lips painted a deep bloody red, and a rose-shaped black beauty spot resting just a few millimetres from these full helplessly teasing lips, Petal was the purest paradigm of the New Sissy.

She opened the door and stepped into the long ground floor corridor of Mistress Dee's marvellous Georgian house, a house that had been her home for nearly ten years.

As she slipped out of her beautiful velvet jacket and hung it up, she thought of the week ahead and the pleasures that she and Daphne would experience.

Daphne was Mistress Dee's First Maid, essentially the senior sissy servant and housekeeper. She was at least five years older than Petal but, thanks to the cosmeticians, looked barely twenty-one. Indeed, all sissies were subject to two yearly body maintenance reviews (or BMRs), and, as the Femocracy had concentrated a huge chunk of its global science budget on feminisation technologies, the cosmetic surgery that underpinned sissification had progressed dramatically. Sissfication of the male begins in earnest at sixteen. As the full tidal wave of late puberty strikes, the male youth is inducted into the local SMC training academy. Using techniques honed over the ten years of the Femocracy and the five years of the Transition, the male is quickly changed into a simpering ultra-feminine slave girl. Mental and physical conditioning, cosmetic surgery and the wondrous impact of Senso on a body already overwhelmed by violent hormonal change ensure a swift transformation. Also, the first sixteen years are spent in a state of trainee femininity carefully prescribed by the Protocol of Change, the formal guidance of the Femocracy on the feminisation of the male. Thus, by sixteen, 'the age of enlightenment', all males are ready to begin their natural role as obedient, highly trained maid servants to the Great Womankind.

And as the sissy slaves progress through their beloved silken slavery, the transformations continue. Determined by fashion and history, each sissy is subject to 'design modification' on a regular basis. And thanks to the cosmeticians, the maintenance of the sissy in an almost pristine state of physical perfection can be guaranteed well into the forties. Indeed, even the decline of the core physical abilities of the human determined by the aging process has been slowed. All sissies are required by law to retire at fifty, yet even at this age they still closely resemble the helplessly beautiful slave objects they were in their early twenties. However, without the constant monitoring and updating of the BMRs, they would soon deteriorate, and the Ecstasy, which must follow within a few days of formal retirement, is seen by the Femocracy as the most humane solution to the consequences of the sissy's removal from the care and attentions of the cosmeticians.

As Petal climbed the stairs to the room she shared with Daphne, she pondered, not for the first time, the mystery of the Ecstasy. She remembered visiting a friend of Mistress Dee, Mistress Lovinia. That very afternoon, the gorgeous black-eyed Eastern Sector mistress was replacing her senior housemaid and there had been a spectacular sissy ball in honour of her fifteen years of service.

'She's been with me since the Transition,' Mistress Lovinia had said, tears in her golden eyes as poor

Betina was prepared for the journey to the Ecstasy Chambers. 'In the Phallocracy, we were husband and wife. We've been together over twenty years. I turned him myself, helped by Senso, of course. And he came into the fold willingly.'

The Ecstasy Nurses were sealing the still very beautiful sissy into the tight Senso pink rubber travel stocking. Betina's mouth was filled with a pair of her mistress's freshly soiled panties and her full recently restyled lips were fastened shut with pink sissy tape. Her very large breasts strained fearfully against the tight rubber stocking and Petal felt her sex strain teasingly against her own tight unyielding restrainer.

Eventually, the head nurse, an Amazonian negress in the terribly erotic rubber uniform of the Ecstasy Nurses, began to pull the Senso pink rubber eyeless hood down over Betina's pretty head. The poor sissy squealed desperately, her final goodbye to her gorgeous, stern but always caring mistress.

Her wide pleading eyes disappeared beneath the soft rubber mask and a small tear dropped onto Mistress Lovinia's alabaster cheek.

They had wheeled Betina to the ambulance and Petal had spent the afternoon giving the two Mistresses a variety of intricate oral pleasurings. As her expert tongue had tickled their shaven clits (all the fashion in 2025) and worked deep into their warm pungent backsides, she had imagined the testing and ultimate pleasuring of the Ecstasy. She knew that poor Betina would never see the light of day again; that she would be kept in the travel stocking all the way to the Ecstasy Chambers on the outskirts of Femdon, a vast complex of underground vaults that contained the rubberised bodies of over five thousand terminated sissies. Here, she would be interned in a small tubular vault. Patches fixed to the front and rear crotch sections of the stocking would be removed. A large ribbed rubber vibrator would be inserted into her well-stretched arse. Her restrainer would be removed and a lighter Senso rubber sheath slipped over its furious tumescence. Attached to the sheath would be a long rubber tube disappearing into the ceiling of the vault. Electrodes would be attached to her nipples and to her testicles. Then the vault would be sealed.

Deep beneath the earth, unable to move an inch, she would then be teased by carefully modulated electronic vibrations, driven to the edge of madness by a constant and intense process of excitation until, after maybe two or three days, her heart would finally gave out. Her final gasp would be into the scented panties of her beloved mistress at the point of an umpteenth orgasm. Her final petit mort would be death itself. Then the tube would be removed and the vault sealed once again. In a few seconds, her body would be turned to ash by ultra-high-powered incineration (UHPI).

Yet no sissy saw this as a terrible thing. All were trained from the very first day of their lives to submit to the will of womankind. A sissy was nothing but the property of her mistress, and, by implication, all women. To live was to experience a gift of the Femocracy. To die was merely another gift. At the heart of their absolute submission was the core of all masochism: the presence of an eroticised termination of life, an ecstatic surrender to death.

Now Petal opens the door to her bedroom and knows she is nothing but the sissy creation of her mistress. This thought is a constant arousing truth for the millions of sissies who service the Femocracy.

She expects to find Daphne in the room, Daphne attired in some suitably erotic outfit; Daphne

89

presenting the image of teasing ultra-femininity; Daphne, her long-time sissy lover, prepared for an evening of wondrous she-male sex. Instead, she finds Daphne attired for something quite different.

Daphne is lying face down on the bed. Yet this is no erotic repose, because she has been placed in tight and stringent bondage. The beautiful brunette sissy, her design as perfect as the day she left the SMC academy, is bound and gagged and squealing helplessly into a fat gag held in place by a very long and thick strip of white sissy tape. Dressed in a very tight black nylon sweater, a short leather skirt, sheer black tights (all Senso by Shelly, SMC), her lovely feet encased in spike-heeled court shoes of gleaming black patent leather, she has been bound in a way that betrays an experienced Dom Male. Her arms are forced behind her back and very tightly bound together at the upper arms, elbows and wrists with white rubber-coated cording. Her long shapely legs, so spectacular in the fetishistic Senso black nylon, are also intricately tied with white cording: at the thighs, above and below the knees and at the ankles. And tied to the cording binding her ankles is another length of cording, and it is this that has been used to force her body into a dreadfully severe and obviously very painful hogtie, the cording pulling her ankles down so far towards her wrists that the heels of the her ultra-sexy shoes are pressed deep into her bottom and her fingers are touching the diamond studded tips of the shoes.

Petal looks at this appallingly kinky vision, this fiendish restriction, and knows that she has been misled. Mistress Dee had promised Petal and Daphne a special week together. Both had thought they would be allowed to explore the delights of each other's sissy forms at a level of detail their servitude rarely allowed. Instead, they were to be placed in the hands of a Dom Male Training Squad.

'Welcome home, Petal. We expected you sooner. Have you been playing naughty games with yourself?'

She recognises the voice and turns to discover Mistress Saturlaine, Mistress Dee's closest friend and long-term lover, a woman the delicate pretty sissy had very good cause to fear.

She is dressed in a spectacular dress of black silk with a tight black leather bodice. The skirt of the dress is wide and beneath it flows a sea of fine black net petticoating. Her long muscular legs, sheathed in black silk hose, slide out of the petticoating down to knee length leather boots with fierce five-inch heels. Around her slender pale-rose neck is a band of black pearls, and her normally long jet-black hair is fixed in a strict bun held in place with a diamond dagger-shaped clasp. Her eyes are the darkest brown, almost black, and they glow with the sadistic intent of a senior Dom Mistress. Her bloody lips curl into a cruel heartless smile and poor Petal knows she will soon be joining her tethered lover on the bed.

'Prepare her,' the startling mistress orders, and then, from the sides of the room, the two Dom Males appear.

Petal cries out in genuine terror and totters towards the window. But before her slender sissy ankles have managed to mince a foot, she is wrapped tightly in the arms of one of the males.

The other then steps forward, armed with cording, tape and a fat sponge punishment gag.

It takes them less than ten minutes to secure Petal on the bed in exactly the same painful terribly strict manner as her sissy friend and lover. She feels as if every bone in her body is a second away from snapping, as if to move even an inch would result in the most appalling physical damage. The sponge gag has been soaked in her Mistress's sex juice, and this only adds to the furious masochistic pleasure that frames her dark very real fear, a fear inspired by the prospect of Dom training.

'I have managed to convince Dee that you two are far too pampered. You are spoilt little rich sissies and this is impacting on your usefulness. She has grown too fond of you, and the training and management guidance of the Femocracy is being ignored. It is time to get you back on track, my darlings. Time for you to remember the true function of your life: to serve and obey without question.'

Petal looks up at the two Dom Males, her eyes wide with fear and desire. She moans into the fat gag and knows the next five days are going to be truly testing. Both Doms are tall, broad and muscular. They are classic examples of the genetically engineered and specially trained male dominants who are the physical power behind the Dom Squads, the civil police who oversee the maintenance of the Femocracy in each of its four global regions.

The Dom Squads' core task is oversight of the proper training and management of sissies. In the Femocracy there is very little crime, and certainly no violent crime. Control of the sissy population is the Dom Squads' single duty, and it is a duty they perform with a zealous energy. Led by Grand Mistress Rosanna, Chief Inspector of Sissies for the Western Region, the Western Dom Squads are by far the most feared of the regional squads, and the British Directorate's Squads, under the leadership of Senior Mistress Saturlaine, are recognised as the most efficient and brutal of the all the Western Squads.

In the Femocracy, the physical power of masculinity has been eradicated except in one very important regard: the legitimate violence of the state. Even before the Transition, the followers of the Bigger Picture included a significant number of non-sissified men, mostly dominants associated with the global S&M scene. This core group was built upon during the Transition, when a small army of specially trained males were used to protect the leaders of the Bigger Picture from attacks launched by the Phallocracy. Since the Establishment, this army has grown into a world-wide force comprising three groups: the Protectors, the Security Guard and the Domination Squadrons (Dom Squads). The Protectors fight the Phallo-Rebels on the Outskirts, the areas that remain under male control around the Eastern and Northern Sectors. Under the command of the Amazonians, the elite military leadership of the Femocracy, they protect the threatened borders. The Security Guard are the intelligence service, protecting the interiors of the Fem Sectors from the on-going attempts of the P-Rs and their deluded female agents to undermine the supremacy of the Femocracy. And then, of course, there are the infamous Dom Squads.

Petal feels an electric shudder of masochistic arousal flood over her body as she stares helplessly up at the two Doms. Both wear the striking black uniform that inspires fear and sexual excitement into every sissy heart. The closest to her is dressed in the standard black leather trousers, black leather boots and black shirt. He is well over six feet tall and has the confident bearing of a hardened solider. The sleeves of the shirt have been rolled up to his shoulders, and the spiked rose branch that is the insignia of the Dom Squad has been tattooed to both of his very muscular arms.

The second is slightly shorter, but with a truly impressive physical design. A hard muscular negro with coal black eyes that burn into poor Petal's helplessly tethered form with a pitiless intensity. Dressed exactly the same as his white counterpart, cruel desire is obvious in his look, but also in the large terrifying erection that presses against the front of his tight leather trousers.

'Eric can concentrate on Petal. Ernst will work on Daphne.'

The sissies' squeals of terror increase in volume as the two Doms reveal their black silk torture sacks. From inside, they take the tools of sissy correction and place them on the floor to ensure that the sissies have a full view of the torments that await them over the next week.

There are the nine-inch vibrators with wicked layers of sharp metal ribbing; the pin-lined penis restrainers; the jars of long-lasting skin irritant that will be teasingly applied to their cocks and arses; the clamps that will leave their sissy arses and mouths stretched wide and helplessly vulnerable to any intrusion the Doms see fit to make; the eyeless rubber hoods with fitted inflatable penis gags; the dreadful seven-inch high-heeled hobble boots; the electric shock-inducing nipple and testicle clamps; the silver cock collars and leashes; the neck binders; the black leather arm gloves that will force their elbows and shoulders together and leave them screaming into an abyss of immobile sissy agony; the punishment bras, with their pin-lined cups; the black rubber Senso body sacks, that will ensure complete envelopment and restriction; the terrible enema apparatus; a variety of paddles and crops. An apparently endless supply of evil weapons of sissy pacification.

And the two helpless beautiful buxom sissies know this is just the surface expression of their guaranteed suffering. They will face hours of psychological torment – including prolonged sensory deprivation, appalling humiliation and will destruction. Worst of all, they know the Doms will make them punish each other; that their powerful sissy love will be so terribly tested by torments each will very willingly impose on the other.

Then, of course, there are the terrible pleasures: the servicing of Mistress Saturlaine and the Doms. They will suck and be fucked; fucked hard and relentlessly. Their heads will spend hours forced deep between the Mistress's broad powerful black nylon-sheathed thighs, drowning in the generous flow of her sex-logged cunt.

'We will start after dinner with the vibrators and the electrical clamps. Then you can fix the mouth clamps and use them in any way you see fit. I suggest you drink plenty of wine. Then give them a good hard fucking, hood and bag them and hang them up in the closet with the vibrators and clamps running full blast. I also suggest liberal application of the skin irritant on their cocks, arses and tits.'

The Doms nod, their eyes glazed over with sadistic desire. The poor sissies squeal helplessly, working their slender ankles furiously against the tight cording, wiggling their pretty, perfectly formed backsides in the tight rubber skirts; sissy damsels in a very real distress whose suffering is only just beginning.

As am I gently fucked by Pansy, I recall the strange torment of that viewing; the bizarre nature of the way I was forced to watch *Visions of the Future*, and the incredible impact this masterpiece of erotic film making had upon me.

Petal was played by Pansy, a marvellously natural and nuanced performance; and Daphne was played by Christina – already a proven and highly skilled actress. Mistress Helen was brilliant as Saturlaine, and Mistress Donna was brief but superb as Mistress Dee. Yet the stars of the show, after the sissies, were undoubtedly Bentley and Taylor – the two striking masters, the paradoxical guardians of the female future that was to be the perfect realisation of the Bigger Picture, a profound, disturbing and deeply erotic philosophy of desire.

The vision itself had been worked out at great expense. A view of the world twenty years hence, the spectacular realm of the Femocracy. However, it was the design of the clothing that completely astonished me. Even as I endured the terrible bondage ordeal of the hoisted sack, as the vibrator buzzed so terribly deep inside me, as the humiliation of the tubes became so dreadfully apparent, my eyes were wide with sissy need and an aroused fascination as I beheld my very own fantasies brought to cinematic life. Here were stunningly beautiful sissies attired in my designs – the clothes that I had drawn during my erotic sessions with the gorgeous and deeply kinky Ms Blakemore. This range of Senso-based attire was to be a pivotal part of the fetishistic transformation of the male and the creation of the Femocracy. Suddenly, even as I reluctantly consumed Annette's most intimate body fluids, I was filled with a helpless pride and a deep, burning excitement: this was how I would serve, this would be my joyous contribution to the Bigger Picture.

That day of great revelation, less than a week away, fills my mind as Pansy so expertly pleasures me. I moan her name and my love as she pushes deeper into me. I give myself so willingly, I surrender absolutely to my sissy needs. I dream of the wondrous future and my progress to full housemaid status. I wonder about the Operation and the period they call Placements, the special training in various 'domestic and related educational environments' and the tests these will pose.

My heart fills with sweet, sexy anticipation and I feel the initial wave of physical vibration from Pansy's gorgeous form – she is about to come. Then, it will be my turn to fill her, to let her drink and to empty myself into her soft expertly widened arse.

As she explodes, as her cries of animal pleasure fill the room, as I recall the detailed images of poor Petal's dark incredibly exciting suffering at the hands of the actor Taylor playing the cruel Dom Eric, the door to the bedroom opens. Our mutual pleasure is interrupted by the arrival of Ms Blakemore, Mistress Helen and Christina.

We separate and pull ourselves up from the bed, startled and rather dishevelled. We curtsey and stare down at our stockinged feet, our freed, damp and carefully decorated sexes rising before us proudly.

Mistress Helen beholds us with a smile of wicked satisfaction.

'You have both done very well in the past twelve weeks. Your progress has been heartening. The processes used to create you will soon be applied on a national basis – through the regional training academies, through the dissemination of Senso and through the political interventions of the Bigger Picture. This is, of course, only the beginning, but within ten years, we are confident the Femocracy will be established over a large part of this tormented world. The rule of the Phallus is drawing to an end, and you, my sissy sweets, can be proud of the fact that you played a crucial role in its much deserved downfall. But there is a little way to go before you are finally ready to play your role. Your training is only half complete. Before formal graduation, you must undergo the training placements. And before that, we need to complete your physical transformation.'

We listen spellbound, our sissy hearts speeding up, knowing that we are on the verge of the next marvellous phase of our sissification. I behold Mistress Helen and I am in holy awe of a true goddess. It is my sole purpose to serve her and all womankind in any way they see fit, and this thought fills me with a deep and highly erotic satisfaction. I look at her superb buxom form and remember the exquisite pleasures of servicing her every need. The taste of her, the feel of her, the smell of her washes over me, trace memories of a divine sexual submission. She is dressed in a tight black nylon sweater, a favoured item of clothing that very deliberately reveals her very large and still firm breasts to maximum teasing effect. A long black velvet skirt runs down to her shins, out of which emerge her shapely black nylon-sheathed legs and feet so sweetly imprisoned in elegant and very beautiful black leather ankle boots with fierce, at least three-inch stiletto heels. Pinned to her considerable chest is a diamond brooch – a sparkling rose, the symbol of SMC and the velvet-gloved steel fist of the Bigger Picture.

'We have arrived at the Operation,' she continues. 'The point at which you will undergo your final and most significant physical changes. During the next eighty hours, you will be given the body that will enable you to fulfil your sissy destiny and experience a physical pleasure previously only dreamed of. Externally, there will be no way of telling that you are in fact she-males; the level of feminine design will be perfect and utterly convincing. Of course, you will retain your male genitalia, but these will be, as they have been, tightly restrained and expertly hidden until required.'

We curtsey our understanding on weak knees and Mistress Helen smiles.

'Good. Now we can continue.'

Christina, stunning and resplendent in her senior housemaid's attire, steps forward. In her hands is a small velvet-lined case. She holds it before Ms Blakemore.

The gorgeous plump negress stares at me. I smile weakly and her amazing honey-brown eyes fill with erotic warmth. I know it is her, more than any other Mistress in this divine cave of sissy delights, who has ensured my progression to this vital point.

Christina opens the case and reveals two small syringes. Ms Blakemore takes one of the syringes from the case and tells Pansy to bend over.

'The Operation will take place in the hospital wing later this evening,' Mistress Helen announces. 'You will be kept heavily sedated until then, and during the Operation itself you will be under a general anaesthetic. A number of minor procedures will need to be performed following the major surgery, so the sedation will continue for at least two more days. The entire process should take no more than eighty hours.'

Pansy lets out a squeal of sissy shock more than pain as Ms Blakemore inserts the thin needle of the syringe into her pert pink left buttock. Within a few seconds, she has fallen face down on the bed, her eyes fluttering, consciousness slipping from her like an erotically removed veil.

Then it is my turn. As the divine ultra-kinky Ms Blakemore prepares the syringe, I consider the events of the past weeks and feel a wave of happiness wash over me. Now, perhaps surprisingly, there is no fear. Now, there is only a supreme sense of rightness, of a destiny in the process of being fulfilled.

After the Operation, there will be the Adjustment – a period of one week where Pansy and I will be trained to come to terms with our new ultra-feminine sex bomb bodies. The thought of having the amazing utterly convincing breasts that Christina and Annette sport with such a deeply sissy pride fills me with joy. At last, I am to be a true sissified servant of the Bigger Picture. And after the Adjustment come the Placements, five two-week 'off site educational experiences', where sissies are made to serve other members and agents of the Bigger Picture. And at the end of the Placements, there is a final assessment and, hopefully, graduation. Then, my return to sweet Aunt Jane and the new West Country branch of SMC.

The needle enters my tender sissy flesh and I moan with a furious masochistic pleasure. Then a vast swirling pool of semi-blackness opens up before me, a pool I fall into helplessly, every muscle in my body relaxing to the point where I feel made of water. I am on the bed, on my back. I am aware of what is happening, but there is nothing I can do or say. I am paralysed.

Despite my physical incapacity, I am stripped naked. Then, to my horror – a horror I cannot express – a further injection is administered, this one into my groin. I try to cry out. But nothing happens. I feel nothing. Mistress Helen appears in my field of vision, a vast goddess of this bizarre and beautiful cult. Then she disappears and I am aware of a wave of truly powerful sexual arousal crashing over my body. My numbness is not total: within a few seconds of this additional injection, my cock is rock hard and I am very much aware of it.

Then a white nylon stocking is pulled over my painfully stiff sex and tied tightly in place around my balls with a pink silk ribbon. Then my body is being sealed inside a pink Senso rubber body glove. Armless, legless, a tool of complete and deeply erotic immobilisation. Then, a fat sponge gag is gently slipped into my mouth. I cannot talk, but I am to be gagged. Then, finally, a matching pink Senso rubber eyeless hood is pulled carefully over my head. Then there is silence and darkness. Then, finally, a deep silence and a vast all-powerful blackness. In my delightful sissy bondage, I slip into a bottomless pool of unconsciousness.

Part Two: Changelings

5

Recovery

I remember very little about the next few days. For most of the time I was either heavily sedated or totally anaesthetised. The physical transformations occurred without any real sense of awareness. I remember the masked faces of doctors and nurses, almost all female. I remember bright blinding lights, momentary explosions of mini-suns cutting into a prolonged blackness. I remember waking in total darkness and realising I was once again in the tight bondage of transportation that was the fat sponge gag and the body glove. I remember a heaviness around my chest and a sudden, incredible sense of physical sensitivity that exploded into awe-inspiring pleasure, only briefly, but enough to warn me of the physical delight that was soon to be mine on a permanent basis.

Then I remember waking in a room, a new room, yet with a very familiar oval design. I was back in the underground training chamber and I was truly changed. And yet I was also more me than ever before.

I was dressed in a pink baby doll of very sheer pink Senso silk, tight pink rubber panties, pink Senso nylon stockings. I was lying on my back on a single bed staring up at a soft pink strip light. A sense of deep unreality washed over me. It felt as if I was observing my own body, as if I had become totally detached from the world as it is. This feeling gradually faded, and, eventually, I had the strength to sit up. And it was at this point that the true nature of my new self became startlingly apparent.

As I hauled myself into a sitting position, I became aware of a new and significant weight around my chest. It was then that I looked down to discover the wondrous vision that was my new more than ample bosom. I squealed with a deep and powerful delight as this masterful addition to my sissified form became apparent to my wide helplessly girlish eyes. And even as I beheld my splendid breasts for the first time, I was becoming very aware of their most arresting feature: ultra-sensitivity.

I moaned with pleasure as the soft silk of the baby doll brushed against their soft flawless pale-rose surface. It was like a thousand delicate kisses were falling on every inch of their curvaceous milky form. I took the breasts in my hands. I weighed them and gasped with satisfied astonishment: they were everything I fantasised they would be and much, much more! The helplessly stiff nipples were a direct response to my furious arousal. I tweaked them with my fingers (whose nails were painted exactly the same shade of pink as the baby doll) and squealed with pleasure.

After maybe ten minutes of fascinated observation and self caressing, I carefully pulled myself to my stockinged feet. The impact of the breasts was immediate: I found myself tipping forward and fought to regain an upright posture. I straightened my back and pulled my shoulders out. The breasts bounced in the baby doll and tears of sissy joy filled my grateful eyes. Then I saw the mirror – at the end of the bed, a full length mirror in an elegant white wooden frame. And then I saw my own incredible reflection.

I walked towards the mirror in a state of awed shock. The beautiful creature before me *was* me, yet more than me. She was my height, with my face and body; yet she was also a stunning sissy sex bomb. I stared at my face in disbelief: surgery had made its already feminine curves softer and slighter longer. My eyes were bigger, or at least had been carefully moulded by plastic surgery to seem bigger. Helplessly doe eyes, eyes that emanated rays of intense and inescapable submission. Then there were my lips. Painted the same colour as my nails, they were much more pronounced, more curved, fuller – utterly voluptuous. My hair remained unchanged, although it had been restyled in a striking Monroe cut, a sea of scented fifties waves that only added to the overall image of a submissive sissy beauty.

My neck seemed slightly thinner and longer, a deliberate illusion that made me appear much younger. Indeed, I now appeared about sixteen years old! I remembered *Visions of the Future*, and realised this was the most striking vision of my own future of absolute slavery to the principles and members of the Bigger Picture.

As well as my amazing breasts, I noticed a thinner waist, yet broader hips. Strangely, my stockinged legs appeared longer and my feet smaller. All, of course, illusions produced by the expert application of the surgeon's kinky knife.

Then the door to the room open and I turned to discover Ms Blakemore standing before me. Gorgeous, ironic, all powerful. I tried to curtsey and nearly lost my balance, tipping forward and nearly collapsing in a sissy heap before her.

She laughed and entered. I regained my balance and stared at her in a state of stunned adoration.

She was dressed in a very tight white nylon sweater and a long black leather skirt with a widened base of lace petticoating out of which emerged feet tied into a pair of five-inch-heeled black leather ankle boots. Her thick coal-black hair was free of restraint and exploded over her shoulders like a waterfall of golden oil.

'You look wonderful,' she whispered. 'We are all so proud of you, Shelly. Of you and Pansy. You are the next stage in the evolution of the Sissy; proof that our feminisation programme will work on a mass production basis. In eighty hours we have created two truly astonishing she-male beauties.'

I looked at her with adoration and longing. I felt my sex fight its restraint and smiled helplessly. Yes, it was still very tightly sealed in rubber and locked in steel. And then I felt the vibrator deep inside my arse, much bigger than previously, and so much more arousing now that I was truly transformed.

'You've noticed the vibrator, I see,' she whispered, moving closer to me.

I nodded, my eyes filled with a savage inescapable need.

'Your anus has been widened to allow thicker and longer intruders,' she said. 'Also, the skin has been made more sensitive. From now on, I think you'll find your arse is an even more pleasurable source of sexual entertainment.'

She was now a few inches from my bosom. She slipped her fingers over the straps of the baby doll and then pulled them over my shoulders. The baby doll fell away to reveal my naked and very considerable breasts. A slight gasp of arousal passed between her glistening blood-red lips and then she placed her hands on them, a hand on each, and I experienced a truly startling sensual pleasure. I squealed with sissy delight and her fascinated smile widened.

'We've spent a long time thinking about what makes the skin sensitive to stimulation. The sensory responsiveness of your new breasts has been trebled by chemicals and artificial skin implants. I'm afraid there will never be a moment when they are not providing you with a powerful physical pleasure. The same process has been applied to your arse and cock. The technology we have employed is far more effective and faster acting than that used with Christina and Annette, so in this respect, as in a number of others, you and Pansy are prototypes'

As she spoke, she lightly caressed my substantial breasts and I moaned my helpless pleasure.

'Of course, you'll need a good firm bra to handle this load. And I've given some serious thought to that.'

She released my breasts and walked over to a relatively small wardrobe built into the curved wall of the room. From inside she took a gorgeous white silk Senso brassiere, its large deep cups decorated with an elegant intricate rose design.

She held it up to me and smiled.

'Raise your arms above your head.'

I did as she commanded and she brought the bra over to my spectacular sissy form before slipping the cups over my ample chest and clipping the bra tightly in place at my back.

The impact of Senso silk on these ultra-sensitive sex orbs was violently immediate. I screamed with a vast mind-crushing pleasure and felt my cock almost burst out of its very well tested restraint.

Ms Blakemore's laugh was long and cruel.

'Brilliant,' she snapped. 'You're completely overwhelmed.'

I fell back onto the bed, stars of unbearable physical delight before my eyes. Ms Blakemore left me wriggling and moaning, returning from the wardrobe with a pair of pink Senso nylon tights and a matching pink leather mini-corset. She held me firmly and managed to get the Senso tights over my legs and pulled tightly into position around my waist. Then she secured the corset around my slender soft waist, binding it with a cruel intent that forced the air from my lungs.

Then she secured me. Using pink rubber-coated cording taken from the wardrobe, my wrists and elbows were tied tightly behind my back. She used a pair of her soiled white silk panties taken from a pocket in her skirt to gag me, sealing them in place with a thick strip of white masking tape. She pulled a cunt-scented white nylon stocking over my head and bound my hosed legs at the knees and ankles with more cording. A final longer length of cording was used to secure my ankles to my wrists, thus leaving me face down on the bed and positioned very uncomfortably in a very strict hogtie.

'The reaction you're experiencing is quite normal, Shelly. It will take a while for you to be able to endure this new heightened level of pleasure. I will come back in about two hours. You should have calmed down by then.'

Then she took a familiar small metal box from the pocket and my eyes, seeing the world through a film of sex-stained white nylon and wild animal desire unleashed from the pit of a crazed masochistic id, widened in terrible recognition. She pressed the red button fixed in the centre of the box and the buzzing deep within my stretched relined arse began.

Ms Blakemore left the room, and I was left with the vibrator, the bra and the terrible ecstatic torture of my re-sensitised body. I cried into the pungent gag, I struggled against the tight unforgiving bonds. The hogtie was strict and severe, and I was its helpless ultra-aroused prisoner.

Soon, the 'I' was gone: I was totally lost in this sex mania; my consciousness its willing prisoner.

By the time the gorgeous black beauty returns, I have travelled a strange and terrible journey from the edge of sexual madness to a state of extraordinary yet tolerable bliss; a journey up a steep mountain of incredible and mind-bending physical pleasure that has reached, near its ego-exploding summit, a plateau of bearable ecstasy.

Ms Blakemore is accompanied by Mistress Helen, Christina and one of the other female maids – Myriam. Christina and Myriam untie me and help me to my feet. In Christina's beautiful brown eyes there is a powerful sissy need and as she pulls me up, she whispers, 'You're gorgeous, Shelly.'

I smile weakly at her and feel the tormenting vibrator lodged so deeply inside my soft ultra-sensitive arse shudder to a halt.

'Without doubt a spectacular success,' Mistress Helen whispers. 'This new process will change everything. To think the changing took less than a week. Quite remarkable.'

Mistress Helen is dressed is a black silk blouse and matching jacket and very tight black silk trousers that display her plump but perfectly formed arse to perfection. Her thick glossy main of dark hair is bound in a tight bun with a rose-shaped clasp. She is utterly astonishing.

'You should thank Ms Blakemore,' Mistress Helen says, addressing me directly. 'She has done you a very significant service.'

I nod and curtsey deeply, trying my hardest to control my balance. Then I thank her and my whole world changes yet again. This is the first time I have spoken since waking from the operation, and now I discover the final touch of genius in my transformation. Suddenly, shockingly, I have the voice of a true sissy; a light, high pitched, deeply feminine and slightly lisped tickle of a voice, a collision between the breathy teasing of a sex bomb and the little girl gasps of a wicked Lolita.

The two women clap and laugh as my voice is revealed. I blush furiously and feel my more than ample chest swell with a bizarre mixture of embarrassment and pride.

As they laugh, my now permanently doe eyes fall upon the striking form of Myriam. I have seen little of her since my arrival at the academy, but now I find myself immediately attracted to her buxom Gallic beauty. With short blonde hair, large brown eyes and very full peach-coloured lips, her striking sexual beauty cannot be denied. She is a petite creature, yet also very full figured. Less than five feet five inches tall, she has her own large bosom, a very slender waist, a particularly shapely bottom and long exquisitely shaped legs. And this perfect form is superbly displayed to highly erotic effect by her housemaid's attire: a tight black silk dress with a very short skirt resting on a cloud of frou-frou petticoating, over which is tightly secured a pretty cream silk white lace-trimmed pinafore. White glacé gloves grace her small elegant hands. Her splendid legs are sealed in black nylon tights, and her small feet rest in black patent leather court shoes, with at least five-inch heels. The tights are delicately and very exactly seamed and map out the perfection of her legs with a strict geometry of sadomasochistic desire.

She was once a French exchange student who worked for a close friend of Mistress Anne's, referred to in one or two overheard conversations as 'the divine Amanda'. Myriam had quickly surrendered to Mistress Amanda's lesbian attentions, and within a few months had been transformed into her sex slave and domestic servant, as well as her employee. Then, she had become involved in the creation of the Sissy Maids Academy, and ever since she had been a willing servant of the Bigger Picture.

Unlike Kathy, the other real girl maid, Myriam seemed to have no distinct 'head' mistress; indeed, her role seemed to be to float between the various mistresses 'as required'.

As I look at her, I feel the immediate and powerful desire I had experienced when I first encountered her during my induction into the SMC academy. In many ways, she is the 'other half' of my primary fantasy of the female. The first half is, of course, the plump mature dominatrix, normally dark haired and dark eyed, and typified by Mistress Helen and my gorgeous Aunt Jane. Then there is the other half: the shapely, delicate and in many ways vulnerable blonde – the cute doe eyed sex bomb into which both Pansy and myself were currently being transformed.

Myriam returns my desiring gaze and I experience a thrill of mutual need. Her lovely brown eyes widen and a slight smile crosses her soft peach lips. I feel my tightly restrained sex twitch and stretch and then feel something else: an immediate and soul-crushing guilt. For as I desire Myriam, I also recall the first rule of my sissification: a sissy shall never sexually encounter a real female unless in the line of her duty of absolute obedience and submission. Any form of penetrative sex with a woman is banned outright. It has been made clear to us that any sissy found breaking this primary regulation will be punished in the most profound and permanent manner: full and irreversible sex change.

I divert my gaze from the lovely French beauty, but feel my desire burn even stronger. Luckily, any further contemplation of the gorgeous Myriam is interrupted by Mistress Helen.

'Now you will be dressed in the formal coming out costume and presented to the other mistresses and servants. Over the next two weeks, you will undergo careful instruction in your enhanced bodies and how to use them to perform your duties. At the end of this period of recovery and discovery, you will be ready for the next part of your formal training: the Placements. However, at the end of the fortnight, the Bigger Picture will, co-incidentally, be holding its annual fund raising dinner at the Academy. This will be a particularly apt venue at which to display our latest creations. By the time of the Ball, there will therefore be a very strong expectation that you will have come to terms with your new physiques.'

I fight to listen to this teasing description of the next few weeks. I try to forget Myriam's dangerously promising smile, and watch with sex-drugged eyes as Christina returns to the wardrobe of kinky delights at the far side of the oval room. Momentarily I wonder whether Pansy is also undergoing such an exciting induction into the delights of her new body. My cock strains and I fight a moan of dark pleasure. The thought of being displayed in this amazingly erotic ultra-feminine condition before the gorgeous females of the SMC and then at an even larger gathering of Bigger Picture notables is almost too much to endure. I feel a high voltage charge of harsh white sex electricity crash through my sissy veins and once again I experience true sexual bliss.

Christina begins to extract the 'coming out' costume from the wardrobe and my eyes widen even further. First, there is the dress, another true masterpiece of ultra-femininity designed by the kinky minds of SMC. It is made from a sparkling pure white silk and covered in tiny perfectly embroidered pink satin roses. It has a very high befrilled neck, with a button-up back that runs from the neck down to the edge of the skirt section. The wide and very short skirt balanced on a thick bed of typically light but also dense frou-frou petticoating, alternating layers of expensive pink and white lace, within which are scattered hundreds of tiny pink and white roses. Its long sleeves are puffed and end in heavily lace befrilled sleeves.

I gasp and the mistresses laugh at my helpless sissy need.

The dress is placed on the bed and I am ordered to remove the teasing pink tights. Eventually, I stand before the gorgeous, clearly very excited Christina in only my tight rubber panties, the teasing mini-corset and the divine Senso bra. Her eyes drink up my amazing breasts and I know she will soon caress them with her beautiful hands and expert tongue. We exchange, once again, a look of intense and unavoidable mutual need.

After the dress, Christina extracts a pair of Senso silk panties and a splendidly elaborate pair of white silk tights. Both these items of fetishistic ultra-femininity continue the theme of the dress: the panties are covered in layers of alternating white and pink lace, and in between each layer is a pattern of the same tiny satin roses that grace the bodice of the dress. The tights are made from the sheerest white silk, and each long semi-transparent leg is decorated with a pattern of white roses that run along elegantly twisting branches from the toes to the gusset area.

I am allowed to sit on the bed to pull the tights up over my long silky smooth legs. As I lean forward, I feel the downward tug of my new large breasts and gasp with pleasure. I raise my bottom up off the bed and slip the tights up around my now broader hips.

The impact on my legs is, as usual, immediate and stunning. I stretch out my toes in a helplessly delicate feminine manner and the smiles on the mistresses' lovely faces broaden. The kiss of silk against my now much more sensitised skin is quite overwhelming. I feel the fat long vibrator, now deactivated, press deeper into my widened anus and fight a louder moan of pleasure.

Then I stand up and try to step into the panties, very much aware of the cool examination of my divine mistresses. I struggle with my balance almost immediately, and Christina rushes forward to prevent an embarrassing fall.

'I think she'll be OK after a few hours,' Mistress Helen says, 'I don't think we'll need the body corset.'

With Christina's assistance, I pull the soft panties into place over the tights and the rubber mini-panties beneath, the outline of my furiously stiff cock still very apparent.

'I think you'll find the erection will now be permanent,' Ms Blakemore whispers. 'Adjustments to the hormonal balance will enable you to remain stiff virtually all the time. This, plus the new improved sensitivity to stimulation, and the increased levels of stimulation, will ensure a state of almost constant sexual excitation. This, in turn, will help ensure our total control over your every thought.'

I look at her in awe as Christina takes up the amazing white silk dress. I behold this startling glorification of ultra-femininity and moan with a total mind-crushing pleasure.

Christina kneels down and helps me to slip my delicately hosed feet and legs into the dress. My eyes fix on her own impressive cleavage and she beholds me with a frank desiring gaze. I smile weakly and she whispers, 'I can't wait, my sissy love.'

Then the gorgeously soft intricate dress is drawn over my sissified form and I am willingly imprisoned inside it. The dress is surprisingly tight, and its bodice seems to be designed to press tightly against my subtly reshaped waistline. The skirt barely reaches my mid-thighs, and the elegantly befrilled silk panties are clearly visible through the mist of intricate frou-frou petticoating.

Christina then carefully buttons up the dress and I am sealed tightly in my divine sissy destiny. As the dress tightens still further, I immediately notice the impact it has on my substantial chest, pushing it upward and outward and thus displaying my impressive bosom in a very deliberate and erotic manner. This brilliant exhibition fills me with a strong sense of sissy pride and tears of joy well in my big blue eyes.

'I do believe she is moved to tears,' Mistress Helen teases.

'Are you happy with your new body, Shelly?' Ms Blakemore asks.

'Yes, mistress,' I respond, my new sissy voice shocking and arousing. 'Very much. Thank you.'

The two beautiful dominants smile. Christina then returns to the wardrobe to extract a silver-coloured shoe box. Returning, she lays the box at my feet and removes the lid.

I look down at a pair of white silk-lined court shoes with striking six-inch spiked stiletto heels. Each shoe has a small silver rose fitted to its pointed toe.

Christina removes the amazing shoes and I look at Ms Blakemore with genuine fear: how, if I can hardly stand, am I to manage to balance in these astonishing heels?

'Over the past few months,' Mistress Helen explains, 'you have learnt all about balance; about the careful counter-weighting that is at the heart of sissy movement and deportment. Now it is time to apply everything you have learnt to this final test.'

Supported by Myriam, I step into the first shoe. Her powerful rose petal perfume is an erotic cloud of dark sexual intent, and as my arm rests on her silk-sheathed shoulder, an electric shock of mutual need passes between us. As I step into the second shoe, she whispers to me in a thick helplessly erotic French accent, 'You are very sexy, Shelly.'

I am too distracted by my sudden and highly precarious elevation to respond in any way to these teasing and deeply provocative words. Suddenly, all I am concerned about is the imminent collapse that threatens as Myriam steps back and I am left to try and judge the counter-balancing of the heels with my considerable and relatively heavy breasts.

'Lean back,' Christina advises. 'Imagine you are leaning onto a wall or the back of a chair. At the same time try and keep your back very straight.'

I follow her advice and find this provides temporary relief from the threat of a humiliating collapse into a heap of sissy pretties. Then I am ordered to take a step.

I look at the women in utter horror. Christina steps forward and slaps me soundly on my right thigh. I squeal with surprise and totter forward. This totter quickly becomes a desperate mincing, for I know that if I stop I will surely lose my balance. Yet, it is this very panic-stricken mincing that allows me to begin to come to terms with the careful subtle art of counter-balance that is at the heart of walking with my glorious new breasts in the highest of sissy heels. I keep my long silk-sheathed legs close together and feel the cheeks of my pert bottom push the teasingly fat vibrator even deeper into my arse. My hips sway and my backside wiggles almost uncontrollably.

The women and their beautiful slaves watch me with an analytical interest. I feel my breasts bounce before me as I totter around the room and a terrible sense of helpless display fires my furious masochistic need. I feel their eyes burn into me and feel how all attractive, buxom women must feel, and I am consumed by a terrible gratitude for my transformation into a chesty sissy slave girl.

After a few minutes, to my surprise, I find that I can balance reasonably well in the heels. My mistresses are also surprised and praise my rapid progress. Then I am made to stand to attention before Mistress Helen.

Christina takes what initially appears to be a maid's cap from the wardrobe, but closer inspection reveals it to be a strange silk and satin tiara-type device coloured the same white as my amazing dress, with my name printed across the front in pink letters.

This is carefully positioned over my thick blonde curls. Then, using familiar white rubber-coated cording, Christina ties my wrists tightly behind my back. Assisted by a clearly aroused Myriam, she then tightly and painfully secures my elbows in a similar manner. This bondage is followed by a very large white rubber ball gag attached to thick white rubber strapping. I gasp and squeal and my mistresses laugh.

'What a pretty picture of sissy perfection,' Ms Blakemore teases and Mistress Helen nods knowingly.

Under Mistress Helen's direct command, Myriam then produces a thick white leather collar from the wardrobe and Christina attaches it around the high neck of the white silk dress. Mistress Helen attaches a silver leash chain to an eye fixed to the front of the collar, and then I am ready to be displayed before the staff and slaves of the Academy.

My eyes meet Ms Blakemore's and I see a dark carefully planned triumph and the contemplation of the rise of the Bigger Picture, a rise I know I must play a key roll in achieving.

Christina tugs on the leash and I wiggle-mince out of the room behind her. As I pass Myriam, she allows her hand to brush against my silk-wrapped thigh and I know something strange and important is beginning between us.

A few minutes later, we enter the library that dominates the lower floor of the mansion house above the training chambers. I have tottered from the lift across wood and marble floors, my tightly pantied bottom wiggling with an uncontrollable enthusiasm, my splendid pristine breasts bouncing excitedly before me. As I mince forward, I am lost in a cloud of pure sexual excitement. Despite reaching a plateau of intense arousal during the earlier bout of very necessary bondage therapy, the highly erotic process of walking with my new body has increased the levels of excitement considerably. This has undoubtedly been made worse by the fact that as soon as we entered the main corridor of the training chambers, the huge vibrator lodged so firmly in my carefully tenderised sissy arse began to throb wickedly once again.

In the library, there is already a gathering of the other mistresses and slaves. As I enter, all eyes turn towards me and a collective whisper of curiosity quickly fills the elegant book-lined room. In the centre of the room is a small white podium. I am led to it and made to stand before the group. I feel a wall of excited eyes burn into me and I stare down at my high-heeled feet. Despite this display of helpless sissy modesty, I feel as if my breasts have been uncovered and revealed to all, for the majority of the eyes are carefully studying my truly impressive bosom.

Then the door to the library opens once again and Pansy enters, dressed exactly as I am and accompanied by Mistress Anne, Annette and Kathy. My eyes immediately seek out hers. But her eyes have already found those that are now the most important. A sense of powerful disappointment strikes me as I see her staring directly at Master Taylor, her eyes filled with a terrible adoration, an almost childish need for comfort and praise. Taylor, in turn, is clearly deeply aroused by the arrival of the latest sissy changeling. His tall broad muscled body, wrapped in black leather T-shirt and matching very tight trousers, fills the room like a terrible aching paradox amongst this beautiful army of determined feminisers. There is a slight smile on his normally hard almost expressionless face, a smile that betrays a genuine love for this gorgeous sissy creature. I am shocked and also aroused. In the incredible video, *Visions of the Future*, Taylor's character, Eric, had subjected poor Petal to terribly perverse and intimate humiliations, but even in the heart of what was a stunningly graphic sado-erotic drama, the mutual pleasure both were taking in this ballet of bondage, domination and fierce control was brutally and beautifully apparent.

The gorgeous freshly transformed sissy is brought over to the podium and made to stand beside me. As she is positioned, her eyes meet mine. Desire and a mutual recognition of our shared fate are instantly communicated. We stare at each other's beautiful ultra-eroticised forms and moan helplessly into our fat ball gags.

Then we are helped up onto the podium by Christina and Kathy. Now, we are truly displayed. The podium is high enough to ensure that everyone present can get a clear view not only of our impressive upper bodies, but also of our finely hosed legs and pretty undies. Bound, gagged and overwhelmed by masochistic pleasure, we sway precariously in our high heels and fight back tears of submissive joy and almost unbearable physical pleasure.

Mistress Helen then steps before us.

'Sisters and slaves, today is a landmark day for the Company, and, more importantly, for the Bigger Picture. For today, we have a very real and impressive vision of the future. In Shelly and Pansy we have the first sissies to be produced by our mass production feminisation process. By the end of the current year, we will be applying this process to sissies across Europe and America. By the end of next year, we will be applying it across the globe.'

The women reward Mistress Helen with a warm loud round of applause and I feel the future surround and envelop me.

'The first regional centres are nearly complete, and the first phase of the Sados complex will be ready by the time the centres produce the first batch of sissy slaves. We will achieve the first target of five hundred sissies within twelve months. This number will have increased to nearly three thousand within twenty-four months. By the end of the tenth year, we will have reached our optimum production capacity of twenty-five thousand sissies a year.'

Again there is loud and enthusiastic applause. I look up from the exquisite humiliation of my erotic display and see the burning eyes of true zealots. The library is filled with the electric energy of the will to power. My fate is in the hands of this furious deeply erotic energy, this powerful female Eros that will spread across the world and do battle with male Thanatos. A true life and death struggle.

Then we are helped from the podium and led through the throng of women. I feel hands brush against my delicately hosed thighs and pantied bottom; I moan with helpless gratitude and drink up the aroused fascinated gazes of the mistresses. Then Taylor steps forward, directly blocking Pansy's path. The poor sissy totters to a halt and looks up at the tall broad cold-eyed master, her eyes filled with awe and fear.

'You said I could have her tonight.'

His words are delivered in a harsh hungry monotone to the women, but it is clear they are aimed directly at Mistress Helen. Shockingly, there is no respect in his voice, just a primitive need.

Mistress Helen moves up behind Pansy.

'Yes. I did. And you can. Do what you please, but don't damage her.'

He smiles very slightly and grabs the leash from Annette. Pansy squeals with fear and desire into the fat ball gag and shakes her new fulsome breasts in a desperate gesture of burning tormenting sexual arousal. Taylor's smile broadens and he tugs on the leash. He leads Pansy from the library like a slave master with a new particularly sexy catch. The rest of us watch with teased eyes pinned to Pansy's desperately wiggling tightly pantied backside, a spectacle of pure she-male sexual being.

Then they have gone and a deep bemused silence, cut through with high voltage sexual electricity, fills the room. What I have just seen seems to go against every rule of the Academy: a male asserting the right of possession; a male dominating with the sheer

123

power of an impressive physical presence. Yet the women accept this without question; indeed, in Helen's eyes there had been a strangely traditional sexual arousal, as if the spectacle of Taylor exerting his 'right' had actually turned her on.

The chain attached to my own collar is then tugged abruptly. I look up at Ms Blakemore.

'He will have his fun, and I will have mine.'

She is my splendid sex goddess and I am her most abject and loving of disciples. I moan with submissive acceptance and she leads me from the library, my sex-soaked eyes drinking up her startlingly well-proportioned and endlessly promising form. My first night as a fully formed sissy slave promises to be a particularly testing and exciting one.

Over the next week, I undergo detailed instruction in every element of my new she-male physique. I am taught to walk and talk, to bend and rise, to perform deep utterly submissive curtsies. I am even taught to dance. Under Mistress Donna's careful instruction, the subtleties of she-male movement are revealed, subtleties I seem naturally attuned to, and which I quickly adapt as core parts of my own physical demeanour. Pansy, already naturally more feminine, seems to need virtually no instruction at all. Although we are trained side by side, I am increasingly aware that she is changing much more profoundly than I. Her femininity seems so deeply engrained that she resembles one of the female slaves more than a sissy. And at the same time as the truth of her rises before my stunned deeply impressed eyes, it becomes increasingly apparent that our deep sissy friendship is drawing to a close. Her heart is now truly Taylor's. Although she remains the property of all women, and Mistress Anne in particular (whom she continues to serve with a truly masochistic enthusiasm), it is Taylor who now commands her true affections. It is him she spends her evenings with, him she serves at weekends. When not being trained, when not serving the mistresses of the house in general work tasks, she is at Taylor's side.

However, we are still allowed nominally to share the same room and, on at least two occasions, have been allowed the mutual joys of our startling sissy bodies, and there is no doubt Pansy has found the times we have been left alone together in the period leading up to the Placements deeply satisfying and highly erotic.

These periods are made even more exciting by the manner in which we are left together and the way we have been prepared for this blissful togetherness, and this in turn is closely related to the strange relationship between the lovely Christina, our senior housemaid, and the beautiful nubile maid Myriam.

An early change in the regime of strictly enforced feminisation has been the increasing presence of Myriam. While Pansy has surrendered to the affections of Taylor, I have found myself increasingly in the company of this beautiful real girl, who, on these occasions, is under the stern instruction of Christina. And it has quickly become apparent why I am so often in the company of the beautifully petite French girl: she is to be an example to me, a paradigm of pure flawless femininity for me to observe and copy. Yet surely she is also an exemplar of sweet submissiveness, for her unquestioning obedience is absolute and constant. She obeys her various mistresses with a graceful enthusiasm that makes my own eagerness to please pale into insignificance.

Yet as well as an example, I suspect the lovely Myriam may also be a test, and a very difficult one.

Why? Because her beauty is almost unbearable, and it is very clear that she is attracted to me. In moments of paranoia, I have taken her frank sexual looks to be part of the test: she is setting me up in some way: if I can resist her considerable charms, I will have passed in the final examination on the road to the Placements.

The relationship between Myriam and Christina is perhaps the strangest and most paradoxical relationship in this gloriously kinky academy. Its model is the relationship between Kathy and Christina and tells very clearly of the flexible notion of female domination at the heart of the philosophy of the Bigger Picture. Christina is very clearly the boss, the dominate maid in any duty or event the two participate in together. Here the real girl is the servant of the sissy. But perhaps this reflects the unique position of Christina within the School. She is very much the First Sissy, the senior housemaid with administrative and operational responsibility for all the maids – she-male and female.

The nature of the relationship between Myriam and Christina has been made most apparent during the two periods of erotic intimacy that Pansy and I have been allowed to share in the period approaching the Placements. It is here that Christina's own ambivalent feelings towards the new 'fully formed' sissies and towards the gorgeous Myriam have found their clearest and kinkiest expression.

Two nights after our formal presentation to the masters and slaves of the Sissy Maids Company, and after a hard day of training, mainly under the strict but compassionate regime of Mistress Donna, we are returned to our shared bedroom. We are led by Christina and Annette, tightly tethered, hobbled and gagged, the vibrators buzzing in our wide sissy arses. We whimper into our fat white rubber ball gags with a furious need, as Christina has promised us both 'a very special treat'. Our tightly restrained breasts bounce helplessly before us and we totter desperately on five-inch high heels, our ankles hobbled with leather shackles held together by a six-inch length of silver chain. Since the transformation, the level of bondage applied to our pretty sissy forms has increased significantly. I suspect this is simply to ensure we are kept under control, for desire, a blinding brutal and all pervasive desire, is our constant companion. Now, more than ever, we see the world through sex-tinted glasses. I have been angrily erect since I awoke from the transformative sleep, and the power of the erection has truly tested the security of my fiendish unforgiving cock restraints. This has created a significant and constant discomfort, which, in the whirlpool of my dark bottomless masochistic desire, has itself only added to the sense of maddening arousal.

Once in the room, the maids untie us and remove the mouth-stretching gags. Then, under their careful instruction, we strip. We undress each other with shaking hands and much moaning, our beautiful bodies and the gorgeous sissy clothing that cover them dreadful provocations to our enraged sexes.

The two maids watch with cruel amused eyes. Since the Transformation, there is no doubt an element of jealousy has crept into our relationship with Christina and Annette. Christina has personally spanked me twice in the last two days for very minor misdemeanours, and during the two nights spent in the 'recovery-room' I have been sealed in a very tight rubber sleep-sack, my mouth stuffed with two pairs of mistress panties held in place by layers of thick silver duct tape, a black stocking pulled tightly over my head, the vibrator buzzing angrily deep within my backside.

So, as well as the helpless sexual excitement that appears my permanent lot, there is also considerable apprehension gripping me as I strip my sissy love. And this apprehension increases significantly when Myriam suddenly enters the room. Yet this is not Myriam in her normal sexy maid's costume. No: this is Myriam clad in a striking white nylon body stocking and the most startling high-heeled hobble boots. Myriam barely able to walk thanks to the curved-front five-inch platforms and the matching razor-sharp stiletto heels. Myriam wearing fingerless white rubber gloves that reach up to her shoulders. Myriam wearing a thick white leather belt with an equally thick connector strip that runs from the front of the belt down between her lovely legs and up via the cheeks of her perfect buttocks to the rear of the belt. Myriam with a look of pure terror cut through with irresistible animal desire; with tears of horror and desire threatening to explode from her gorgeous honey-brown eyes.

'Myriam will be joining you for the evening,' Christina says, her sultry voice cut through with cruel sarcasm. 'As an observer.'

While we stare in helpless astonishment at the fetishistic beauty of Myriam, Annette retrieves two more sheer nylon body stockings from the wardrobe. These are very similar to the body gloves employed by Ms Blakemore and Mistress Helen, with strategically positioned lace-edged holes at the front and rear of the groin area, and fingerless hand coverings seamlessly attached to each arm.

Before being ordered into the body stockings, the tight rubber restrainers and the cock rings are removed with the usual theatre of helpless sissy squeals, and we are allowed a full view of our sissy cocks for the first time since the Transformation.

Both are still dyed a bright hot pink, and we both retain the gleaming silver rings attached to our pierced scrotums. Yet, although it is hard to believe, we both notice a distinct increase in length.

The senior maids titter girlishly at our surprise and Myriam stares at our stiff elegantly curving cocks with a dark unyielding hunger.

'A slight extension, courtesy of Ms Blakemore.'

Despite the fact that Christina had already taken me on the first night after the Transformation, she has never removed the restrainer. Indeed, I was very tightly bound and gagged and face down when she took me, and my sole function had been to be the tormented receptacle of her own considerable sex.

As soon as the restrainers are removed, we are ordered into the teasing body stockings. The extra sensitivity imparted by the Transformation makes the kiss of soft white nylon on our expertly sissified bodies all the more delightful, and we both squeal with helpless pleasure as we wiggle into the stockings. This pleasure is made even more acute when we are ordered to pull each other's sexes through the lace-edged holes, so that our new improved cocks and the fat almost bulging balls that accompany them are fully exposed. We stare into each other's wider, more doe-like eyes with a terrible passion as we gently guide each other's rock hard cock into position.

Then we are made to lie on the bed face down and a new bondage sculpture is prepared. Using the familiar white rubber-coated cording, our wrists are crossed and tightly bound. We moan with masochistic pleasure as our elbows are then tied tightly and very painfully together with yet more cord. Our legs are then similarly secured at the lower thighs, above and below the knees and at the ankles. Then, a final familiar touch: a longer length of cord is attached to the cording binding our ankles and pulled tightly up our nylon-enveloped bodies before the free end is tied to our tethered wrists. Thus we are both secured in a very tight and severe hogtie. It is at this point that the vibrators still lodged deep inside our arses begin to buzz angrily at full blast and we fight screams of insane sissy pleasure.

Once tied, we are turned to face the side of the bed where the maids and Myriam are standing. Being hogtied, we have to pull our heads up quite painfully to get a reasonable view of what happens next.

Before our straining sex-maddened eyes, Myriam is prepared for her role as 'observer'. Her wrists are fitted into hard pink rubber shackles. The shackles are then attached to lengths of slender silver chain, which are pulled behind her back and attached to an eye bolt fixed into the room's rubberised flooring, bending her body back painfully. A white leather collar is fixed to her neck and a further length of silver chain is attached to a metal loop at its front. This, in turn, is connected to a further eye bolt positioned in the floor directly in front of her, providing a counterweight to the pressure exerted on her back by the rear chains and thus holding her in a painful upright position.

Tears of pain begin to trickle from her eyes: she knows there will be no mercy this evening.

A very large white rubber ball gag is then stuffed into her soft sexy mouth and strapped tightly into place at the base of her slender neck. Her eyes widen further, her splendid breasts rise and fall rapidly in their tight nylon prison with a girlish fear, and the two maids admire their kinky handiwork, both very clearly aroused by the sadistic power they possess over Myriam and the two helpless ultra-horny sissies.

Yet the French beauty's sufferings are far from over.

As soon as Myriam is secured in this terribly uncomfortable standing position, Annette extracts a small metal box from the bedside table and takes it over to the stretched French beauty. She opens it teasingly beneath the lovely girl's eyes and Myriam immediately begins to squeal with genuine terror into the fat gag and shake her head rapidly.

It is only when Christina extracts two golden nipple clamps that we understand the reason for her reaction. The poor girl squeals furiously as the sharp teeth of the first clamp are stretched open and then applied to the long stiff nipple of her left breast. Anger and pain fill her dark sexy eyes and her damsel in distress squeals rise an octave as serrated and finely sculptured metal bites into tender damsel flesh. Without batting an eyelid, Christina then applies the second clamp, leaving the gorgeous slave girl struggling desperately and very erotically.

The senior housemaid then steps back to admire her cruel handiwork, a sadistic smile on her beautiful face, her own dark eyes filled with a sinister sexual arousal.

'There – all ready for a night of considered contemplation.'

The two sissy maids then turn their wicked attentions to us.

First, we are turned onto our sides, and then two more metal boxes are extracted from the bedside drawer. Almost immediately we begin squealing with our own very real fear, knowing exactly what is inside and thus the torture that awaits us.

Christina applies the clamps to my large perfectly formed breasts as Annette works on the lovely helpless Pansy. Soon, the two of us are wiggling and squealing with a terrible desperation. The heightened sensitivity of the breasts makes the teasing pain of the clamps even more apparent, and the tortuous consequences of this are soon apparent in our wide tear-soaked eyes. Yet our sissy mistresses show no mercy, and we are very quickly positioned so that I am directly facing Pansy's huge angry cock and she is facing mine. This is a position previously employed by Aunt Jane and Ms Hartley, and the night of pleasure this brought us was a very important turning point in our relationship as sissy lovers.

Yet whereas that splendid night was an evening of voluntary pleasuring, tonight's bondage sculpture will be designed to ensure only enforced sexual torment. For no sooner are we facing each other, our beautiful new breasts so cruelly tormented, than Annette is slipping what appears to be a bright pink rubber eyeless hood over Pansy's head. Yet what is very unusual about this hood is that there is a very obvious mouth section that has been lined with a thick ring of white rubber, and as the hood is pulled tightly into position, it becomes clear that the ring is designed to fit inside the mouth and force it wide open, thus creating a bizarre mouth gag. And seconds later, I too am being plunged into a very similar ultra-kinky hood, and very soon my own sissy mouth is forced painfully open and I am gasping with fear and deep discomfort. Yet this is not the end of our torments.

Lost in a world of rubberised silence and darkness, I feel a thick collar being attached to my neck. A chain or similar leashing device is attached to the collar and then my head is pulled violently forward. I feel Pansy's hard hot cock press against my cheek and then I feel my head being manipulated so that her substantial phallus is gradually forced into my helpless mouth. And at the same time as this dreadful humiliation is being visited on me, so exactly the same fate is being visited on poor Pansy. We are to be hogtied together, hooded and forced to spend the night sucking on each other's permanently erect sissy cocks.

I feel my own cock press against the roof of Pansy's mouth and make a strange squeal of despair into my own widened cock-filled mouth. Then there is an odd stillness and I know that our wicked captors have left us to our awfully kinky fates. And I know that poor pretty Myriam will not be freed from her dreadfully uncomfortable 'viewing position' for the rest of the night, and that the belt secured so tightly around her waist and between her legs holds two large vibrators, one lodged in her sex, one forced deep into her arse, and that both are now buzzing furiously and she is screaming her agony and ecstasy into the fat ball gag without any hope of release for at least the next eight hours.

And as we all writhe furiously and helplessly, the victim of the senior sissy maids' dark jealous plotting, we learn something fundamental about the Bigger Picture, something that the Mistresses, the Masters and the other sissies will never admit to: at the heart of its intricate history of desire is the frailty of human need and the hunger for power through aggression; that the society of the Bigger Picture painted so carefully in the startling *Visions of the Future* video, is little more than a picture of another form of totalitarian state, a dictatorship of women, a sado-state rather than a Femocracy. And in this way, what Lady Ashcroft and Mistress Helen and the illustrious Eleanor Groves plan is just a variation on the classic theme of the human will to power. Yet to me, even in my state of ultimate torment, this is merely the way of things, and the society offered by the Bigger Picture clearly has many advances over the various patriarchal dictatorships (and so-called democracies) that have dominated world history for over a millennium. And then there is my own deeply masochistic sissy desire. Although, even in the heat of the strongest need, I can contemplate political philosophy in a bizarrely abstract way, there is no escaping (mentally and physically) the overwhelming erotic truth of my own sexual drives, my own massive masochism. And this is demonstrated so very clearly by the helpless pleasure I am now finding in this latest torment. As I suck on Pansy's cock, and as she sucks on mine, and as we work each other towards the first of many explosive orgasms, I realise there is a profound truth at the heart of the Bigger Picture that lurks in all fascist ideologies: the love of submission, the need to surrender your very desire to live to the Bigger Picture.

6

Discovery

Despite the challenges posed by the mistresses and their other lovely slaves, the rest of the two weeks of adaptation are filled with pleasure, excitement and revelation.

As we are trained to adapt to our glorious new forms, as each day brings us closer to the true nature of she-male femininity, my emergence as a figure of note within the spectacular conspiracy of the Bigger Picture continues.

We are less than a week away from the Annual Bigger Picture Fundraising Ball. Then the spectacular manor house will be returned to one of its key historic functions: the hosting of major social events. At the Ball, the slaves will serve not only the mistresses and masters of the SMC, but the increasing army of wealthy influential female supporters of the Bigger Picture. Here they will hear a keynote speech from Ms Eleanor Groves, the ex-First Lady of the United States of America, a controversial figure following her very public divorce from the President, and also a rumoured presidential candidate in four years' time.

In her speech, Ms Groves will outline the remarkable progress that has been made and plans for the next year, the most crucial year so far for the Bigger Picture.

I have been privy to much of the planning for the event, thanks to my selection, along with Christina, as a joint secretary to the Bigger Picture Strategy Committee, a group of the key mistresses: Lady Ashcroft (in the Chair), Mistress Helen, Mistress Anne, Ms Blakemore, together with a number of key figures associated with the Bigger Picture outside of the UK – Celine Cherisse (an American business-woman), Sophie Berri (a famous French intellectual who has held a number of important positions in the French Government) and, most impressively, the divine Ms Groves.

The Committee has previously been serviced by Christina alone, who was a senior administrative manager in her male life, and possesses many of the skills required to make the committee function at an operational level. I have been brought along for another reason – the design of the new generation of Senso clothing. Christina accepts my presence at these meetings without comment. Indeed, as we approach the Ball and the Placements, her feelings of jealously towards me seem to have faded considerably.

When Ms Blakemore told me I had been selected for a new, much more responsible role, I was filled with a strange mixture of pride and fear, especially when the membership of the Committee was revealed. I was to meet Eleanor Groves, one of the most famous women on the planet. Yet by the time I am led down the ground floor corridor of the mansion house on the actual day of my first meeting, my sissy heart is thumping with a desperate terror and a terrible arousal.

To my astonishment and deep pleasure, we have been freed from our more overtly sissy maid attire and presented with what Ms Blakemore describes as 'office sissy' wear. In my case, this is a very tight white

Senso nylon sweater which extenuates my generous and perfectly curved bosom to perfection, a black Senso rubber micro-mini that barely covers the tops of my black Senso nylon-sheathed thighs, and stiletto-heeled court shoes of jet-black patent leather. My hair is bound in a tight bun, with the standard rose-shaped diamond clasp. My lips are painted blood red, with a hint of pink rouge on my cheeks. I feel fantastic. I take small expertly feminine steps. I feel my buttocks wobble and my breasts bounce. The vibrator buzzes at a low but deeply teasing level, and I walk confidently beside the gorgeous Christina.

Christina is dressed in a very tight silver blouse made from Senso satin, a grey pinstriped micro-mini cut from expensive Italian cloth, silver-grey Senso nylon tights, and exactly the same court shoes as myself. She looks utterly stunning, especially with her hair styled loose thick and long, and with her lips painted a hot pink.

Christina knocks on the door to the Committee room and the familiar sharp voice of Mistress Helen snaps 'Enter!' I feel my pounding heart slip into my mouth and follow Christina into the room.

A large circular table dominates the room. Around it sit the most senior women of the Bigger Picture. Christina and I perform our deepest most submissive curtsies and face our divine mistresses.

Our eyes fall with helpless fascination onto the form of Eleanor Groves. I find it hard to believe I am standing only a few feet from the woman who was the First Lady of the United States for eight years.

She rises from her seat as we rise from our curtsies. 'Introduce us, Helen.'

Her soft precise American voice fills the room without even trying; the voice of profound and absolute authority. Helen smiles and guides her towards us, a strange, almost maternal pride in her large dark-brown eyes.

Ms Groves is dressed in a splendidly elegant and highly fashionable two-piece suit of a creamy yellow silk. Underneath the pearl-buttoned jacket is a high-necked white silk blouse. The skirt falls just above her knees to reveal long shapely legs sealed in white silk hose. Her shoes are white silk-lined, five-inch stiletto-heeled pumps.

At fifty, she looks barely forty. Her blonde hair is cut very short, and her striking pale-blue eyes regard us with a gaze trained in the art of objective observation. I avoid this unnervingly frank look and consider her splendid almost voluptuous figure, re-membering how the press had initially worshipped this woman as a form of sex siren. Indeed, during almost the entire period of her husband's presidency, she remained, for whatever reason, more popular than him. And looking at her now, it is easy to see why.

'This is, as you know, Christina,' Helen says, inspiring the lovely Christina to perform an even deeper knicker-flashing curtsey.

Ms Groves smiles gently. 'Yes, I remember her well. The first born.'

Christina swoons with a very feminine admiration and blushes furiously at these teasing words.

'And this is Shelly.'

Ms Groves turns her stunning gaze directly upon me and I feel close to losing consciousness. A soft cloud of rose petal perfume suddenly torments my nostrils and, as I breathe in her beautiful aroma, I perform my own deep and utterly submissive curtsey.

'Shelly,' Ms Groves whispers. 'Your latest creation. She's gorgeous, Helen. Utterly gorgeous.'

Now it is my turn to blush. I press my knees together and sway on the high, high heels. I feel my chest rise and fall with a helpless sissy desperation. I am complete as never before. I am in a state of almost transcendent bliss.

'Bring her to me later on.'

Mistress Helen smiles and nods and I look at her in amazement.

'You should be deeply honoured, Shelly.'

I nod and curtsey my startled gratitude. I am to serve Eleanor Groves in the privacy of her own apartments.

I am made to sit next to Ms Groves, while Christina sits by Mistress Helen. The two main items on the agenda are the introduction of my Senso designs into the 'fashion chain' and the upcoming annual fundraising Ball. However, Mistress Anne almost immediately insists that a third item be discussed, an item that sends a cold shiver of pure fear down my sissy spine.

'I really think we should talk again about the issue of TSC.'

Mistresses Celine and Sophie nod their agreement and Helen mumbles a slight 'Yes, it's time we decided exactly what the position is on this.'

Lady Ashcroft smiles wearily. 'I thought we had agreed what the position was.'

'No. We argued and then walked away from a decision.'

Mistress Anne's voice is filled with a typically unforgiving hardness and Lady Ashcroft visibly flinches at the redhead's abrasive tone.

'We'll discuss it under any other business. Until then, I suggest we stick to the agenda.'

And so TSC is left for later and we begin a discussion about the distribution of Senso.

It quickly becomes apparent that sole responsibility for the introduction of the Senso fabric in Northern

America will rest with Celine Cherisse, while in Europe, this role will be undertaken by Sophie Berri.

Like Ms Blakemore, Mistress Celine is a striking black American. However, she is younger and leaner than the wondrous Academy matron, and is dressed in a black silk suit with no blouse, and stiletto-heeled black patent leather court shoes. Her black hair is cut short and worn in a natural 'Afro' style. She has a powerful frame, and is an ex-national and Olympic judo champion. She has a cool precise and very businesslike manner. There is none of the humour or generosity of spirit that makes Ms Blakemore such an extraordinary mistress. Yet I have been led to believe that the two women are more than close friends.

Sophie Berri is also a cool hard-eyed beauty. She is dressed in a below-knee-length tweed skirt, seamed black silk stockings, modestly heeled black leather court shoes and a semi-transparent cream silk blouse. Her thick abundant jet-black hair is held in a loose bun by a black wooden hair pin. Her eyes are a dark blue, her lips a gleaming strawberry red. She has a very firm and surprisingly buxom figure. She wears grey steel-framed spectacles, with harsh rectangular frames and has the air of a Left Bank intellectual. Yet, despite the fact that she is one of France's most famous philosophers, she is also Chief Executive of a fashion house inherited from her mother, and an ardent supporter of the Bigger Picture.

So these are the beautiful powerful and senior members of the Bigger Picture, a group overseen by the regal figure of Lady Emily Ashcroft, whose own ice-blue eyes are now drinking up my form with dark gulping looks of sadistic desire.

'Utterly splendid,' she whispers.

I blush before this stunningly gorgeous aristocrat.

'You are the model we will use to change the world.'

And for the next two hours the group begin to plot exactly how this takeover will be managed. Christina takes detailed notes of the discussions and I, perhaps strangely, have little to do, other than to serve the tea when it is delivered by Annette and guide the mistresses through a book of my latest design drawings put together by Ms Blakemore. However, I am far from bored: the detailed discussions regarding the preparations for the Ball and the 'roll out' of Senso are utterly fascinating. I am also constantly aware of the closeness of the beautiful Ms Groves, both through her obvious magnetic presence and also by the fact that, throughout the meeting, she caresses my nylon-sheathed inner thigh with a long warm hand. The pleasure this produces is considerable, and I find it difficult not to release a loud moan of embarrassing confession. However, somehow, I find the resilience to endure in relative silence and to concentrate on the discussions.

Eventually, the discussions on Senso and the Ball end and we reach the terrifying 'any other business'. A renewed quiver of fear passes over my elegantly sissified form as I contemplate TSC, or 'Total Sex Change'. At the moment, this is only a punishment for the naughtiest of sissies – those who foolishly break the fundamental rule denying absolutely sexual congress with a female. But within the Bigger Picture, this is not a view shared by all. Indeed, there is a school of thought that argues using male desire to control the sissy once full sissification has been achieved is flawed. This view, held by a minority group who have been christened 'the Radicals', argues for total sex change once the point of complete transformation has been reached. The phallus, the Radicals argue, is a tool of oppression, and a Femocracy that allows its survival will inevitably be destroyed. True control can only be ensured by a policy of systematic and full sex change.

I listen in horror as Mistress Anne argues for a full and proper discussion of TSC. She wishes it to be used, at the very least, as a back-up policy in the event of organised male rebellion. To my surprise, she is supported by Mistress Helen, together with Mistresses Celine and Sophie. Momentarily my eyes meet Mistress Anne's and I behold a terrible hatred of the male sex, a hatred that informs her dark and deeply sadistic imagination.

Despite the support of Helen, Lady Ashcroft is reluctant to renew a discussion that has clearly been had on more than one occasion. She is known to be a firm supporter of the 'Moderate Majority' and a key force in controlling the Radicals. I have noticed her bumpy relationship with Mistress Anne on more than one occasion, but never before have I seen evidence of a tension between Helen and the gorgeous mature aristocrat. Indeed, it is clear that Lady Ashcroft is surprised by Mistress Helen's support of Mistress Anne.

Luckily, the discussion dries up very quickly. Lady Ashcroft's authority is supreme in the committee and it also becomes clear that Ms Groves, who appears bored by the tension created by the discussion, is firmly on the moderate side.

'Please, ladies. We've had this tedious argument on too many occasions. Let's just agree to disagree and pursue the strategy we've approved. If we don't, we'll lose too much support outside.'

Her wise words help bring the meeting to an end, although Mistress Anne, clearly very annoyed, makes it very clear this is far from the end of the matter.

By now I am in a state of quite unbearable arousal and, as Christina and I totter sweetly from the room, Ms Groves takes me to one side.

'I look forward to meeting you again this evening, Shelly.'

I curtsey and smile modestly. I feel her hand run across my tightly skirted bottom and a quiver of utter delight pulses through my body.

Her stunning ice-blue gaze stays with me for the rest of the day. In her eyes I see a new level of power, a terrible familiarity with absolute control that burrows deep down into my soul and establishes an erotic and very firm anchor.

After the meeting, Christina returns me to the room I nominally share with Pansy. I fear some kinky punishment born out of a renewed jealously, but once the door to the large oval bedroom is closed, she embraces me and plants a long hot quite desperate kiss on my soft strawberry lips.

I totter backwards on my heels and grab her tightly to maintain my balance and also to communicate a shared sexual need. She grasps my tightly skirted bottom. I gasp as her hands slip under the skirt and she sinks her nails into my panties and hose. There is sadistic intent and angry passion. I respond by begging her to hurt me.

She pushes me onto the bed.

'Mistress Eleanor is a demon,' she whispers, her voice thick with sex need.

I stare up at her, my legs akimbo, my skirt pulled up over my thighs, exposing my panties. My bosom heaves with helpless fury and I feel my tightly secured cock strain painfully against its ever-present layers of cruel and deeply exciting restraint.

'Tonight you will suffer, my sweet.'

My eyes betray the erotic impact of her teasing words.

'And Taylor will help her.'

Arousal fades, quickly replaced by fear. Christina smiles and I feel my heart skip a beat.

'I'm sure she'll want something really imaginative and bizarre, and I'm pretty sure Pansy will be involved.'

My look of concern deepens and she laughs.

'Oh, Shelly – you are such a terrible tease! You know you'll love every second of it!'

I ask her if she has serviced Mistress Eleanor.

Her smile fades and she nods. 'Yes, on one or two occasions. She is a very special mistress, Shelly. You will never forget tonight.'

She then leans down and very slowly slips the sweater over my head. With a loving gentleness, she then unhooks my brassiere and lets my wondrous breasts loose from their teasing Senso silk prison. I cry out with a shocking and immediate physical pleasure as her lips brush against my long hard ultra-sensitive nipples. Then she is sucking hungrily on my left breast and I am screaming helpless love.

As we are both tightly restrained, oral pleasuring is about as far as this heated session can go; but given the heightened feeling built into our marvellous chests, this is enough to produce a mind-bending pleasure.

Eventually, Christina pulls herself off me and tidies her clothing before leaving, her face flushed with frustrated desire, her chest heaving with a terribly erotic desperation. I drag myself up from the bed and wonder at the divine sex madness that fills every inch of this glorious she-male academy.

Soon after Christina's departure, Annette enters the room and helps me prepare for my afternoon movement and dance class with Mistress Donna. She notices my obvious dishevelment and teases me as I am helped out of my 'office sissy' attire and into a pair of opaque white nylon tights, a matching leotard and a pair of five-inch-high stiletto-heeled court shoes. My hair is combed up into a tighter bun and then pinned into position with the classic SMC rose-shaped clasp.

The tight white nylon very provocatively reveals the full erect length of my tightly restrained cock, and Annette, who has sampled its delights on more than one occasion, is obviously impressed.

'A beautiful cock and a beautiful pair of tits. The best of both worlds, without a doubt.'

Her hand runs over its restrained form and I release a high-pitched moan of pained pleasure.

'Mistress Eleanor will have plenty of fun with this tonight, my sexy little petal.'

I look at her and remember the intimacy of our sufferings during the perverse projection of *Vision of the Future*. There is nothing we can hide from each other now, and in the look that passes between us, I see both a teasing cruelty and a very definite warning. In Christina's voice there had also been a hidden concern. Tonight will be a very real and harsh challenge, perhaps the final test before my entry into the more prolonged test of the Placements.

Annette then ties my hands behind my back and uses a fat white rubber ball gag to silence any further speculation on my part.

A collar and leash are attached to my neck. This bizarre ritual of bondage is unusual for a trip to Mistress Donna's dance studio, but I accept bondage like I accept food and drink: with an instinctual gratitude.

Before we leave, Annette cannot resist spending a few minutes teasing my nylon-sheathed breasts with her hands, leaving me once again squealing and wiggling. She laughs as I struggle and a helpless anger fills my carefully constructed doe eyes. Then anger fades and I am, once again, lost in an addictive pleasure.

Eventually, I am led from the room and out into the corridor that leads to the dance studio. I wonder why Mistress Donna, always the gentlest and the kindest of the mistresses of the SMC, has deemed it necessary for me to so tightly secured. Then I enter the studio and realise it is not Mistress Donna who has ordered my latest ordeal by bondage; for standing in the centre of the room is Mistress Anne and Celine Cherisse. And standing next to them is Myriam.

My eyes widen with surprise, especially given that the two mistresses are dressed in costumes that indicate they have more than movement training in mind. Mistress Anne is attired in a black latex cat suit, a jet second skin that reveals every detail of her impressively shapely form. This amazing costume is complemented by a pair of near-thigh-length black leather boots with fierce seven-inch heels and a thick leather belt strapped tightly around her slender waist from which hangs an ivory-handled riding crop. Black latex rubber gloves are stretched across her hands, and a choker of black velvet with a bloody ruby centrepiece is wrapped tightly around her slender pale neck.

Yet it is not this costume in particular that inspires shock and surprise. It is what is positioned between her legs; for rising out of the crotch area of the cat suit is a large strap-on dildo, a shiny black rubber cock with layers of glistening ridges. I stare at this and moan with an amazed fear into my fat ball gag.

Mistress Celine wears a red leather satin-panelled basque, black nylon stockings held in place by long black silk and elastic suspenders, and five-inch stiletto-heeled ankle boots. Added to this are a pair of elbow-length black leather gloves. She too is wearing a thick black leather belt, attached to which is a leather paddle and a vibrator control box. And between her legs is her own strap-on dildo, almost exactly the same as the one between Mistress Anne's legs, but this one coloured a bloody red.

I look at the two women in a state of absolute shock and Annette tugs violently on the leash. I totter forward, my breasts bouncing helplessly. Suddenly, I feel terribly exposed. Then I look over at Myriam and feel a sickening fear grip my heart.

The petite French beauty is clad in a black rubber body glove, a single sheath of skin-tight Senso rubber that runs from her feet up her neck and, like Mistress Anne's cat suit, reveals every luscious contour of her perfect form. A thick strip of black masking tape holds a fat gag in place and her tear-filled eyes are wild with a terrible need, betraying the fact that vibrators are busily tormenting her arse and pussy.

At first, I think she is balancing on her own, yet close inspection reveals that she is positioned on a circular metal platform and secured by means of more masking tape to a thick silver pole that runs parallel to her tightly cocooned form.

The point of this strange bondage and humiliation escapes me, yet it's very pointlessness warns me of the cruelty waiting here, a fact made even more apparent by the look of sadistic arousal that the two mistresses share.

'We thought you would appreciate a little variation on your deportment training this afternoon, Shelly,' Mistress Anne whispers, her voice a terrible erotic tease.

I am brought before the two women and then made to kneel down before them, my face only inches from Mistress Celine's giant terrifying black rubber cock. The sudden brutality in Annette's movements betrays her own role in this cruel conspiracy. Her earlier kindness was merely a front. Now, she intends to have her revenge against me.

'Wait in the corner,' Mistress Celine snaps at her. 'Facing the wall, hands behind your back. We will deal with you in due course.'

A look of sudden fear and betrayal fills Annette's beautiful green eyes.

'What?' Mistress Celine snaps. 'You thought this was all we required of you . . . bringing the sissy to us? No, my sweet flower, you'll also entertain us.'

Annette curtsies deeply and minces over to the corner, tears of terror already beginning to trickle down her elegant marble cheeks.

'Perhaps we should begin with a little softening up,' Mistress Celine continues, taking the vibrator controller from her belt and pointing it down at my shaking ultra-sissified form.

She turns the dial on the control and within seconds the low level buzzing that is my arse's almost constant companion begins to increase in ferocity. I moan deep into my mouth-stretching gag and soon realise that I am to be very sorely tested by these two experienced and deeply perverted mistresses, for within less than a minute, the vibrator is running at a pitch I have never previously experienced. I squeal helplessly with a terrified pleasure as the vibrator seems to bore deep inside me. A high-pitched electric humming fills the room and I feel the cheeks of my backside begin to wobble uncontrollably. The pleasure imparted by this new level of vibrational intensity is soon replaced by a jaw shuddering discomfort. Mistress Anne demands that I lean forward so that my wobbling buttocks are stretched taut against the fabric of the leotard. As I do so, the two women position themselves so that they have a perfect view of this bizarre display.

My squeals of genuine discomfort increase and I feel the vibration in my buttocks begin to travel up my body. The laughter of the two beautiful and quite wicked mistresses fills the room. Then, the vibration washes over my breasts and I beg for release from this terrible humiliation. However, there will be no mercy this afternoon; and as soon Mistress Anne notices my helplessly wobbling breasts, she orders me to sit back up on my knees. As I do so, I feel the terrible power the vibrations have over my so intricately and expertly feminised body, and tears of utter degradation spill from my eyes as my breasts bounce before the mistresses like two cats trapped inside tight rubber sacks.

They watch this cruel spectacle for maybe ten minutes, teasing me with dark mocking compliments. I try my hardest not to feel anger, to understand the nature of my absolute and eternal submission, to see this as a further test of my true sissy being. But in their eyes I see only a stark unforgiving contempt. Their pleasure is my pain – a pure, simple sadism.

Eventually, Mistress Celine turns the vibrator down to a level that is nearly tolerable. By the time I am unceremoniously pulled to my feet, my breasts feel quite numb and my anus feels a foot wide. Yet even this is only the beginning of my suffering.

As I struggle to find my balance in the high heels, I instinctively take in the surroundings, and almost immediately I begin to recognise things have changed.

Although the basic layout of the studio is as it always has been, a number of interesting and worrying additions have been made to the furnishings. For a start, there is a large, silver-coloured exercise bike a few feet from the mistresses. Also, there is a long leather-covered exercise bench. Beyond the bench is a gymnastic horse. My eyes widen in astonishment as I notice that instead of handles, the horse has three hard rubber phalli rising out of its main body – one on its own and two positioned very closely together.

The mistresses laugh at my look of fearful incredulity.

'This afternoon, we're going to concentrate on sissy gymnastics,' Mistress Anne teases.

'Yes. We've got off to a good start with the individual floor exercises,' Mistress Celine adds. 'Now it's time to move on to the team event.'

I am led across the room to the exercise bike, and as we move closer to it, I notice that it too has been erotically customised. On the face of it, the bike is a typical exercise machine – except for one crucial and highly kinky addition: a single hot-pink hard rubber phallus that rises out of the centre of its black leather seat.

Mistress Celine orders me to bend forward and I feel her hands slip between my legs. There is a strange tearing sound, which I recognise as a Velcro strip being pulled free, and then I feel the vibrator being slowly eased out of my arse. I squeal with helpless pleasure and receive a very hard smack to my backside. I try to remain silent and still as the rest of the wicked intruder is pulled from my back passage.

And once it is free, I know that things can only get worse.

'Annette – come here!'

The terrified sissy turns from the wall, performs a brief bob-curtsey and then rushes over to assist the mistresses in any way they command. As it turns out, her role is relatively simple: to help Mistress Celine pick me up and place me onto the exercise bike, so that my poor tormented back passage is positioned directly over the long hard phallus. Then I am released. The tip of the phallus quickly slips inside my arse, and within a few terribly arousing and terrifying seconds, I am completely impaled on this new tool of dark intrusion.

I squeal with fear and a terrible all-pervasive pleasure. I feel as if I am being split in two, rent asunder by the force of the phallus and the terrible white-hot pleasure it brings.

And no sooner am I locked so intimately and tightly onto the exercise bike than Annette is tying my bound wrists to a small metal eye positioned at the rear of the bike with a white nylon stocking. I feel my body pulled backward and whimper with helpless sissy fear. Yet even as I am being pulled one way, Mistress Anne is arranging for me to be pulled the other in a most uncomfortable and disturbing manner. I look on with a sense of increasingly eroticised doom as she extracts a pair of golden nipple clamps from a pocket built into the side of the bike. Her eyes sparkling with a cruel arousal, she holds the clamps inches from my tormented face.

'I know you've felt the bite of the clamps before, mon ange; but I suspect the little torment I have in mind will be a slightly more refreshing experience.'

I shake my head angrily and squeal loudly into the fat white rubber gag. Mistress Anne laughs and very slowly, with a teasing sadism, slips the brutal teeth of the first clamp over my nylon sheathed and very stiff left nipple. As it bites into me, I unleash a somewhat melodramatic scream that attempts, in its pathetic way, to hide the dark pleasure this elegant and vicious torture inspires.

The second clamp is attached and my pleasure is doubled; then it is trebled for, as soon as the clamps are in place, Mistress Sophie takes the golden chain leash attached to each clamp and pulls it forward. There is a terrible and immediate counter-pressure.

This is increased as the leash is slipped through a small metal hook fitted to the handlebars of the exercise bike.

Thus I am held fast in counter-pointed bondage. My high-heeled feet are then slipped onto the pedals of the exercise bike and secured in place with Velcro strapping.

Mistress Anne steps back and admires her ultra-kinky handiwork. At the same time, Mistress Celine and Annette move the platform containing the im-mobilised and utterly gorgeous Myriam so that she is directly facing my perversely tethered form.

Mistress Anne moves closer to Myriam and says something to her in a low aroused whisper. Myriam's beautiful brown eyes widen in horror and she begins to struggle in the unyielding and exciting rubber body glove. I stare at her with a helpless fascination. I watch her tightly rubberised breasts wobble angrily and then notice an electrical wire running from between her legs and down onto the metal surface of the platform, where it is fitted to a small three-pronged plug.

'At the heart of movement is energy,' Mistress Celine teases, as Mistress Anne takes up the plug and fits it into a matching socket set into the front of the exercise bike. 'And all energy is ultimately desire – the desire for movement.'

I ponder these opaque words with some difficulty, as I am aware of a growing heat in my back passage – the phallus is beginning to warm up.

'I suggest you start pedalling, Shelly,' the gorgeous black beauty says, her dark eyes filled with a cruel amusement. 'There is an electrical heating element built into the core of the phallus, and it will soon become painfully hot. By pedalling you will open a diversion circuit and allow electricity to flow into another circuit that runs through Myriam's body glove. This will effectively turn off the heating element and turn on the massage sensors in the suit and our pretty little French pet.'

I squeal and begin to pedal desperately. Almost immediately, the phallus begins to cool. Yet, at the same time, poor Myriam begins to moan violently into her thick tape gag and struggle pointlessly against her utterly unyielding bondage. I watch her large perfectly formed breasts bounce angrily and realise that, thanks to my own panic-inspired efforts, she is undergoing a terrible sexual torture.

'The body glove is pure Senso rubber,' Mistress Celine explains. 'It is also fitted with a number of very powerful stimulation devices, positioned against all the key female erogenous zones. Also, as I am sure you have noticed, she is fitted with arse and cunt vibrators. These have been buzzing away merrily for the last hour or so, but are now positively exploding inside her. While this is rather exciting for a few minutes, I am afraid it will become quite unbearable for anything above this short period. However, if you stop, I am afraid the pain will be considerable, and thanks to your bondage, quite inescapable. So, it is your pain against hers, my pretty little sissy whore.'

I look at Mistress Celine in absolute astonishment: what have I, or Myriam, done to deserve this awful sadistic punishment?

'You have done nothing,' she says, her telepathy disturbing and arousing. 'It is not a question of punishment, Shelly. It is a question of entertainment.'

And so I pedal on desperately, my eyes wide with fear and anger, but also with a helpless arousal. My thighs work with a fearful determination, my breasts tug painfully against the brutal clamps and I feel the phallus sink deeper inside me. Yes, once again, the wicked mistresses of the Bigger Picture are demonstrating painful inescapable truths. As I watch the beautiful French blonde wiggle, bounce and squeal, as I watch tears of utter horror and dreadful sexual discomfort pour from her honey-brown eyes, I cannot escape my own sadistic pleasure: I am pedalling not just to escape pain, but also to induce it. And when my eyes meet Myriam's, I see something quite amazing: a recognition of my pleasure and an acceptance of it; I see the look she gave me as Christina and Annette took their cruel revenge on myself and pretty, dainty Pansy – a look of deep attraction; a look that holds a deadly consequence for me if I am foolish enough to return it. But I do return it. Yes, I am interested in her in a way that totally contradicts all the rules and regulations of the Sissy Maids Company and the philosophy and principles of the Bigger Picture.

As the bizarre spectacle of our deeply ambivalent torment unfolds, I cannot help but notice that the two beautiful merciless mistresses have now focused their attentions on Annette. The gorgeous red-headed sissy has been taken to the side of the studio and is now being forced to strip. Tears of divine humiliation flood from her pretty green eyes as she slips reluctantly out of her lovely maid's attire, and very soon she is standing in a sexy pile of satin, silk and nylon, stripped down to a splendidly intricate black silk teddy, black silk stockings held in place by red silk-lined garters, and her very high open-toed black leather mules.

She looks stunning, and blushes furiously as the two mistresses tease her about one rather striking aspect of the sexy and very tight silk teddy – the fact that the crotch section is essentially a semi-transparent silken flap that can be unbuttoned (there is a row of neat tiny pearl buttons) to enable access to Annette's large hard tightly restrained sex.

As Mistress Anne proceeds to bind poor Annette's long bronzed arms behind her back at the wrists and elbows with white rubber-coated cording, Mistress Celine teasingly unbuttons the flap and then pulls the sissy's impressive cock out with her rubber-gloved hands.

Annette squeals with frightened pleasure and wiggles her pretty, silk-sheathed bottom. Mistress Anne delivers three very hard slaps to this near perfect behind and a look of intense masochistic arousal fills Annette's striking emerald eyes.

Mistress Celine fondles the sissy's sex, only adding to the ballet of helpless arousal. The sissy's cock is huge, sealed tightly in shining black latex rubber. It is a work of dark sissy art, and at the base of the scrotum hangs a golden ring, a ring to which Mistress Celine now attaches a silver leash.

Poor Annette watches this fiendish intervention with terror-streaked eyes and a moan of desperate need slips from her strawberry lips.

Mistress Celine then tugs on the leash and the sissy releases a cry of pain and pleasure.

'Gag her,' she orders Mistress Anne.

The older French beauty smiles and nods. She pulls from a small side pocket in her startling cat suit a pair of white silk panties.

'A little present from Myriam,' she whispers. 'Taken off her just over an hour ago.'

Mistress Anne steps forward and unceremoniously stuffs the panty gag into Annette's sweet sissy mouth. As she does this, Mistress Celine produces a thick roll of black masking tape. Annette's eyes widen with a very obvious sexual pleasure as the pungent panties are forced home, and she whimpers with a delightful sissy pleasure as Celine proceeds to tape them firmly in place.

The gorgeous red-headed sissy is then led by the leash towards the leather-backed training bench. Her perfect buttocks wobble uncontrollably and her significant perfectly sculpted bosom bounces with a gloriously erotic enthusiasm. Despite her fear, she is clearly very excited, especially since the gagging.

By this point, my desperate peddling is becoming a significant challenge. My legs are heavy with effort; huge pools of sweat have gathered under my arms and tormented breasts. My face is soaked in a film of hot pungent sweat. My breathing has become extremely laboured and there is no doubt that I am beginning to cross the border between consciousness and unconsciousness.

Poor beautiful Myriam is now also at the very edge of breaking, her eyes filled with a pleasure that has smashed through its own barrier into a realm of real and terrible pain; yet, even in the heart of this bizarre discomfort, her gaze is still filled with a hunger for me, an obvious unyielding need which is both mystifying and truly amazing.

I feel my tired legs slow and the phallus heats up. I squeal for help, a useless demand. My mistresses are far too preoccupied with Annette's fate to take any notice of my sufferings.

They have made the gorgeous well endowed redhead stand directly in front of the leather-covered gymnastic bar. Then she is ordered to lean over it, so that her stomach is resting on the bar, her large breasts and head are draped over one side and her bottom is hauled up into the air by the weight of her upper body. Then the leash attached to the scrotum ring is removed and the joined end of the other leash that runs from the two brutal nipple clamps is attached to the ring. This has the effect of creating a fiendish and very painful counterbalance leaving her swaying over the bar. Her arms are then pulled out at exact right angles to her body, so that they run along the length of the bar. They are then strapped tightly into position at the wrists and elbows and poor Annette is immobilised and exposed. This exposure is made so much worse when Mistress Anne steps forward and begins to unbutton a second flap that covers the space between Annette's exquisitely formed buttocks.

Once the flap is pulled aside, a perfect few of the sissy's exposed arsehole is provided, a view made much better by the fact that her bottom is now directly beneath one of the powerful white strip lights that illuminate the studio. The pink tip of her vibrator is clearly visible – indicating a depth of intrusion into the anus that excites my own masochistic cravings, despite the increasing discomfort caused by the phallus inside me. I increase the volume of my well-gagged pleas for mercy and release, and still there is no response from the beautiful cruel and imperial mistresses.

Mistress Celine steps forward and carefully works the long hard vibrator out of poor Annette's well stretched and trained arse. A smile of sadistic amusement lights up her sharp-featured and still strangely girlish face. And as soon as the vibrator is pulled free, she steps back to give Mistress Anne access to this pretty sissy orifice.

There are no words exchanged, just a cold knowing glance between these expert and deeply perverse mistresses, and then Mistress Anne takes her dark unforgiving pleasure, plunging her phallic intruder deep into Annette's arse. The sissy unleashes a squeal of utter outrage and agony into her fat pungent panty gag, another melodramatic cry that inspires Mistress Celine to burst out laughing and remove the vicious-looking riding crop from her thick black leather belt.

Annette continues to buck and squeal as she is anally raped by an obviously very excited Mistress Anne.

'Ride 'em, Cowboy!' Mistress Celine shouts.

Anne then suddenly withdraws from her sissy prey and Mistress Celine steps forward to deliver five hard painful cuts of the crop to Annette's helplessly exposed behind. The sissy screams into her gag in agony, fighting uselessly against her kinky bonds. And the more she struggles, the more pain she imparts, thanks to the evil manner in which her clamped breasts have been attached to her scrotum!

Then it is Mistress Celine's turn to violate the gorgeous deeply tormented redhead. And as she does so, Mistress Anne turns to me, her wicked smile a warning of a truly mercilessly heart.

'Better let you cool down or you might explode,' she whispers, leaning forward and pulling the plug out of the exercise bike. She then flicks down a switch close to the plug and almost immediately the phallus begins to cool.

I look over at Myriam. The torments of the vibrators had begun to lessen as soon as I began to run out of energy, so she has now managed to recover an element of sanity. She looks at me and Mistress Anne through a film of sweat, her gag-packed cheeks crimson, her eyes wild with sex hunger, her body still vibrating erotically to the memory pulse of her sinister and brutal intruders.

Mistress Anne turns to face Myriam and whispers soft teasing words in French. Unlike their last conversation, Myriam responds with a moan of pleasure and a helpless nod.

'She likes you,' Anne says, turning back to me. 'A little more than she should. But you are rather lovely, my little sexy petal, so we must try and forgive Myriam her weakness. And, to be honest, she has suffered for her art this afternoon. So perhaps now it is time to give her a little reward.'

Mistress Celine has withdrawn from poor Annette, leaving the sexy sissy a simpering wreck of hopeless and eternal masochistic need. As her large, crystalline tears strike the rubber-matted floor of the studio, the two wickedly imaginative mistresses begin to free me from the deeply testing and perversely arousing exercise bike.

By the time I am lowered onto my weakened worn-out legs, I am at least half returned to normal consciousness. I feel my hard tightly imprisoned cock press into my stomach and I know I am still alive. Desire is the engine of everything, the machine that drives us through the chaotic jungle of life. And I, like all human beings, am merely its helpless agent.

As Mistress Celine helps me take a few tentative pained steps forward in the high-heeled shoes, Mistress Anne begins to remove the layers of thick black tape securing poor Myriam to the mobile pole.

As Annette continues to sob and whimper, I cannot help staring at her crimson striped backside with a sadistic pleasure.

'You enjoyed watching her suffer, didn't you?' Mistress Celine asks, her dark eyes filled with an amused curiosity.

I nod and her smile widens.

'Yes, of course you did. We all did. You are part of something beyond yourself, Shelly. Like we all are. A terrible, vital power. One or two of our sisterhood try to pretend this power is a perversion of men. But we know better. It is the power of the human being itself, my sexy sissy slut; the power to control, to manipulate and to destroy. Its tool is desire, its product is domination.'

Myriam, covered in sweat, her eyes wide with a fierce blinding arousal, is helped down from the platform by the gorgeous wicked Mistress Anne, who whispers sensually dark and deeply perverse French lullabies of cruelty and control.

Then a bizarre, even comic moment: Myriam is made to hop across the room to me, her large perfectly formed bosom bouncing uncontrollably, every inch of her buxom Gallic form exposed and extenuated by the tight black Senso rubber of the body glove – a sight that fills the eyes of the mistresses and myself with a helpless endless longing.

Myriam is in her late teens and a vision of ample loveliness; her ripeness, the fact of her perfect sexual timeliness, is at the core of her attraction. Yet this is framed by the naivety of her gaze, by the innocence of her desiring look. I know the women find her helpless naturalness, the total lack of reflection or cunning, another essential facet of her appeal. To overwhelm and control this innocence, to defile it with a fascist enthusiasm, is undoubtedly a vital part of the pleasure they take in torturing and humiliating her. And, strangely, I can sympathise with them while also envying her. At these moments, I am lost in a grey space between sadism and masochism, between utter submission and the bloody hunger for control. It is, perhaps, the natural space for me – the locus of absolute ambiguity.

'We have to finish off Annette and then prepare ourselves for an evening engagement,' Mistress Anne says, inspiring a moan of erotic terror from the tethered, prone she-male beauty. 'So, we thought you two should have an opportunity for a little relaxation.'

Mistress Celine takes the leash around my neck and leads me towards to the far wall of the studio. Mistress Anne taps Myriam on her rubber-sealed bottom with the crop and she hops rather absurdly after us.

By the wall, we discover a narrow cupboard door. Mistress Celine opens it to reveal a small closet, of the kind normally used to store brooms or ironing boards. As we stare fearfully into this dark space, Mistress Celine produces rolls of black masking tape again and I stare at Myriam with a sense of exquisite anticipation. She returns my gaze with a look of dizzying adoration. Her need is like a blow to the heart, a need that is also a terrible pain, the self-destructive essence of desire.

We are forced tightly together. Our large carefully moulded breasts are pressed together and my sex is forced up against the hot rubber-sealed space between her long sexy legs. She cries into her gag with a furious pleasure – a dream, made reality, a fantasy exploding through the fragile surface of the illusion of the real.

Our faces are only a few inches apart – the saliva-coated edge of the fat white rubber ball gag touches the tape sealing her soft full lips. Our eyes fill with visions of the other. Mistress Anne then begins to bind us together: pulling a length of tape from the thick roll but not tearing it free, she pastes the length against our slender feminine ankles and begins to wind it slowly, carefully and expertly up our hot tormented sexually enraged forms, a looping motion of utter enveloping – a joint and highly erotic mummification.

While Mistress Anne consumes us in soft sado-erotic tape, Mistress Celine prepares two black stockings, taking them from a drawer built into the wall by the closet. She pulls them taut and slowly runs them, one at a time, between her legs, so that they slip between the slender gap between the basque and her left thigh. A look of brief but very real arousal fills her emerald eyes. She then spreads the first stocking into a wide bowl and begins to lower it over Myriam's head.

The French beauty's attention is dragged from contemplation of my buxom sissy form and her eyes fill with fear. Mistress Celine smiles.

'You really are the perfect damsel in distress, Myriam,' she whispers, pulling the stocking tightly down over the sexy slave's lovely face as she squeals fearfully into her highly efficient gag.

Myriam's struggles are lessened by the fact that Mistress Anne's erotic mummification has now reached our waists and we are subsequently held very fast. As she wiggles and squeals she rubs helplessly against me, causing great arousal. Soon I am moaning with the pleasure of her inadvertent caress. And as the stocking is pulled tightly into place, as I find myself facing a new nylon-distorted Myriam, Myriam as a fetish doll girl toy, Mistress Celine begins to pull the second stocking over my head, just as Mistress Anne's fiendish mummification reaches just below our substantial breasts.

As I am plunged into a world of hazy sensual black nylon, the scent of Mistress Celine's cunt fills my nostrils. I whimper with a helpless sissy pleasure and feel myself pulled closer to the gorgeous rubberised figure of Myriam. As the tape progresses up over our chests and towards our necks, my sex is pushed even harder into the delicate space between her legs. She squeals with a dreadful frustration and I beg for release into my own inescapably cruel ball gag. And it is as the tape reaches our shoulders that a panting

162

highly aroused Mistress Anne finally ceases her intricate and ultra-kinky mummification.

Then, to our mutual horror, but surely not to our surprise, we are picked up by the two beautiful wicked dominants and placed inside the closet space, a space that only just accommodates our tightly sealed forms.

'Someone will come and dig you up . . . eventually,' Mistress Celine teases, as we squeal with fear and a dark dreadful sexual excitement.

The door to the closet is closed and we are plunged into an absolute darkness. Almost immediately, I can feel Myriam's heart racing furiously, driven by desire and terror. I try and comfort her, moaning softly into my gag. She quietens slightly and then moans back. I try to wiggle my body slightly so that my nipples flick against hers and my cock teases the taped edge of her own stuffed sex. And it is as I do this, and she moans her own desperate appreciation, that the vibrators begin to buzz once again, in my expertly stretched arse and in her sex and her own highly trained anus. And now our moans of fear turn into well-gagged cries of sudden and terrible pleasure. And soon we are both wiggling helplessly, a wiggling that becomes a deeply erotic ballet, that becomes a confession of powerful shared attraction.

Is this the nearest I will ever get to a woman? This evil teasing is yet another black expression of domination, an absolute demonstration of the control that is wielded over the two of us by our mistresses, by *all* the mistresses and masters of the Bigger Picture. Yet it is a control we desire without question, a control that is assured by our need for its brutal yet sensual embrace.

And as we struggle so intimately in total darkness, our gagged breathing and moans of pleasure the final communication of a growing feeling that moves beyond mere sexual attraction, we can also hear the women complete their terrible tormenting of poor lovely Annette. The sound of the crop, her gagged pleas for a mercy that will never come and is in fact not wanted, a further play rape, a descent into a cruel but mutually assured ecstasy – all provide the soundtrack to a profound communication between this gorgeous innocent French beauty and my helplessly sissified and deeply masochistic self, the discovery of something that is moving closer and closer towards a strange irresistible love.

7

An Evening with Mistress Eleanor

We are left tethered so tightly and sweetly together for maybe an hour, maybe longer. By the time we are extracted from the closet by Kathy and Christina, time has lost its meaning. The intimacy we have found in each other's sexy bodies in the red hot torment of a most intense and relentless restriction has left us both stunned and madly aroused. As the maids free us from this latest bondage ordeal, we moan with a deep, deep pleasure, actually begging to be left sealed tightly in the erotic darkness of the closet.

But then we are freed and I face Myriam through a film of boiling sex sweat and behold her form in desiring astonishment.

I stare at her perfect breasts with awe-filled sex-hungry eyes. She smiles slightly, happy to be before me, proud of her gorgeous ample form.

'You are to be cleaned and delivered to Mistress Eleanor,' Christina says to me, her voice filled with amusement and arousal.

I am hardly interested in her words, my attention kidnapped by Myriam's large perfectly formed breasts. Her long hard nipples beg to be teased by soft ruby-red lips. My desire to place soft sissy kisses upon them is almost overwhelming.

'You are to be sent to Mistress Helen for the evening,' Christina continues, addressing Myriam.

Suddenly Myriam's attention is diverted. Her eyes fill with a new sexual anticipation, a dark masochistic pleasure. I feel a pang of jealousy as I see that the prospect of spending the evening with the buxom fiendishly perverse Mistress Helen fills my gorgeous French angel with a dark pleasure.

Kathy then leads Myriam from the room. My eyes fix onto her broad hips and surprisingly large – but still perfectly proportioned – backside, its teasing wiggling a subtle goodbye.

Through all of this, both of us have remained gagged. I also remain collared and leashed, my arms tied tightly behind my back. Christina, dressed in her classically beautiful and wildly sexy Senior Housemaid's costume, takes up the leash and leads me from the room. I follow her down the corridor back to my room, just as I had followed Annette to the studio, my eyes pinned with helpless need to her long perfectly shaped black nylon-sheathed legs.

The bizarre adventure with the gorgeous Myriam has inspired new levels of powerful sexual stimulation, and the sense of frustration is now quite unbearable. I need relief from this boiling desire like a heroin addict craves a final fix. Desire is the weapon of choice for the Bigger Picture and, as it tortures my mind and body, I know it is the most powerful of all weapons. With it, this society of utterly unyielding and fiercely determined women will surely sweep all men aside; with it, the Femocracy will become a terrible wonderful reality.

Yet my desire – the desire for the lovely soft doe-eyed Myriam – is a strangely double-edged sword. For within the totalitarian framework of the Bigger Picture, it is illegal desire, a clear flawless heterosexual desire that seeks neither domination nor submission. It is a desire that I am familiar with and which my training has sought to destroy totally. It is my desire for my Aunt and, perhaps more importantly, my desire for the startling regal Justine. I am astonished and excited by it; I am also deeply concerned. After so many weeks of careful indoctrination in the sexual politics of the Bigger Picture, it seems that I am, despite the terrible fundamental pleasure I get from my feminised submission and my intricate sissy transformation, still a desiring male.

Eventually, I am returned to the room once shared with Pansy. As I look at the neatly made bed, I remember our eager exploratory love-making with a slight sadness. Now, more than ever, Pansy is surrendering to the desire programme demanded by the Bigger Picture. Her masochism is informed by a surprisingly powerful homosexuality, and she has willingly become Taylor's sexy little she toy.

I am undressed and Christina allows herself five cruel minutes teasing my rock-hard rubber- and steel-imprisoned cock, making sure not to remove the mouth-filling and now very uncomfortable gag.

She wallows in my sissy squeals of angry need, her eyes burning into mine. I fill my nostrils with her powerful rose perfume and beg her for forgiveness and release. Instead, she releases her hellish grip on my sex and guides me to the shower room. Here, under her watchful eyes, I am made to wash myself very thoroughly with scented sissy soap. My silky smooth body is, of course, a source of further arousal. Christina insists that I spend a number of deeply tortuous minutes soaping my ultra sensitive breasts, and I continue to squeal with a dark painful passion as this forced caress drives me quite mad.

Eventually, I am dragged in a state of semi-delirium from the shower and very carefully and intimately tried by the senior housemaid. As the thick soft scented pink towel is carefully guided over my sex toy form, I moan with pleasure. I feel the soft teasing silk of Christina's exquisite dress brushed against my so terribly sensitised form, the sheer electric nylon of her tights kiss my legs and thighs. My rubberised cock inadvertently brushes against the fluffy layers of frou-frou petticoating that maintain the ultra-short skirt of her maid's dress at a near 45-degree angle. Her silk-gloved hands traverse my tight helpless petite buttocks with a fiendish teasing intent and I squeal my angry appreciation. She laughs and promises me a sound spanking. I moan into the fat ball gag, begging her to carry out her erotic threat as quickly as possible.

By the time she returns me to the bedroom, I am mad for her, my mind a sex mush, my body a device to torture itself beyond the edge of sanity and into the black lands of the absolute id.

She grabs me by the hair and pulls me with her onto the bed. Within seconds I am held over her nylon-sheathed knees, my cock held tightly between her warm hosed thighs, and a rain of hard mocking blows are falling on my buttocks. I cry out a confession of intense pleasure into the ball gag and her own desperately excited breathing rings in my sissy ears.

After twelve hard merciless and utterly wonderful slaps, I am thrown off her knees and told to stand to attention before her with my hands behind my back.

My cheeks flushed, my substantial bosom rising and falling desperately, my cock rearing up before her like a black sex sword, I await my fate with an ecstatic trepidation.

Christina looks into my eyes and I see a burning dark passion. As the heat in my bottom turns from pain into a warm teasing pleasure, I know that my suffering will never end and neither will my desire for it.

'As much as I would like to put you through your paces, my sexy little minx, I am afraid Mistress Eleanor has demanded your presence by no later than 7.00 p.m.; so let's get you prepared.'

She rises from the bed and indulges herself with a last, teasing caress of my incarcerated cock. I moan and her smile lengthens into a grin of sadistic pleasure. Then the new dressing begins.

From the wardrobe, this strange, apparently bottomless wardrobe, this garden of fetishistic delights, she takes a pink Senso latex rubber leotard and sets it down on the bed. I look at it with aroused eyes. It is incredibly thin and slight, almost a piece of artificial skin. I feel my cock twitch at the thought of this slender highly erotic garment resting against and teasing my own skin.

The leotard is followed by a pair of pink Senso silk tights of a denier so fine it seems that what Christina is holding before me is carefully shaped pink mist. I moan with appreciative pleasure at the sight of this ultra-sexy hose and watch carefully as Christina then pulls a pair of pink patent leather ankle boots from a drawer at the bottom of the wardrobe. The boots have startling seven-inch stiletto heels with silver tips and a large glass rose has been positioned on the sharp point of each toe. Pink silk ribbon laces run through silver buckles, and a row of tiny bells are attached to the top of each ankle.

The boots are placed by the bed and then more kinky fetish wear is extracted from the wardrobe.

First, a striking pink Senso latex rubber hood, an extraordinary device with no mouth piece, but with two eye sockets, each covered by a fine film of transparent pink-tinted plastic. This is followed by a pair of pink Senso latex rubber fingerless mittens, a very wide thick pink leather belt complete with attached rubber shackles, and a strange pink Senso latex rubber sheath.

Before I am wrapped in this bizarre and exciting costume, I am led to the small dressing table just beyond the wardrobe and carefully made up. Since the Operation, there has been little need for any significant make-up, as my face has effectively been carefully tattooed to produce permanently cherry-red lips and flawless alabaster skin; and indeed, it is not my face that concerns the lovely senior housemaid. My naked body is covered in a thick mist of powerful musk perfume and my thick, now very long blonde hair is carefully brushed through and then bound in a tight bun with a pink elastic pom-pom band. I behold my reflection with a familiar fascination, even now startled by the power of my transformation into a beautiful sissy slave.

Then Christina takes up a large pink rouge stick and adds a further kinky touch. I squeal with a savage sexual pleasure as she proceeds to apply the stick to my nipples and also to a large area at the front of each large breast, creating two sexy pink targets.

Once so intimately rouged, I am led back to the bed and the next stage of this deeply perverse and awfully exciting dressing.

We begin with the tights, the beautiful ultra-fine silk tights. Christina orders me to sit on the bed and draw the delicate sensual hose up my legs. I obey without a second's hesitation, feeling my sex dig painfully into my stomach and my painted breasts

170

pull down against my ribs as I do so. The vibrator is pushed deeper into my arse and I release a well gagged moan of delight. My arousal is absolute; I am enslaved by myself, by the desires programmed and the desires extracted from the depths of my subconscious.

As I very carefully draw the tights up my legs, I experience a new level of fetishistic pleasure. This is a truly astonishing tactile torment, one which I accept with a gasp of deep and helpless gratitude.

'Yes,' Christina whispers, her own arousal very apparent in wide sex tortured eyes, 'they're really lovely. I wish I could wear them tonight.'

As I draw them up over my angry tightly imprisoned sex, I notice a small hole and soon realise this is to accommodate said member. As I stare down at this kinky addition, Christina steps forward and takes the edge of the tights and pulls it up snugly around my waist. As she does so, my cock falls against the hole and, almost of its own desperate volition, begins to force its way forward. Christina quickly slips her long blood-red-nailed fingers around the rubberised head and then pulls the whole organ through, quickly followed by the bulging testicles. I moan with a familiar outraged excitement, and watch, stunned, as she then proceeds to draw the pink rubber sheath over my already tightly sheathed sex!

To my surprise, the sheath is actually made of a far tougher harder rubber than the Senso latex. Indeed, it is more a plastic cover, with its own rigid unforgiving form, than a rubber sheath. It is pulled over my restrained sex and then secured in place against my lower stomach via adhesive tape that runs around its inner rim, leaving my rubberised testicles trapped beneath. It is now as if I have a huge metal cigar rising up from where my sex had been.

I moan with delight and surprise into the still firmly secured fat rubber ball gag. Christina then takes up the stunning pink rubber leotard and orders me to step into it. I obey without the slightest hesitation, and soon I am drawing this highly erotic article of fetish wear up my delicately hosed legs. As I pull it up over my thighs, Christina again steps forward to help with the challenges posed by my rampant sex organ. And it is only now that I see there is a small slit in the front of the leotard, and it is through this that the gorgeous highly aroused senior maid pulls my entombed sex. As she does so, I notice that there is hardly any feeling – the hard cover protects my sex from the stimulation of Christina's elegant expert hands; and as soon as I realise this, a sense of dreadful disappointment washes over me. Now I am to be denied feeling in the most erotically sensitive part of my body.

My cock pops out of the front of the leotard which is then pulled up over my gloriously ample breasts and then up over my shoulders.

The leotard is a startlingly arousing piece of dark Senso genius. It spreads over my buxom sissy form more like hot pink paint than a material, revealing every curve and sensual bump, including precisely detailed re-readings of my large firm breasts. I moan with a terrible deep pleasure into the ball gag and watch the sex light burn even brighter in Christina's gorgeous dark-brown eyes. There is a slight film of sex sweat on her pale chin and glistening erotic moisture on her full blood-red lips. Her own substantial chest rises and falls with the heightened beating of her sissy heart and she pushes her sheer nylon-sheathed thighs tightly together in order to push the vibrator permanently inhabiting her expertly trained arse even deeper into the sensual darkness of her most intimate region.

'God,' she whispers, her normally high-pitched voice lowered two octaves by the madness of a fierce and utterly unforgiving sexual arousal. 'Oh God.'

Then, with a slight shake of her head, she returns from the pit of all-consuming desire and attempts to continue with this highly exciting and ultra-kinky task.

After the leotard come the matching fingerless mittens. They are strikingly petite and, as they are applied, quickly and very effectively immobilise my hands. The sense of helplessness this immobilisation creates is quite wonderful and I whimper my masochistic pleasure, a pleasure that is given even greater force when Christina attaches the thick pink leather belt around my slender sissy waist and then slips my rubberised wrists into the tight rubber shackles, pinning my arms to my sides and leaving me deliciously exposed to her wicked and wildly perverse attentions.

Next comes the hood. Christina picks it up and holds it before my fascinated fear- and desire-filled eyes. I whimper pathetically into the ball gag and she smiles cruelly.

'You make such a lovely damsel in distress, Shelly. No wonder Mistress Eleanor is so keen to play with you tonight.'

She pulls the mask over the top of my head, slipping it carefully across the tight bun and then pulling it down over my face. The soft ultra-clinging fabric of the hood quickly consumes every inch of my face and I am plunged into a pungent rubber darkness from which I slowly emerge as the plastic covers set across each eye allow me a strange view of the outside world. The plastic covers are a light shade of pink, so suddenly the room beyond is seen through a sissy haze. I moan into the gag and I see Christina say something, but I can't hear her; indeed, it is quite impossible to hear anything through the hood – now I am deaf, dumb and my vision is reduced to a pink mist.

In this state of severe sensory deprivation, I am helped into the very high-heeled boots. Christina kneels down to tie the silken laces tightly in place. As she does so, I watch the short skirt of her pretty senior housemaid's dress rise up on a wave of delicate frou-frou petticoating and reveal the most luscious and shapely of thighs tightly sheathed in the softest sexiest black nylon. But this is a pink-tinted dress and these are pink-tinted black nylon tights.

Eventually, Christina climbs to her wondrously high-heeled feet and stands back to observe her highly kinky handiwork. I wiggle with pleasure as she drinks up my sexy tethered sheathed form. Her eyes widen with a fresh violent desire and I beg her through my utterly silencing gag for a kiss or a caress. She laughs at my sex suffering and delivers another very hard blow to my rubber and silk covered backside. As my arse vibrates with the sensual force of the blow, Christina produces a pink leather leash and teasingly fixes its metal eye buckle to the ring fixed to the base of my scrotum, which has been pulled through the slit in the leotard along with my tightly rubberised testicles. Then, taking up the leash, she guides me from the room.

As we mince into the corridor, I am aware of the bells brushing against my ankles. The surrealism of this latest humiliation is almost too much to endure: each ultra-high-heeled step I take is no doubt producing a sweet sissy tinkling, yet I am unable to hear it.

I am led by the leash down the long corridor that traverses the underground training chambers to the elevator. Eventually, with some hesitation, I totter inside the narrow metal cube, receiving another hard eroticised slap as punishment for my lack of enthusiasm. I watch the world through the distancing film of pink plastic and suddenly I am very much more aware of my body and its outrageously erotic form. I feel my large ultra-sensitive breasts bounce inside their tight rubber prison; I feel my perversely imprisoned sex sway inside its capsule-like restraint and my fat bulging balls vibrate beneath its hard unforgiving length. As we enter the elevator, I notice Christina slip a vibrator control box from a pocket in her elegant silk maid's dress. Within seconds my arse is being tormented by the high-pitched vibrations of the evil intruder fixed almost permanently in my backside. I squeal into my gag and hear my head fill with a strange high-pitched wail of sex distress, but outside, in the elevator, I know there is hardly any noise – only my wiggling helplessly sexy deeply tormented form.

I feel my stomach turn as the elevator climbs up into the main body of the Ashcroft manor house. The metal doors part and I am led, still squealing in irresistible ecstasy, down a dark corridor towards the main entrance hall.

We walk out into the well lit beautifully designed foyer area. I know my heels are striking shining marble stone and echoing furiously. But I still hear nothing except my own heart beat and amplified squeals of pleasure.

Then I see Mistress Helen. She is standing talking to Ms Blakemore. The two beautiful buxom women turn to face my noisy sissy form. I see their gorgeous faces light up with cruel amusement. Ms Blakemore, my stunning elegant mentor, claps her hands with joy. Christina curtsies deeply and says something. The women laugh and Ms Blakemore waves at me as at a man locked in a sensory deprivation tank. She then strolls over to look more closely at my tethered rubberised form, her eyes filled with dark mocking arousal. I feel her hands run over the ultra skin-tight rubber of the leotard and moan with terrible pleasure. I watch her grip my sex, but, thanks to the nature of the sheath, I feel nothing. Then her left hand idly strokes my backside and I beg her through the gag for some form of release from this terrible relentless utterly exquisite torment. But she, of course, hears nothing. Then, I am led away.

I turn to watch her through the permanent pink haze. She waves and gives me a gentle amused smile. A whimper of terrible disappointment escapes the fat rubber ball gag.

Christina leads me up the spectacular winding staircase towards the Mistress Chambers. Each step is an erotic tease and a fearful adventure. Thanks to the shackles and the intricacies of balance demanded by my ample figure and the precariously high heels, I have to watch every tottering ultra-sissified step very carefully, a task made much more challenging by the hood and pink plastic eye coverings.

Yet, perhaps amazingly, we get to the top of the stairs without any major balance incidents. Then I totter along behind gorgeous Christina towards the VIP quest quarters and the startling Eleanor Groves. As we get nearer to her, I feel my heart quicken, my breathing deepen. I remember her long elegant hand on my nylon-sheathed thigh and a quiver of ecstatic anticipation shoots across my body. Then I remember the strange costume I am trapped within. I know it is Mistress Eleanor who has demanded this perverse and ultra-erotic outfit, that this is all part of her own darkly kinky intent. This evening, I am to be her sex toy, and the thought fills me with the most delightful anticipation.

By the time we reach the door to the guest quarters, I am almost dizzy with nervous arousal. Christina seems to tap very lightly on the door and then, as if of its own volition, the door opens. Christina tugs firmly on the leash and I follow her into the room beyond, my bottom wiggling, my breasts bouncing, my heart pounding.

I am in a very large room, a room dominated by a huge bed covered in silver- and cream-coloured sheets of purest silk. Yet this is by no means just a bedroom. On one side of the room there is an oval dining table laden with food. There are four elegant wooden chairs tucked beneath it. On the other side of the room is a black leather sofa, two matching arm chairs and a glass-topped coffee table. Built into one entire wall of the room is a massive entertainment centre housing a large widescreen TV, plus a DVD and an expensive mini hi-fi system. A large walk-in closet dominates another wall, and in the far corner of the room is a doorway through to the bathroom.

Mistress Eleanor is standing by the bed. Christina immediately performs a deep loving curtsey. Thanks to my bondage and costume, the best I manage is a bob-curtsey, but, under the circumstances, I feel this is a commendable effort.

I notice a slight smile cross Mistress Eleanor's cherry lips. She examines my bizarre hyper fetishistic appearance and then nods slightly. Then, to my surprise, she leans forward and places what seems to be a small piece of circular metal – like a watch battery – against my rubber covered left ear. It sticks firmly to the shiny deceptively soft surface. She then steps back and addresses Christina.

'A very fine effort, Christina. You know me too well.'

I look up, astonished – the metal device is obviously a transmitter that allows me to hear through the hood.

A flicker of pride crosses Christina's lovely dark eyes and she bob-curtsies as meekly as possible.

'Taylor!'

Christina's look quickly changes to one of abject fear as Mistress Eleanor shouts the name of her long-time slave and male lover.

Taylor emerges from the walk-in closet. He is dressed in a black silk shirt, matching leather trousers and black leather motor cycle boots. He regards us with a vague curiosity.

'I think Chrissy has done a wonderful job with Shelly . . . don't you?'

Taylor thinks about his mistress's words and eventually nods slightly.

'And I think she deserves a reward for her efforts . . . don't you?'

A very slight smile quivers across Taylor's thin almost bloodless lips.

Christina's eyes immediately widen in utter terror.

'Please, mistress,' she whimpers. 'I have other duties this evening . . . with Mistress Anne.'

Eleanor laughs, amused by the sissy's terror and her foolish attempt to create an excuse.

'Well, Anne will just have to wait. I'm sure she'll understand.'

Christina momentarily takes a step backward, tears already welling in her beautiful doe eyes. But then she stops, realises the terrible inescapable fact of her fate, and performs a deep submissive curtsey.

'Of course, mistress – I am yours to do with as you please.'

In her words there is a helpless finality. As an SMC sissy, and a servant of the Bigger Picture, she will accept anything, do anything, be anything for her mistresses. This is the absolute and final truth of our silken servitude.

'Taylor, I suggest you get Christina with Pansy together and we'll join you later. But feel free to start without us.'

I listen to these strange words, my eyes widening with fascination at the mention of Pansy's name.

Taylor steps into the room. He takes Christina by the hand – a surprisingly gentle gesture – and then leads the already sobbing sissy to her no doubt dreadful fate. A familiar sadistic arousal grips me as I watch this gorgeous busty she-male wiggle-mince into the large walk-in closet and then disappear very mysteriously.

It is only as I turn back to face the incredible Mistress Eleanor that I begin to look at her in any detail. For these first few minutes, there has only been the spectacle of her being, the mystery of a global celebrity. But now I find myself beholding not just a woman of incredible fame, but a very beautiful mature female and a dedicated member of the Bigger Picture.

She is dressed in a very tight black nylon sweater that displays her still firm and considerable bosom to a striking and highly erotic effect. Beneath the sweater is a short grey pinstripe skirt that rests a good two inches above her knees to reveal long very shapely legs wrapped in sheer black nylon hose and feet encased in five-inch-stiletto heeled court shoes of a gleaming black patent leather. Her lips are painted a bloody red and there is a hint of pale-blue eye shadow on her long-lashed eyelids. She wears simple but clearly very expensive diamond stud earrings and around the high neck of the sweater is a band of sparkling white pearls.

With her short blonde hair adding the final touch of dominant precision, Ms Eleanor Groves is undoubtedly a very impressive and beautiful woman.

Yet it is more than beauty that makes her so special. There is in her, more than any of the women I have had the pleasure to serve since being so carefully feminised by my wondrous Aunt, the fire of power, an aura of absolute, unquestioned authority that radiates out from her impressive form and over my so perversely costumed and mutated body.

Mistress Eleanor moves closer to me. A heavy musk perfume somehow seeps beneath the hood and my eyes widen as she runs a long finger over the sealed shaft of my cock.

'A terrible torment – immobilising and de-sensitising your cock like this. But also . . . amusing.'

Her precise American accent, with its perfect diction, only serves to emphasise the absolute nature of her authority. Her eyes stare at the capsule-imprisoned dick and seem to consider the possibilities for torment and sadistic pleasure.

'I hear you spent the afternoon with Celine and Anne.'

I nod warily and she smiles, almost gently.

'Yes, they can be rather extreme in their methods. Poor Annette will have to have a few days off. I hope Helen understands.'

I look at her through pink-tinted plastic – confused, frightened . . . helplessly aroused.

'Oh don't worry: I don't go in for all that melodramatic stuff. I leave the others to do that for me. No doubt Taylor will have dreamt up something utterly appalling for you and the others, but for now you're perfectly safe.'

She walks over to the dining table and begins to select a variety of buffet snacks and place them on a small light-blue china plate. I watch with a sudden realisation of my own terrible hunger. I hear my stomach rumble loudly in the echo chamber that is the hood.

She takes up a fork and begins to eat the food, a terrible wicked torment. I wonder if she realises I have not eaten since breakfast time. I wonder if she even cares.

As she eats, she continues to talk.

'You probably know more about the workings of the Bigger Picture than any of the other slaves – she-male or female. I suppose there is an irony here somewhere. But you are one of a kind, Shelly. Without doubt our most successful prototype. Also, you have provided us with a fascinating and absolutely essential insight into the sissy mind. With your designs and Senso, we have a key to the feminisation of a million males.'

I can't help giving her a disbelieving look and she laughs.

'Even through the hood, I can see you don't believe me. Well, that's understandable. But I assure you it's true. Of course, Pansy is as important on the physical level – you are both startling examples of the second generation sissification technology. But Pansy has surrendered to a truer, deeper-rooted nature. Her homosexuality – if we can use such a word when talking about a sissy – precedes any masochistic inclination. With you, the desire to submit is most certainly the fundamental sexual driver. Even now, as you watch me, angered by your hunger and my utter indifference to it, you wallow in your suffering, you extract a fierce sexual pleasure from the torments I impose.'

I moan into the fat gag filling my long-tortured mouth and imagine the taste of the savoury snacks she is eating with such a sadistic abandon. Yet, despite this craven cruelty, I know every word she teases me with is utterly true. Even now, my eyes are overwhelmed by her dominant beauty. As she eats, she crosses her legs and allows, no doubt for my benefit, the grey pinstripe skirt to rise up her thighs and reveal virtually the whole length of her perfect black nylon-sheathed legs, a gesture deliberately designed to stress her absolute authority over me and my dark need for it.

'On Saturday, you will be properly revealed to the sisters of the Bigger Picture. We have had our own very pleasurable "coming out" event here, of course, but the annual Ball will be attended not only by sisters from across the globe, but by many women who are yet to buy into our plans. It is these women you will impress, Shelly. After they have seen you, we believe they will sign up not just with kind words, but with real promises of support, with money and other vital resources. It is they who will fund the major expansion of our activities – the development of the regional and national centres and the completion of the Sados facility.'

I listen and fight a dizzying sense of disbelief. How has this happened? How have I travelled from the warm embrace of my Aunt's scented undies to become the sissy icon for a global conspiracy of supremely powerful and utterly determined women?

'In five years, we will have established the Bigger Picture as the primary global vision of the future of humanity. We will, of course, face considerable resistance. As the project of modernity fades, as the illusion of male reason collapses under the weight of relativism and the self-destructive fantasies of liberal equality, we will return to the true state of male rule: warfare. Essentially, a war between two primitive and deeply related religious ideologies: Christianity and Islam.

'We can already see its beginnings. The primitives are already in control, my pretty sissy flower, and their reign will end in global catastrophe. Not necessarily a nuclear war and annihilation; but rather an anarchic collapse – a process which is also visible as I speak. The superpower model of global power balancing has already broken down. Over the next five to ten years, the world will degenerate in a vast collection of warring tribes and mini-states. Even well established power blocks – the USA, Europe, China and South East Asia – will fall apart under the contradictory pressures of globalisation. And that will leave only the grotesque truth of primitive male religion. The Phallocracy, as it sinks under the tidal wave of history, will cling even more desperately to its Bible and Koran. And the evidence of the failure of the civilisation that emerged from these backward self-serving fantasies of a phallic God will be the chaos he has created. And that, my sweet, will be our moment.'

I listen to her in amazement, enthralled and appalled, aroused and utterly terrified. In her beautiful pink-tinted, ice-blue eyes, I see a vision to challenge the corruption of male dominance, but still a vision of dominance, an ideology of power.

'Yes, I can see what you're thinking,' she continues, although how she can see anything other than the surreal eroticism of my ultra kinky costume is beyond me. 'This is just another totalitarian ideology of absolute control – replacing one fascism with another. And maybe you're right. But this is a global movement in the truest sense of the word, Shelly – a movement that will cross all national boundaries, all races, all primitive selfish interest groups. And it is also a movement of women that has found a clear place for men and which recognises the furious and unavoidable power of male desire. We don't want to stop men desiring, to resist the workings of the male body. We want to harness and control their desire.

These two factors – a global alliance and a philosophy of desire – will allow us to seize the moment provided by the collapse of the Phallocracy. And yes, as you have seen, the Femocracy will be a dictatorship, a global regime rooted firmly in a politics of power. But this is the nature of our being, Shelly. It is the nature of Nature.'

She wipes her fingers on a cream-coloured napkin and then uncrosses her legs. Her eyes appraise my unsteady rubberised form and a smile crosses her grease-stained blood-red lips.

'I am not a lesbian, at least not in the way that Helen and the others so clearly are.'

A sudden and perhaps shocking change of subject. My eyes widen with a helplessly erotic interest.

'They enjoy your oral pleasurings, but ultimately your sissification is part of their own desire – for the feminine, for the obvious pleasures of the feminine form. And I understand that. But I'm afraid the thought of fucking Celine, or Helen, or any of them ... well, it kinda leaves me cold. Which is a bit strange, perhaps – given that my husband was so goddamned useless in the sack. But then I always had Taylor, and the other agents that passed my way. And they were always more than happy to do my bidding. So I guess that makes me a little old fashioned; even, within the context of the Bigger Picture, a little perverse.'

I wonder if she can see the look of total astonishment in my eyes.

'But the funny thing is, the really weird fucking thing is ... I find the sissies really rather sexy; especially the ones who have been ... transformed. And you, Shelly; well, you are the cherry on the cake as far as sissification is concerned. With those incredible tits and that lovely substantial dick. Jesus, I'm

getting wet just looking at you. And yep, the rubber
. . . all my idea. Rubber and sissies. I confess to all
my terrible dark crimes of desire. Rubber, sissies and
dick. Always plenty of dick.'

She laughs and I whimper with shock and astonishment. Her urbane, East Coast accent has suddenly
mutated into a thick Arkansas drawl. Originally from
Little Rock, the truth of her is very much in this
husky raunchy country tone.

She straightens her skirt and stands up. I glare at
her through the hood and hear my heart pound with
an appalling desire.

'Of course,' she continues, 'the sisters don't want
sissies fucking real girls; and that makes plenty of
sense to me – on a political level. They fuck each
other and serve women without question. But on a
personal level . . . well, it's a real shame. So I've come
up with this little "get out of jail free" costume. Now
I can do what I like – you don't get to come or
experience any direct stimulation, and the protocol is
satisfied. Of course, if I were to snap and let that
naughty pecker out of its prison – well, then you'd
end up with a complete sex change and I wouldn't
have a dick to tease.'

She strolls over to me and takes up the fiendish
leash. I whimper into the fat gag and realise that I
have been transformed into a human dildo: my sole
function is to give this startling woman pleasure
without being able to experience it myself.

She tugs playfully on the lead and I totter forward
fearfully, wiggling my rubberised bottom with a
helpless sissy femininity. My large firmly secured
breasts wobble before me and a feeling of total
submission grips my girlish heart. I stare longingly at
Mistress Eleanor's splendid shapely black nylon-
wrapped legs through a film of pretty pink and my

long-imprisoned and tormented cock demands an impossible release. The vibrator buzzes in my expertly widened arse and a squeal of profound sexual need slips past the fat wicked ball gag. I am hers. I am theirs. I belong as a simple desiring sex machine for these women. For all women. I am, thanks to my training and my deep subterranean masochism, the perfect sissy; the paradigm of submission and sweet scented surrender.

At the bed, I am told to sit. My buttocks, soft pert prisoners of an evil rubber prison, rest on the cream silk sheets. My harshly punished cock presses into the wall of my stomach. I feel my breasts pull down against the equalising pressure of the rubber leotard. My fetishistic entrapment in rubber and the finest nylon is almost unbearably pleasurable. But this is nothing compared with what is to come.

I watch, increasingly amazed, as Mistress Eleanor begins to pull her sweater from beneath the belt of the sexy grey skirt.

'I'm 51 next month, Shelly,' she whispers. 'So I take it you will be impressed by what I'm about to reveal. I feel better now than when I was 31. And I think I look better, too.'

I remember the pictures of her as a young woman, before she was first lady, when she was first associated with the state governor who would become her husband and, improbably, the President of the United States of America. She was certainly nothing special then, a heavily be-spectacled pullover-wearing woman in her late twenties. A lawyer by profession. But time and the acquisition of power had transformed her into a stunning exemplar of dominant confident womanhood.

'It's power,' she continues, pulling the sweater up over her head in one swift teasingly precise gesture.

'It's kept me young. That and money. That and the best fucking hairdresser in Arkansas.'

I stare at her with renewed astonishment and adoration. As the sweater is thrown casually onto the floor, my plastic-covered eyes behold a perfect athletic torso and large still firm breasts tightly imprisoned in a striking black silk brassiere with elegant lace trimming around the top of the well-filled cups.

As I moan with admiring pleasure into the ball gag, she begins to wiggle out of the grey skirt, her eyes pinned to mine with a hard simple desire.

'Not long now, sissy,' she says.

I look down at the gusset of her ultra-sheer black nylon tights and see a large circular stain. She smiles and lets the skirt drop to the floor. Her arousal obvious, she kicks off her heeled shoes and moves towards me on stockinged feet.

I squeal with a terrible unrewarded desire as she proceeds to alternately caress and pinch my rubber-sealed breasts. I feel the vibrator slip deeper inside me as my buttocks instinctively press into the bed. I close my eyes and see a black eternity filled with exploding silver stars.

Then I am being pushed onto my back and pulled by strong muscular arms so that I am laying face up along the length of the bed.

I smell her sex juices and moan with thirsty need. She uses white rubber cording taken from the beside table to bind my ankles and knees very tightly together and I moan my delight yet again.

'So many sissies love bondage,' she whispers, tying the knots. 'I need to spend more time practising my rope work.'

Then I am prone and helpless, and thus ready for her kinky attentions.

She pulls off the damp tights with an animal eagerness and then, to my further astonishment, rips away the bra to reveal her breasts in all their impressive mature glory. Then, standing back from the bed to provide me with a cruelly tantalising view, she wiggles out of the black silk panties.

And here she is: one of the most famous, powerful women in the world, stark naked before me. A truly beautiful sight; an image of firm, carefully preserved and deeply erotic maturity.

I stare at her wet glistening blonde pubic hair and gasp with a frustrated anticipation into the ball gag. She laughs and then virtually jumps onto the bed. In a few seconds, she has straddled my helpless co-cooned form and, her thighs carefully parted, is lowering her sex over my capsuled cock.

Is this losing my virginity? Is this contravening the strict laws of the Bigger Picture? As my sex slips inside her, I feel nothing. A furious sense of injustice floods my tormented sissy mind, but even in the midst of this righteous anger, I know I must accept, that I must obey without the slightest hint of a question.

And soon she is riding me, her thighs pumping her body like powerful pneumatic pistons – up, down, up, down. Faster, faster.

'Oh yes,' she begins to moan. 'Hard and fast. Hard and fast.'

I can do nothing but look up at her through the slender film of pink plastic, my eyes wide with desire and unfulfilled need, eyes pinned to her bouncing bosom, a bouncing whose frequency and power builds up and up towards the point of profound female release.

'Hard and fast, you beautiful sissy cunt,' she snaps, her teeth grinding together, her eyes tightly shut.

A film of hot sex sweat soon covers her rocking pumping body. Her mouth is open in a grimace of pleasure pushing towards a transcendent pain and back again towards ecstasy. Suddenly she leans forward and grabs handfuls of bed sheet on both sides of me. She lowers herself so far that our breasts touch and I squeal with a desperate need to exploit this moment of semi-tactile pleasure to the full.

Then she sits up, preparing herself like a rocket for blast off. She presses harder. A series of guttural grunts fills the room. It is almost as if she is de-evolving into some kind of sexy simian from the golden blackness of pre-history.

As she comes, screaming and bucking insanely, the sweat pouring from her marvellous body and flowing in small sensual rivers over my tight erotic second skin of fine latex rubber, I squeal my own helpless, desperate frustration, begging, after this day of sexual suffering, for a release of my own, a release denied so cruelly in the ordeals that have been carefully and sadistically created for me by the wicked and gorgeous mistresses of the Sissy Maids Company and the Bigger Picture.

But, yet again, there is nothing here for me but further repression of need and a dreadful all pervasive re-affirmation of my absolute objectification and unending and complete submission.

Mistress Eleanor pulls herself off my arching permanently hard cock toy. She looks down at me with a strangely gentle deeply satisfied smile and climbs off the bed.

I lay helpless and useless and she extracts a short black silk robe from the closet. She pours herself a large glass of golden-coloured wine. She drinks it in two coarse gulps, sighs contentedly and returns to the bed.

'Right . . . let's go see what Taylor's up to.'

She unties my legs and then helps me to my unsteady high-heeled feet. I look down at my

189

capsuled cock. It glistens with a thick film of sex juice. The powerful fundamental stink of her cunt seeps through the wicked rubber hood and I feel a quiver of olfactory pleasure pass through my rubberised and tightly tethered form.

Mistress Eleanor takes up the terrible cock leash and I am led across the bedroom and into the mysterious depths of the walk-in closet.

Suddenly, I am in a valley of deeply fetishistic pleasures, walking very tentatively between two rows of Mistress Eleanor's clothes, her considerable travelling wardrobe. A vast array of splendid dresses and blouses, formal skirts and trouser suits, beneath which run two rows of elegant sexy footwear – shoes, boots, sandals – every one marked by wickedly high heels.

A variety of strong sensual smells fill the closet, perfumes lingering, the cock-teasing aromas of feminine power mixed with the still very strong scent of her sex. Then we come to a door, its outline marked in the darkness by light bleeding from the room beyond. Mistress Eleanor opens it and we walk into a large perfectly square white-walled room, a room whose function is quickly made apparent by the squeals of fear, pain and anger mixed with reluctant pleasure that immediately flood the amplification transistor connected to my ear.

Even by the standards of the Sissy Maids Company, the room offers a bizarre and disturbing spectacle. My eyes are automatically drawn to the gorgeous spectacle that is Pansy. Pansy, once my lover and fellow trainee sissy, the sexy she-male created with me in the deeply erotic heat of my Aunt Jane's kinky imagination. Now, she is Taylor's sex slave, his adoring sissy lover; his gorgeous utterly submissive object.

She stands a few feet from me dressed in a lovely and quite outrageous red gingham dress. Her beautiful blonde hair has been bound into two little girl pigtails with strawberry-coloured silk ribbons; her striking ice-blue doe eyes, wild with a pained arousal, behold me with a dark teasing delight. If she is smiling, I cannot see, for her always full and voluptuous lips are obscured by a thick strip of red duct tape. Her red-rouged cheeks bulge with some large fiendish gag. A large diamond stud has been inserted into the left nostril of her small girlish nose, and a small golden ring is fixed to the right. The dress itself is very short, its skirt and attached frou-frou petticoats barely reaching beyond her upper thighs. The front of the dress has been cut away to reveal a pair of beautiful white silk panties against which the full rigid length of her sex is fully visible, including the wicked cock rings that ensure absolute obedience to her handsome harsh master. Her long perfectly proportioned legs are sheathed in white nylon stockings and held in place at her thighs with striking red silk elastic garters. Her small sexy feet are imprisoned in a pair of red leather ankle boots with striking red silk laces. The arms of the dress end in puffed lace-trimmed sleeves and glacé gloved hands. The high neck is also trimmed with delicate French lace. Yet, by far the most striking part of this kinky outfit is the chest, for her large breasts are exposed to the eyes of all who can see through a film of very sheer white nylon that covers the entire chest area of the dress.

I look at her and gasp into my gag. I feel my deeply pained cock strain even harder against its rubber and steel restraint. I want her so very, very badly.

She moves past me with a look of equal need, a slight sissy moan escaping her expertly secured gag. I follow her as best the perverse hood will allow and then I find myself staring at Taylor. He is sitting on a large black sofa, his legs crossed, drinking casually from a bottle of Japanese beer. The silver metal fly of his black leather trousers is open and his huge hard cock is fully exposed.

Pansy curtsies deeply before him and then kneels directly in front of his striking sex weapon.

As all this is revealed, I am constantly aware of a very high-pitched and desperate squealing, a noise that gradually forces my attention towards the opposite side of the room and a sight that fills me with an instant dread followed quickly by a disturbing sexual arousal.

As Taylor leans forward and brutally tears the strip of duct tape from Pansy's soft sissy lips, I behold Christina, or a being I take to be Christina. A figure sheathed in black Senso latex from head to toe, trapped inside a seamless ultra-erotic body glove of simmering rubber. Armless and legless, with an eyeless hood fixed into the very fabric of the glove, the only part of her body visible is a pair of full strawberry lips stretched wide by a large pink rubber phallus attached to a metal post a few inches from her hooded face, a phallus plunged deep into her mouth and which she is sucking upon quite helplessly. Indeed, as I examine this kinky scene more carefully, I begin to understand that her whole precarious balance depends on her continuing to suck on the phallus. This is because her feet are clamped inside a devilish single shoe, a tight leather boot that consumes her feet and runs up to the middle of her knees, and which balances on a single seven-inch-high silver stiletto heel. And even this is not the final cause of her true terror-filled distress. This is because her sex, also sheathed seamlessly in Senso black rubber, which emerges from between her rubber legs like the long rigid stalk of some bizarre sex flower, is fixed via a leather shackle wrapped around her bulging rubberised balls and a six-inch length of silver chain, to a metal link fixed into the side of the pole.

A loud buzzing emanating from her backside betrays a particularly wicked anal intruder, and a painful-looking silver clamp has been fixed to each rubber-covered nipple of her large, firm and very beautiful breasts.

The poor tormented sissy wiggles and gags on the fat rubber cock, knowing that if she releases the perverse tool of torture, she will most probably lose her balance and her whole body weight will fall on her imprisoned balls.

As I behold this terrible sentence of balance torment, I hear a gasp of pleasure from Taylor. I turn back to see that Pansy has now taken his long hard red cock in her mouth and is eagerly teasing him towards orgasm.

Mistress Eleanor is watching this spectacle with wide sex drugged eyes and a partially open mouth. She shifts nervously on her feet. I stare down at her blood-red toenails and then look up and catch her gazing at me. She smiles and in her smile I see a shocking and wonderful confession: envy. She is clearly envying Pansy! Then her smile widens and she stares at Taylor. He meets her eyes with his usual frank arrogant indifference and seems to read her mind.

'Do it,' he snaps, between increasingly short breaths. 'Do it now!'

She nods and turns towards me. Then she grabs me by the arm and leads me to the centre of the room so that I am just a few feet from the imperilled helpless Christina. She kneels down before me and begins to work free the dreadful desensitising capsule. I squeal in astonishment and her wicked coarse laughter fills the room.

I can only stare down at her in utter astonishment as she removes the cock rings and then works free the tight rubber restrainer. I gasp with an animal relief and excitement as my cock is exposed to the cool air of this dark satanic chamber.

Then the unthinkable: with a brazen desiring smile, she takes hold of my long-tormented penis and begins very gently to lick its bulging purple head. I squeal with amazement and instantaneous violent arousal. A film of moisturising spittle soon covers the head and the full length of the rigid aching shaft. This highly erotic lubrication is undertaken with a deeply revealing expertise, and as Mistress Eleanor takes my cock fully into her warm mouth, I fight to remain upright, my knees buckling under the startling electrical stimulation of every pleasure cell in my helplessly and joyously sissified form.

I explode within two minutes, an eruption of thick creamy come which she accepts with an obvious and, within the context of the philosophy of the Bigger Picture, utterly baffling pleasure. My eyes, sheathed in pink plastic, behold her pumping head and guiding hands, they feast on her large firm breasts, now fully visible as the silken robe has fallen open in the midst of her erotic teasing. I see all of this and feel my body split apart under the appalling pressure exerted by a volcanic eruption of come, a seismic orgasm well off the sexter scale.

As she drinks my helpless offering, a sudden brutal dizziness washes over my rubber-sealed body and I feel myself fall away from her erotic grasp. The pink haze turns red and then black. I collapse onto the ground, and the last thing I see is Mistress Eleanor standing over me, her hand wiping come from her bloody lips, her smile utterly sluttish.

When I wake, I am face down and lying on a hard surface. Or rather: secured tightly. Almost immediately, I become aware of the fact that my torso has been strapped tightly to a table top of some kind. The rubber leotard and hood have been removed, as have the silken tights. I am dressed in a white Senso nylon body stocking. Thin leather straps hold me tightly to the table top at just above the buttocks, the waist and chest. My arms have been pulled very painfully behind my back and secured in a pink rubber bondage glove that runs from my hands up to my shoulders. As I struggle to understand this latest kinky ordeal, I become aware that I am, in fact, bent over the table, and that my legs have been strapped to what seem to be its metal legs at the ankles, upper calves and thighs. The table legs appear to move away from the actual table at a slight angle, so that my own nylon-sheathed thighs are in fact spread quite widely apart. Also, I have been secured in such a way that my cock and buttocks are actually over the edge of the table. More bizarrely, I am gradually aware of the fact that the vibrator has been removed from my long-tormented arse and that a rear panel fixed to the stocking has been removed to leave my back passage completely exposed. And, on top of this, my cock, which has been resealed in its rubber restrainer and tightly re-ringed, has been secured, via the fiendish collar fitted around my scrotum and the silver leash attached to it, to a hook fixed somewhere beneath the table, thus pulling it very tightly straight forward. This ensures that even the slightest movement results in a painful tug to my sex. Also, I am, to my surprise, completely un-gagged. Yet when I manage to look up, I suddenly begin to understand why the gag has been removed, for standing directly in front of me is Pansy. She is dressed in a powder-blue body stocking, exactly the same in design to the one teasing my own sissy form. She is standing bolt upright. This is due to the fact that she is strapped to a thick metal pole similar to the one that was entertaining Christina. Yet rather than facing the pole, her back is pressed tightly against it and she is held in place by thick white leather strapping wrapped around her ankles, her knees, her thighs, her stomach and her neck. Her arms have been forced behind her back and tethered tightly with powder-blue rubber-coated cording at the wrists and elbows. A powder-blue stocking has been stretched tightly over her pretty head and through the thin film of soft nylon it is possible to see a strip of thick white masking tape spread firmly over her soft strawberry lips. Her bulging cheeks betray another fat panty gag, and a high-pitched buzzing betrays a new deeply positioned anal vibrator.

Her rigid crimson and totally unrestrained sex rises out of the lace-edged hole positioned between her legs. It is only a few inches from my face and I stare at its imposing tumescence with shock and helpless arousal. Then the teasing voice of Mistress Eleanor fills the room.

'You obviously needed milking quite badly, Shelly. Taylor has suggested that the three of you spend the night together, and I am happy to oblige. I'm sure you'll appreciate the little ménage-à-trois we have arranged.'

I hear a squealing behind me and manage to tilt my head around to see Christina positioned directly between my legs. She has been freed from the awful pole-based penis gag and re-tied to the pole in exactly the same way as poor Pansy. She remains encased in shimmering black Senso rubber, but her very considerable and highly excited sex has been freed from its wicked restraint and is now only inches from my helplessly exposed backside.

The fiendish cunning of what is about to happen hits me hard. As poor Christina moans with furious excitement into her eyeless rubber hood, her mouth now filled with a large black rubber ball gag, as her ample breasts bounce in their tight rubber prison, as her own anal vibrator drives her mad with dark sex need, I see very clearly the wicked plan Mistress Eleanor and Master Taylor are about to put into kinky operation.

Mistress Eleanor comes briefly into view behind Pansy. The poles are affixed to solid metal stands, which are themselves on small rubber wheels. Mistress Eleanor slowly pushes the stand towards me as Taylor takes up position behind Christina and begins to push her stand towards my exposed arse.

'Open wide!' the gorgeous American beauty snaps.

Suddenly, Pansy's cock is brushing against my lips. Instinctively, I open my mouth and it slips slowly inside. I gag and moan, and then feel Christina's tremendous sex begin to work its way into my expertly trained anal passage. I am to suck and be fucked, to be part of a sissy sex triptych.

Eventually, Pansy's cock is forced deep into my mouth. It is then that Mistress Eleanor reveals a thick leather collar secured to my neck, with two lengths of white leather running from it. She takes up the lengths of white leather and pulls on them hard, forcing Pansy's body to press against my face. She buckles the straps together just beneath Pansy's pert helpless wiggling buttocks, and thus ensures we are very intimately tied together.

As I suck helplessly on Pansy's hard boiling cock, Christina's sex slips deeper into my rectum as Taylor wheels the gorgeous buxom she-male into position. I whimper with an intense double pleasure as she presses deep into me and experience a new level of masochistic pleasure.

Held rigid by the straps, I am a helpless receptacle of cock. Almost as soon as Christina is fully inside me, she begins to pump her sex, setting up an erotic fucking rhythm. This is in part created by the fierce vibrations travelling from her arse and across her tightly rubberised form. A similar vibration is being transmitted via Pansy's hot moist cock, and soon my own body is shaking helplessly and my own cock is being tortured as it tugs helplessly against the chain holding it firmly in place beneath the metal table.

And this is how we are left.

I hear Mistress Eleanor move closer to me and then a warm hand is stroking my buttocks.

'You are the perfect specimen, Shelly,' she whispers. 'And your cock is quite beautiful. Tonight, you will pleasure your dainty companions while I fuck Taylor. Think of me as you fill with come.'

I hear Pansy's moans suddenly increase in volume and realise that Taylor is, in some kinky terrible way, teasing his pretty ultra-sissy to the edge of masochistic ecstasy.

Then the hands are gone, the moaning lowers to a background hum accompanied by the wicked buzzing of the vibrators, and I feel Pansy's cock begin to press harder into my mouth. The vein in her sex throbs and the bulbous head bangs mercilessly against the back of my throat. Her moans transform into squeals of furious sissy pleasure and I respond by sucking harder. Then, after a sudden well gagged wail of ecstatic pain, she explodes into my mouth, and I struggle to swallow her thick hot salty come without choking. Tears pour from my eyes, my tightly bound, sheer nylon-sheathed body quivers with serious nerve-tingling pleasure and, within seconds of swallowing the last drop of Pansy's sex nectar, I feel Christina push that little bit harder into me and I know she too is about to achieve a volcanic orgasm.

It will be a long, testing night, a fact made clear when the powerful strip light that illuminates this strange terrible chamber is switched off and we are plunged into a complete and utter darkness. I remember the feel of Mistress Eleanor's own soft lips around my now cruelly imprisoned sex and realise this is my punishment. I remember Myriam's gorgeous soft hungry form pressed so tightly against my own, and realise this is the price I must pay for a day of subversion. Yet even as I suffer this prolonged sightless torment, I am overwhelmed by a dreadfully deep-rooted and powerful sexual arousal. I am riding the endless roller coaster of sadomasochistic desire that frames every decision taken, every word spoken and every movement made in the kinky academy of the Sissy Maids Company.

8

An Interlude with Myriam

The next few days are easily the busiest and most
exciting of my delightful stay in the academy, for
these are the two days before the annual fundraising
Ball, a key event in the calendar of the Bigger Picture
organisation which, this year, will also include the
formal graduation of the newest Sissy Maids, Pansy
and Shelly. But we are to be displayed publicly not
just for ceremonial purposes: the newest model of
sissy, of which we are the spectacular prototypes, will
be used to convince the doubters amongst those
present, those with significant influence who remain
on the periphery of the Bigger Picture, that the vision
of a global Femocracy is a viable one, that the future
can be feminised and a dictatorship of all powerful
women established. There will also be a vital keynote
speech by Mistress Eleanor, a speech which will set
out the Bigger Picture in a detail previously unheard
or impossible. This will be a most important night,
and the academy buzzes with a highly erotic and
deeply invigorating excitement.

In our beautiful sexy scarlet trainee costumes,
Pansy and I totter hastily about the Ashcroft mansion under the strict but fair command of our
mistresses and the senior housemaids, Christina and
Annette. Mistress Helen is in overall charge of the

arrangements for the Ball, which will be held in the vast banqueting room, which takes up most of the ground floor of the north wing of the house, and which is accessed via the large beautiful ornate entrance hallway and foyer.

As the percussive ring of stiletto heels striking marble and wood fills the house, I am suddenly aware of the beauty and history of this grand country residence. The Ashcroft family has been associated with the house and the county since the Civil War, and 350 years of history, which has been carefully hidden by the SMC occupancy, is suddenly returning to the formal elegant rooms, rooms previously used to entertain kings, queens and a vast array of other dignitaries.

Overall control of the operational aspect of the event is devolved by Mistress Helen to Christina. At first, I am shocked to learn that she will be in control not only of the sissies, but of the female maids and the small army of female catering staff who have been brought in to support the event. Yet Christina's administrative skills are considerable, and she quickly demonstrates why she is the Senior Housemaid and the most trusted of all the SMC sissies.

In her striking black silk dress, sheer, delicately seamed black nylon tights and five-inch-heeled black patent leather court shoes, her gorgeous silken jet hair bound in a tight bun, a cream silk pinafore tied tightly over her dress and accentuating her buxom figure, she is a vision of paradox: power and submission, control and absolute subjugation.

Pansy and I are directly under her control, and we are quickly reacquainted with a simple and very painful fact: Christina is a particularly hard task mistress. Punishments for the slightest infraction or error are frequent and harsh, and after a few hours in her brutal care our shapely sissy bottoms and thighs are stinging from the determined application of an ivory-handled riding crop that is permanently fixed to a leather belt worn beneath her gorgeous silk pinafore.

Our own sheer red nylon tights soon rather ineffectively hide the cherry-red welts that criss-cross our upper thighs and buttocks. Our cries of protest and pain are quickly silenced by fat cherry-red ball gags, and we spend much of the time with our mouths painfully filled and tears of genuine pain filling our wide sissy eyes. Yet even as she so cruelly punishes us, we secretly beg for more. This is our reason to be: to suffer and serve in the name of the Bigger Picture and the divine sisterhood that is at its unyielding gorgeous heart.

Yet it is not only Pansy and me who suffer. The lovely incredibly desirable Myriam is assigned to our work team and she too must endure the constant painful encouragements unleashed by the cruel gorgeous she-male. Dressed in her own sexy black silk housemaid's dress, her own soft strawberry ripe lips soon framing a fat black rubber ball gag, she works alongside us with a graceful patience, putting our own masochistic acceptance to shame with her resilience and tolerance of abuse.

And then there are her stunning honey-brown eyes and the way they constantly seek out mine, the way they subtly attempt to recall the glorious illegal intimacies of our time bound so tightly together in the erotic darkness of the movement studio's tiny storage cupboard. And then there is my helpless response, to return her frank desiring look with a furious confession of deep need. Yes, the confession of a true and irresistible need, and further proof that the indoctrination of the SMC academy has, in one key area, failed: despite my sexual attraction to all the lovely sexy sissies, I remain at the very most a bisexual, and most likely still a heterosexual sissy, a woman-loving transvestite, whose body has been clearly and ruthlessly transformed, but whose soul, while willingly bound to the service of all womankind, is still very much the soul of a male. As much as I love my feminine frillies, my sheer nylons, my tight silken panties, my startling high heels and, most importantly, my splendidly large and perfectly formed breasts, I still remain sexually oriented in a profound psychological manner towards the female.

During the build up to the Ball, we work punishing twelve-hour days cleaning, washing, ironing, arranging guest quarters and setting out tables and chairs. All twenty of the en-suite guest rooms are to be used for this major Bigger Picture event, and the mistresses demand that each one is prepared to the highest standards of cleanliness and general suitability for a powerful influential woman.

And then, on the Friday afternoon before the day of the Ball, something truly remarkable and shocking occurs, something that was perhaps inevitable, given the constant presence of the beautiful Myriam and the terrible relentless temptation she poses to me, something which is to change everything in a dark, terrible and tremendously exciting way.

We are assigned guest room twelve, just the two of us, by Christina. I look at her with a hint of doubt and she places her silken-gloved hand threateningly on the painfully familiar riding crop. That morning, Mistress Helen left suddenly on business associated with the guests and Mistress Anne has been placed in overall control of the arrangements. There is a sense that we are behind schedule, and the atmosphere amongst the slaves has become far more intense, inspired no doubt by the fact that Mistress Anne has already made a sadistic and deliberate point of thrashing her personal tutee, Pansy, in front of the rest of us, simply as 'an inspiration'. And it is she who has taken Pansy and Annette to room thirteen, leaving Christina to manage the preparations of rooms twelve and fourteen.

Luckily, I am yet to be thrashed today, although poor Myriam has already been given a sound spanking by a clearly aroused Christina. Both of us are ungagged, and, due to the nature of the work, both of us are fetter free. I am, of course, dressed in my helplessly erotic cherry-red junior's attire – a gorgeous red silk dress that fits tightly across my buxom sissy form, and over which a white silk lace-trimmed pinafore is tightly tied. My legs are sheathed in sheer red seamed nylon tights and my feet are held erotic captive in beautiful black patent leather court shoes with reasonably manageable three-inch heels. My hair is bound tightly in a strict bun and held in place with the stylish diamond rose clasp that so many of us in the forced employ of the Sissy Maids Company are required to wear. Beneath this sexy ensemble, I am wearing a tight rubber mini corset, a teasing white silk-lined lace-frilled brassiere that is constantly caressing my ultra-sensitive breasts and a pair of white silk heavily befrilled panties, beneath which my poor, constantly hard sex is trapped in its prison of tight teasing rubber and brutal cool steel. A fresh extra-large vibrator has been slipped into my arse and is buzzing at a relatively low level of maddening stimulation as I struggle eagerly to fulfil my sissy duties.

Myriam is clad, as usual, in the uniform of a fully qualified housemaid – a virtual mirror of my own sexy costume, but coloured jet black except for the white silk pinafore and a very dainty white silk maid's cap with long silk ribbons that run down the back of her tightly bound hair. From the distracted look in her beautiful honey-brown eyes, I know that she has been fitted with the special 'ecstasy belt' that Mistress Anne had demonstrated so cruelly and erotically during our recent kinky adventure in the movement studio.

Christina leaves us alone in the room and we set about our duties with a significantly reduced enthusiasm, our bodies tired and tormented by the powerful sexual desire that is now a constant and unyielding companion, our minds unable to focus on the tasks at hand. And soon we are looking at each other with wide sex-addled eyes.

'I want you,' Myriam whispers, as we make up the large double bed.

A silk sheet rises and falls and suddenly our faces are inches apart.

'I can't. If we're caught, I'll be changed ... completely. I've never been with a woman. They like that. They want me to be a virgin.'

She smiles gently. 'I want you, Shelly. And you want me. We are fighting the inevitable. And no one need know. Christina has left for at least an hour – she has gone to play with Annette, to relieve her suffering for a little while. Now let us relieve ours.'

'But Mistress Anne ... she's in the next room!'

'She is watching Christina and Annette fuck. Then they will pleasure her. We are the only ones on this floor working, my love.'

She moves closer, her perfume a powerful soul-weakening tease.

'But the belt, the restrainer.'

'I can remove yours and you can remove mine.'

Then she kisses me, a long deep hard kiss that leaves my heart fluttering furiously and turns my delicately hosed knees to useless jelly.

I am utterly startled. This is nothing like kissing a sissy. There is a softness here, an all-consuming gentle embrace; she is taking me and giving herself completely at the same time.

And then we are kneeling on the bed. Despite my doubts and fears, I know I can no longer control myself: I must have her, I have to complete what we began in the sweet darkness of the closet and what has been in the many looks of mutual need that have passed between us in the last few, so terribly exciting weeks.

I feel her small soft perfectly formed hands press against my breasts and I cannot resist allowing my own hands to fall onto her hosed thighs. I feel warm firm skin through the erotic film of sheer nylon, and my hands inch gently beneath a sea of lacy frou-frou petticoating.

'Feel me, Shelly. Feel the core of me, my pretty sissy petal.'

Yet when my hands finally reach the top of her thighs and move toward her nyloned sex, I encounter Mistress Anne's wicked, so sensual ecstasy belt. I press against a nylon-sheathed hard rubber panel and Myriam squeals with pleasure. I know that fitted to this panel is a large ribbed vibrator and that it is now locked deep inside her cunt, and as I push against the panel, it digs deeper into her long-tormented sexual heart.

'Take it off and fuck me. Please . . . *please!*'

I kick off my high heels. She does the same. She turns her back on me to allow the removal of her soft cream-coloured pinafore. Then I am unbuttoning the large white pearl buttons that run the length of her perfectly shaped back, from the high neck of the maid's dress to the befrilled edge of the wide very short skirt. Then she slips the dress over her shoulders and lets it collapse down her body. I gasp with pleasure as a gorgeous red and black striped basque-style corset is revealed.

'It unclips,' she whispers, her eyes wide with furious angry helpless need.

My hands shake almost uncontrollably as I unclip the metal eyes that hold the corset in place and then pull the two whaleboned side panels part. The ridges of her spinal column set out a ladder towards a very dangerous ecstasy, and as she pulls the corset free of her body, I know I am surely doomed.

She turns, topless, to face me. My eyes fall on her breasts and I experience a strange collision of artistic appreciation and dark male desire. Her bosom has a striking perfection – natural proportion and simple elegance. Her breasts are large, but firm. She is perhaps 21, maybe 22 years old, and her body betrays a physical excellence that inspires a terrible moan of unbearable envy and need.

She takes my head in her hands and guides my face towards her breasts, and in a few seconds I am covering these exquisite pale rose orbs of silken flesh in delicate sissy kisses and she, my gorgeous needful Myriam, is purring with a deep irresistible sensual pleasure.

Eventually, she pushes me away. I slip off her soft scented tights and white silk panties to reveal the ingenious and utterly wicked Ecstasy Belt, basically a classic chastity belt design of hard black rubber, whose front and back panels are fitted with two long ribbed and remote controlled vibrators, designed to bore deep into her and provide variable levels of a very permanent physical pleasure that can quickly become mind bending and utterly debilitating.

'There are times I cannot think, that I cannot remember who I am,' she says. 'She is so cruel. I am tied, gagged and left with these boring into me at the highest frequency. Normally, she has beaten me, attached clamps to my nipples, even smothered the vibrators in skin irritant. She is cruel and perverse, and so terribly imaginative. Pansy and I have suffered so much, and enjoyed it even more.'

She smiles gently as I seek out the hidden metal clip at the top of the rear panel. It is sealed beneath a flap of softer black rubber placed just between the buttocks and is impossible to remove by the unfortunate wearer. I pull back the flap and release the eye clip, and suddenly the fiendish ecstasy belt device loosens. A gasp of delight slips from between Myriam's beautiful rose-red lips, and then, with her help, I gently ease the belt free of her gorgeous long-tormented body, in the process slowly slipping the vibrators from her arse and cunt. She squeals with a terrible pleasure and a furious relief. Her large ripe breasts bounce enthusiastically as she demands I speed up our erotic preparations.

'Now it is your turn, Shelly – undress for me.'

Desire is now my all-powerful god. I am beyond fear of the potentially appalling consequences of my actions. I stare at Myriam's perfect form and know there is only one way forward. I climb from the bed and stand before her, my eyes pinned hungrily to hers. She smiles encouragingly and lets a hand slip between the lips of her silken sex. As she teases herself, I undress, a slow, graceful and deeply feminine striptease that, judging from her breathing and the increased efforts of her fingers, excites her terribly. And, eventually, I am down to my restrainer, the cock rings and the anal vibrator. I stand before her proud and angrily aroused, my imprisoned sex hard as the steel binding it, my generous chest displayed brazenly for her erotic entertainment. She beckons me back onto the bed. I kneel before her on the silken sheets. We are so close that our hard painfully erect nipples rub together. I squeal with a deeply girlish pleasure. She takes my tormented sex in her hands and then leans forward and places a long soft kiss on each of my considerable breasts. A squeal mutates into a long slow guttural moan. She carefully unclips the steel cock rings and then very gently teases the rubber restrainer off my balls and cock. I cry out with a mixture of powerful sexual arousal and brutal relief. Then, my pink-dyed cock pops up before her, a startling sissified phallus – the perfect symbol of my bondage and the philosophy of the Bigger Picture.

Never taking her beautiful golden-brown eyes from mine, she then begins to caress my cock. I moan and cry, I beg her for release. I feel her warm soft fingers run gently across the boiling achingly rigid shaft of my sex and I whisper her beautiful name helplessly. She leans forward and we kiss, long, hard, desperately. She then leans down between my legs and gently kisses my sex. Memories of Mistress Eleanor and Pansy come flooding back. I recall the ministrations of Christina and realise that this is the desire that the Bigger Picture plan for all sissies, this and the painful pleasures of anal penetration. We are programmed to suck and fuck ourselves into a she-male homoerotic oblivion, and yet here I am about to go against the cardinal sanction of the Bigger Picture – the most complete and perfect manifestation of the sissification process is about to betray her mistresses in the most intimate and profoundest of ways.

'Call me "Mon Ange",' she whispers, momentarily leaning back from her ministrations. 'My Angel.'

I whisper these simple French words, trying my hardest to imitate her husky southern pronunciation.

Her lovely, always girlish and slightly innocent smile widens.

'Perfect,' she whispers, helping me to lie down on my back across the bed and then positioning herself so that she is straddling my body, her dripping hairless sex directly above my desperate so long denied cock.

Then, with a slight high-pitched moan of pleasure, she lowers herself onto me. I look up at her in awe: again I am worshipping a mistress. Yet this is a form of worship banned by the official church. I am a heretic – a blasphemer.

Myriam: the first woman I penetrate, the first woman and, perhaps, the last. Her eyes close as I slip deeper into her soft warmth. She cries out as I instinctively raise my back and push my sex forward into her, towards the very edge of a splendid and highly dangerous abyss.

I am surprised how easy it is – in the end. In only a few minutes we have established a powerful natural rhythm and she is riding me like a huntress atop some strange sissy steed. My wide helplessly doe eyes drink up the startling vision of her vibrating sweat-soaked form; her large perfectly shaped breasts bounce furiously and specks of hot sex sweat fly from them and strike my own shaking bosom. I feel the muscles in her sex grip my sex tighter and gasp with a shocked pleasure: it is as if I have been lured into some dark pungent cave and now a trap has been sprung to keep me locked safely and helplessly inside.

She comes a few seconds before I do, screaming her joy at the top of the fierce relentless rhythm that has built up between us, a synchronised sex beat shattered into a million fragments of intense wordless pleasure at the moment of fundamental orgasm.

I explode in a way I have never exploded, shouting 'Mon Ange' over and over as I fill her, as I pour my hot salty love into her.

Then she falls forward onto me and I grab her, holding her soaking form hard against my own, my cock still deep inside her, our wet breasts rubbing together with a most erotic friction.

Eventually, she pulls herself up. I am still rock hard inside her and, thanks to the physical and chemical alterations of my changing, I know I could fuck her again within seconds. But she slowly withdraws from me, a strange look now in those pretty Gallic eyes, a look of very significant sadness.

'I am so sorry,' she whispers, tears beginning to trickle from her eyes. 'I have ruined you. But please understand, my love, I had no choice. And also, please remember that I do love you . . . so very much.'

I look at her with genuine concern and deep puzzlement. She very rapidly gathers up her clothes and then, still naked, flees the room. I call her name, pulling myself up onto my elbows, feeling the deeply pleasurable weight of my perfect bosom as I manage, finally, to sit upright.

I dress in a stunned concerned silence cut through with a wonderful sense of physical release. And at the heart of my concern is a feeling I first experienced in Pansy's gentle arms, a feeling of intense and unyielding love, a powerful adoration that goes beyond my sissy sadomasochism. I have been taken in a most erotic manner by Myriam and in this taking has blossomed the love that began to develop in the dark pleasures of the movement studio. Yet at the core of this love there is a strange doubt, a doubt emerging from her guilty tear-stained eyes.

Almost unaware of my dishevelled state, I quietly and quickly begin to dress, pulling the restrainer back over my hard, still hungry sex and clipping the cock rings in place with a sense of sadness and a very powerful arousal.

In the bathroom, I carefully reset my hair and then I totter, in my sexy junior's attire, from the room, unsure of where I am going and what I am doing, lost in a haze of desire and fear.

9

The Ball

The guests begin to arrive on Saturday afternoon and the maids, she-male and female, are kept very busy from just after lunch to near tea-time, tottering desperately back and forth with cases and bags, eager to serve the many mistresses delivered by taxi and private car to the large entrance of the spectacular Ashcroft mansion.

Dressed in my gorgeous Senso silk junior's costume, I wiggle-mince in five-inch-high black patent leather stilettos up and down stairs, across the marble hallway and through long elegant corridors, carrying hand luggage and leading guests to their rooms.

Despite my outer cheerfulness and the intense pleasure I take in exhibiting myself in this most ultra-feminine of conditions before so many beautiful women, some of whom are very famous, I remain deeply concerned by the events of the previous day. My initiation into the most intimate delights of the female form, my wildly illegal adventure with the glorious sex kitten Myriam, is constantly playing on my mind. The strange nature of her departure and the tearful apology keep replaying in my mind, a sinister loop at the heart of which is a terrible truth that I need very urgently to discover.

Yet all these worrisome thoughts are quickly blown into a fine immediately forgotten dust as I totter back to the hallway to collect the latest mistress, for it is here that I discover my wonderful gorgeous Aunt Jane. My heart swells, my finely hosed knees buckle with a deeply erotic weakness and tears of genuine happiness suddenly fill my girlish and helplessly doe eyes.

She is as beautiful and impressive as ever. Dressed in a knee-length black leather skirt, a tight black nylon sweater and a black leather jacket, with sheer black nylon hose and high-heeled black patent leather mules, her thick black hair bound in a tight bun, she is a vision of truly dominant womanhood. Standing by her side is Justine, dressed in a black silk trouser suit, her own long straight blonde hair cascading over her broad athletic shoulders like a stream of golden water, her blue eyes pinned with a cool fascination to my approaching ultra-sissified form.

I draw to a giddy halt a few feet from Aunt Jane and perform a very deep panty-flashing curtsey and whisper a desire-ridden 'mistress'.

Her imperial smile widens. 'It's so good to see you again, Shelly. Three months have made a lot of difference. You look . . . quite incredible.'

I smile shyly and bob-curtsey my thanks.

'I am your creation, mistress. Here I have learnt that and much more.'

'So I hear. Helen and Emily have given me very good reports of your progress. And of the greater vision. It's almost too good to believe.'

Strangely, there is a hint of irony in her voice and, as I look deeper into her eyes, I see something doubtful, questioning. There is a lack of conviction, a lack of true belief. This has, undoubtedly, always been there. I hear this irony and immediately think of

214

Ms Blakemore. Yes, again I get the impression of the two camps, the moderation of Ms Blakemore, Mistress Donna and, perhaps, Mistress Eleanor, and the cruel determination of Mistress Helen, Mistress Anne and Mistress Celine.

'Do you like your new body, Shelly?' Justine asks.

I look at her and remember my helpless desire for this beautiful, graceful and erotically aloof woman. Young, yet wise beyond her years. Cool, yet incredibly sexy. A stern, sensual ice queen. I behold the two beauties – maybe thirty years separating them – and remember the various ways in which I have served them, the places my tongue has been, the secrets that float effortlessly between us in each sexually charged look. I remember the loving cruelty of their control, the expert and inescapable nature of their bondage, the perverse enthusiasm at the heart of their erotic imaginations. Yes, they are very much the same, these two women. A tall glacial blonde and an ample dark-eyed brunette. The same and yet different; a perfect and intersecting contrast rooted in the same shatteringly simple truth: the affirmation of the feminine will through the subjugation of men.

'Yes, mistress,' I reply, my voice a powerful demonstration of the truly profound nature of my alteration.

I pick up a single black leather bag at Aunt Jane's side and ask them to follow me.

As I mince forward, I am aware of their eyes feasting on my buxom sissy form, and I make sure I wiggle my tightly pantied bottom in as ultra-feminine a manner as possible.

As we climb the stairs, I try to determine exactly what it is about Aunt Jane and Justine that has changed. As they stare up at my red nylon-encased legs, I contemplate a reserve in their voices as well as an irony. It is almost as if they are here for a secret reason. There is a touch of duplicity about them, of disguise.

These thoughts are soon dispelled when we arrive at the room allocated by the red number pinned to their bag. And it is only as we enter the guest suite that a sudden and quite shocking fact makes itself known: before me is one of the giant double beds reserved for mistresses . . . and their lovers!

I place the bag on the bed and, with shaking knees, turn to face the two women, suddenly painfully aware of the new nature of their relationship, trying to hide a strange mixture of sexual arousal and intense, if ill-defined jealously.

'Yes, Shelly: I'm afraid Justine and I are more than just good friends now. The last three months have brought us together in a rather more intimate manner.'

Aunt Jane's words, delivered with renewed irony, are followed by a somewhat theatrical embrace between the two women and a long passionate kiss.

I watch in astonishment. The two most important women in my life (before I met Myriam) have become lovers.

'Don't worry about the bag,' my Aunt adds, sitting down on the bed. 'But you can give me a foot massage.'

She kicks off her shoes and stretches out her long elegant legs. I feel my sex engage in another useless struggle with its layers of rubber and metal restraint, perform a deep curtsey and kneel before my most revered mistress.

With hot shaking hands, I lift her left foot and then begin, very gently, to massage the instep. Aunt Jane sighs with a deeply aroused relief and I look up at Justine with admiring, yet also deeply curious eyes.

She releases one of her very slight half smiles and then removes her silk jacket. Beneath, she is wearing a beautiful white silk blouse with a very low neck line.

'Kiss the foot,' she says suddenly, coldly, a voice distant and frightening.

I lean forward and kiss Aunt Jane's nylon-sheathed toes. Aunt Jane moans with pleasure and Justine laughs, a clipped cruel sound that echoes throughout the room.

Then, to my surprise, Justine unbuckles her thick patent leather belt and lets her black silk slacks fall to the ground. Beneath she is wearing sheer black nylon tights. She kicks off her high-heeled ankle boots and then steps out of the trousers. She strolls over to the bed and sits down next to her lover.

'When you've finished with Jane, do me.'

I nod fearfully and realise that both women require not just a massage, but the kinky delights of full foot worship. Soon I am smothering Aunt Jane's feet in kisses and caresses and, as I do so, the two women kiss and cuddle and Justine lets her own feet run up between my legs. The next fifteen minutes are a strange three-way sex game that aptly illustrates the history and nature of our relationship. I service my two mistresses with absolute commitment as they moan in each other's arms. I have known for some time that Aunt Jane is a lesbian. Previously she had been involved with Ms Hartley, Pansy's guardian, and Ms Hartley's absence from the Ball strikes me as unusual. I assume she will appear later and continue my erotic ministrations.

Eventually, I am told to stand to attention before the women with my hands behind my back. I present myself eagerly, yet also hesitantly. I am unsure of my ground now: so much seems to have changed between us in the last few months, yet so much is the same.

'We're both very impressed by what the SMC has done to you, Shelly,' my Aunt says, as Justine strokes her hair with a lover's gentle admiration. 'I hear you have met Eleanor Groves. I hear that she was more than a little taken with you. Eleanor is a wonderful inspirational woman, and she has played a major role in pushing forward the global agenda of the Bigger Picture. As you no doubt remember, my sweet sissy, this is not an agenda that I was immediately taken by. I sent you here to free you of your male weaknesses, to allow you to develop your femininity to its highest level. You have clearly achieved this, but at what cost? I can't answer that question yet, dearest. But what I can tell you is that I have begun to doubt the wisdom of the Bigger Picture and the motivation of many of those who lead it. Eleanor appears increasingly a figurehead, a useful tool to access power, influence and finance. Emily Ashcroft is a moderate and, ultimately, she is in a weak position. She is supported by others – Donna, Amelia Blakemore. But these are in the minority. The true leaders of the Bigger Picture are emerging. These are the hardliners. You have seen their fascist vision, the totalitarian paradox of the Femocracy. A world where sissies are little more than toys to be deposed of at will. A world built on a sado-erotic philosophy of female power and domination. A world really no different to the one we have now. A world controlled by women like Mistress Helen and Mistress Anne, and others, even more extreme. Indeed, in the hands of these women, the Bigger Picture will be even more of a fascist enterprise. I have been given access to secret documents from an internal pressure group, documents insisting on the forced castration of all sissies, of an abandonment of the principle of a self-controlling male desire in favour of its total eradication. These

218

same documents insist on the mass extermination of all males who refuse to undergo this most radical of treatments. It is little more than a cracked feminist Nazism, and it will fail miserably.'

I listen in horrified astonishment. I listen and begin to understand the core of the tensions I have witnessed over the last few months. The sect within a sect. The arguments at the steering group. The random cruelties of Mistress Anne. The kindness of Mistress Donna. The ironic and gentle attentions of the wonderful Ms Blakemore. The brutal indifference of Mistress Helen.

'The radical vision is doomed to failure because no man will allow himself to be utterly destroyed, Senso or no Senso. Never mind who is running the country or the world. Extremism will always breed resistance. Always. And the moderates? Well, history has shown that, if they don't act, they too will be destroyed.'

And it is at this exact point that the door to the large elegant room opens and Lady Ashcroft enters. Aunt Jane immediately falls silent and rises from the bed, a brief look of concern transforming into a broad generous smile. The two women embrace and I watch Lady Ashcroft's hand pass in a lingering fashion across my Aunt's tightly skirted, generous and very shapely behind.

They kiss and part.

'Three months is a surprisingly long time,' Lady Ashcroft says, appraising my Aunt carefully. 'You haven't been returning my calls.'

Aunt Jane smiles weakly and nods. 'I've been out of the country. On business.'

There is a moment of tense silence. Lady Ashcroft's beautiful pale-blue eyes narrow. 'Business,' she whispers, a hint of suspicion, a touch of doubt in her deep clear voice.

Aunt Jane ignores Lady Ashcroft's change of tone and turns away from her, talking as she does so, her eyes fixed in a cold and meaningful way on the semi-clad Justine.

'A little modelling work. In America. For one of Celine's companies, actually. A very interesting experience.'

'She never mentioned it.'

'I doubt very much if she knew.'

'You didn't tell her?'

'It didn't seem particularly necessary. And anyway, none of us know everything about all the members . . . do we?'

Aunt Jane arrives at Justine's side and sits down on the bed next to her so that she is, once again, facing Lady Ashcroft.

'Helen has done a marvellous job with Shelly. Surely the best yet.'

The subject changed, Lady Ashcroft's look of distrust fades and a smile returns to her beautiful face.

'Helen's determination and Amelia's genius. Now we have the basis for a true mass production. With this and the completion of the Sados facility . . . well, there's no stopping us.'

'I hear Senso is about to be injected into the American market. With this and the support of Eleanor . . . we are facing the first major expansion.'

'Within a year, the Bigger Picture will be a global presence.'

'But is it a coherent Picture, Emily?'

This sudden question wipes the smile off Lady Ashcroft's full strawberry-painted lips.

'What does that mean? You're certainly full of mystery today, Jane.'

'It means that Celine has a different view of things. That the American message is too extreme. That the conservatives clearly have the upper hand in our biggest expanding market. They're already talking of castration camps.'

Lady Ashcroft's eyes widen. There is real anger in her voice as she virtually spits her response.

'That's utter rubbish. We have agreed the middle way. The Steering Group is fully agreed –'

'And Anne and Celine? They're openly plotting behind the back of the Group, and Helen is helping them.'

A sudden sadness washes over Lady Ashcroft's face.

'Yes, I know. I know all about the plotting, the back-stabbing . . . the factionalism. And I have to fight it every day. We have to keep to the middle way or everything will be destroyed.'

The sense of depressed resignation in Lady Ashcroft's tone seems to have taken the wind out of Aunt Jane's sails.

'Yes,' she whispers. 'I'm sure you're right.'

Lady Ashcroft smiles weakly. 'Now . . . get yourself ready. Drinks will be served at 7.00 p.m. And let me have Shelly back . . . she's needed downstairs.'

For the next two hours, I continue to assist with the arrivals and associated preparations, my mind filled with erotic thoughts of my Aunt and Justine and more considered speculations on the nature of her visit. There is a split in the Bigger Picture. My Aunt, introduced to the sect only three months ago, is now warning of its downfall in a manner that is more in tune with a seasoned and ultimately betrayed veteran. The mysterious conversation with Lady Ashcroft has only added to the sense of unease about my role and the future direction of this strange and kinky society of female dominants, a direction that will very much be influenced by those who are now arriving, a striking array of the rich and the powerful, many of whom I cannot help but recognise. I assist some of the world's most powerful businesswomen, politicians, sports personalities, television chat show hostesses, actresses, even a famous and highly controversial woman priest. I feel their eyes fall upon me, mostly looks of fascination and desire, but in some cases fear, envy and disgust. I know that tonight I am to be 'publicly unveiled' in a no doubt very humiliating manner, and the thought fills me with a terrible mixture of trepidation and intense masochistic arousal.

As well as the maids – she-male and female – there is a small army of young female catering staff, provided by Mistress Celine. Each one is no older than twenty, and all are strikingly good looking. They are dressed in very sheer black nylon tights, black micro mini skirts and cream-coloured silk blouses. Each one looks uncomfortable with the spectacle that is revealing itself before their eyes, particularly the elaborate costumes and ultra-buxom figures of the sissy maids. Even as the guests are arriving in the large entrance hall, the catering staff are walking amongst them with glasses of expensive white wine set on silver trays. On tables lining the far wall of the foyer area, there are more bottles and glasses. On more than one occasion I have noticed the propensity for alcohol and the connection between the high spirits it inspires and the increased suffering of the sissies.

Just before 7.00 p.m., Annette appears and ushers me into a side room just before the vast library. Here I find myself standing before Ms Blakemore and Mistress Donna. Standing next to Mistress Donna is Pansy, dressed in her beautiful junior's costume.

I haven't seen my beloved Ms Blakemore for over a week and the sight of her dressed in a gorgeous black velvet evening gown, with a plunging sensually revealing neckline, a dress that runs to the tops of her black nylon-sheathed ankles, is a sight to bring a helpless smile of absolute joy to my cherry-painted sissy lips.

She steps forward in five-inch-high stiletto-heeled court shoes and I perform a deep loving curtsey, making sure she gets the fullest view possible of my red nylon enveloped thighs and heavily befrilled white silk panties.

'You look marvellous, as usual, Shelly.'

There is the usual hint of ironic tease in her sultry American accent and I smile shyly, the memories of our exciting days together washing over me like a shower of liquid gold.

'But now it is time to make you look even more spectacular.'

She steps back to reveal a table laden with sissy delights.

'You will go to the ball, Cinderella,' Mistress Donna teases.

I turn to look at her and find myself remembering beautiful mysterious Myriam. Like Myriam, she is a petite blonde with striking blue eyes. Unlike Myriam, Mistress Donna has the exact precision figure of a trained athlete, a figure tonight expertly displayed by a tight white nylon sweater, a pink leather mini skirt, white nylon tights and pink patent leather ankle boots with striking six-inch heels.

There are two dresses – one for Pansy and one for myself. My dress is snow white; Pansy's is a delicate powder blue. I stare at Pansy and see the fierce bottomless need burning in her large eyes. She smiles slightly and I remember the love and intimacy we have shared.

'I suggest you begin by undressing each other.'

I curtsey my understanding and mince towards Pansy. Our eyes meet again and a powerful electric charge of animal desire flows between us. I remember our last erotic adventure, a night of helpless oral pleasuring, a night of her tightly gagged moans of uncontrollable pleasure and repeatedly violent orgasm. I drank deep of her that long, sexy night, and in this dark teasing consumption our love, always so powerful – my first sissy love – had once again blossomed. She smiles slightly, her body quivering with the terrible sexual need that is our constant companion. I behold her marvellous form and fight off a moan of savage sex hunger. Her long blonde hair is bound in a delightful schoolgirl ponytail with a white silk ribbon which itself is bound in a fat sissy bow. Her gleaming white silk pinafore strains in a deeply erotic manner against the pressure of her buxom sissy form and the tight red dress beneath. Shelly knows Pansy is very tightly corseted – Mistress Anne insists on an elaborate and constant array of foundation wear – the 'discipline of body restraint'. She also knows the corseting has the quite deliberate effect of pushing the sissy's already considerable bosom forward in a most provocative and sensual manner.

Pansy's cherry-red lips glisten promisingly in the striking sunlight that bleeds into the room and her perfect snow white teeth – another product of the transformation – sparkle briefly as her tongue slowly crosses her lips.

I stand a few inches from her and swallow hard. Her smile broadens. There is a confidence in her eyes that I lack. A purity of purpose. An acceptance. I know that at the core of this confidence is her utter devotion to the sexual fascism of the Bigger Picture.

She has adapted in a way that I now know I never can to the demands of sissy love.

'Turn around,' she whispers. 'My love.'

I smile shyly and turn. I feel her hands gently untie the bow binding my own silk pinafore in place and sigh with a deep sexual pleasure.

In a few incredibly erotic minutes, I am stripped down to just my ever-present restrainer, my rock hard sex rising before my mistresses like a sex rocket long delayed blast off. The women behold my perfect sissy form with tormented eyes, paying particular attention to my proud firm large breasts. I look into Ms Blakemore's eyes and see a terrible need only just resisted.

'And now Pansy,' she whispers, her voice lost deep in the sex trance.

Soon, we are both naked except for our restrainers and standing before the table upon which our ball gowns are set out, our junior maid's uniforms piled at our dainty sissy feet.

'Tonight will mark the successful completion of the second phase of your training,' Mistress Donna explains. 'On Monday you will begin formal placements as qualified housemaids. However, the full status of SMC housemaid cannot finally be granted until you have completed the Placements. It is here you will act as independent maidservants to a variety of highly demanding mistresses outside of the SMC training academy. It is here that what you have learnt in the past few months will be fully and thoroughly tested. And if you pass, my sexy little flowers, then the next stage of the great adventure will begin. Pansy will remain here as a training maid, working on the next generation of sissies which will begin to flow into the academy from the regional centres. Then, once the regional training centres have been established in their own right, she – along with the rest of us who remain in the HQ – will relocate to Sados. And Shelly – once you have graduated, you will return to the West Country with your Aunt and establish the first fully fledged regional training academy.'

We listen, entranced, to this gentle reaffirmation of our sissy futures; yet even as the lovely mistress sets out these futures, there is doubt in my mind, doubt inspired by the bizarre events of the last two weeks and the increasing sense that all is not well amongst the Bigger Picture's senior sisterhood.

Then, finally, we are allowed to dress. Pansy is assisted by Mistress Donna and I, to my utter delight, am aided by Ms Blakemore. The elegant plump black beauty holds up what initially looks like a cream-coloured ball gown made of beautiful shimmering silk and covered in sparkling sequins. However, closer inspection reveals that the gown has been very elaborately customised for sissy use. Indeed, its key function seems to be to ensure that the paradoxical nature of the sissy form is displayed to full and very apparent effect.

The dress has a narrow central bodice that widens into a chest section of a much finer transparent white silk of the type used to make stockings. The long skirt of the dress runs only down the sides and back, with the front section completely open. Beneath this startling construction, I am to wear only a white rubber mini corset and a pair of white nylon tights, plus a pair of stunning white silk-lined court shoes with testing five-inch heels.

But before any of this gorgeous attire is allowed near my body, Ms Blakemore, a wicked excited smile lighting up her gorgeous face, leans forward and begins very gently to remove the cock rings.

I whimper with intense brutal pleasure as the rings are unclipped and then perform a helpless dance of frustrated ecstasy as the plump dusky beauty teasingly unrolls the fiendish rubber restrainer. Then, once again, my cock is free. I remember the second before I entered Myriam, the instant of masculine need, the bizarre collision of my desire and my form. I blush helplessly, a terrible confession of my guilt.

'This should amuse you,' Ms Blakemore says, taking a sheer white nylon sheath from the tabletop. My eyes widen and she smiles.

'Yes, a little piece of teasingly soft decoration for the party.'

Then she slowly slips the cool scented sheath over my hard boiling sex and I lose control completely. As she guides it along the crimson length of my cock, I moan and squeal with a furious pleasure. And soon, thanks to Mistress Donna's own erotic ministrations, poor Pansy is doing exactly the same.

'I told you we should have gagged them,' Mistress Donna snaps, very obviously enjoying herself.

Once the sheath has been pulled tightly in place over my bulging aching balls, it is secured with a pink silk ribbon tied in a suitably fat sissy bow.

The kiss of soft Senso nylon on my tormented granite sex is almost unbearable and tears of terrible frustration are soon building up in my large doe eyes. And no sooner has this wonderful torment been completed, than Ms Blakemore takes up the white nylon tights and orders me to put them on, an order I obey without question. I slip the sheer deeply fetishistic material over my silky legs and a smile of deep dark pleasure once again crosses my face. Of all the fabrics and materials that have possessed my sissified form over the past months, it is surely the sheer nylon of tights and the various kinky body stockings that has brought the most immediate and powerful sensual pleasure. This pleasure has of course been doubled by the impregnation of cell-tormenting Senso, and as my body once again reacts to the fiendish irresistible chemical, I know that whatever happens, I will never be able to kick the addiction of ultra-femininity, the super drug that has swallowed my mind whole.

Like many of the body stockings, the tights are fitted with a strategically placed hole through which Ms Blakemore slips my sheathed cock and balls once I have managed to pull the hose into place around my waist. As she adjusts the ribbon, my watering eyes turn to Pansy. The poor sissy is wiggling and squealing angrily as Mistress Donna pulls her own rigid sex through the lace-frilled hole. Her tormented gyrations cause her large pale rose breasts to bounce with an almost hilarious fury and her bottom to wriggle in a most beautiful and arousing manner. Mistress Donna, angered by this teasing display, administers two very hard slaps to the sissy's pert backside, and although this succeeds in slightly stilling Pansy, it is quickly clear her sexual excitement has only increased.

With the tights positioned, it is a relatively simple task to wrap the mini corset tightly around my already strictly trained waist and clip it into position. As Ms Blakemore lovingly ensures that the clips fit into the row of eye sockets that ensure the tightest fit, my back arches inward and my breasts jut forward. The gorgeous black beauty laughs teasingly and compliments me on my spectacular bosom. I smile shyly and feel my unrestrained sex strain desperately in its ultra-soft nylon prison. Then, to my shock and deep pleasure, Ms Blakemore leans forward and gently caresses my tormented sex shaft with an elegant milk chocolate hand. I squeal with pleasure and her smile broadens.

'I miss our little chats, Shelly.'

'I do too, mistress.'

'Don't worry, though – there will be plenty of other opportunities. Perhaps sooner than you think.'

Her words perplex and arouse, but before I have a chance to consider their true meaning more fully, Ms Blakemore has removed her teasing hand and set about fitting me into the elaborate evening gown.

She carefully unzips the shimmering masterpiece of ultra-femininity and helps me step into it. A quiver of delight ripples across my sissy form as the dress is pulled up my finely hosed legs and over my tightly corseted waist. Ms Blakemore slides the dress up over my straining sensitised breasts and a whimper of painful arousal escapes my glistening cherry lips. Then I am inside it and my delectable African Queen is slowly pulling up the silver zip that traverses the dress from the waist to the high neck. And as the zip progresses up the curving line of my spine, the dress seems to close around my body and reveal its true, spectacularly erotic nature. As I suspected, the lower half of the dress is entirely open and my erect nylon-cocooned sex is fully exposed to view. The sides, back and bodice section of the dress are made from a skin-tight sequin-covered silk that hugs my figure like an erotic body glove. The chest section, as has been noted, is made from a much finer transparent silk and both manages to support my breasts and display them in a most enticing manner.

As soon as the dress is properly fitted, Ms Blakemore takes up a white-lace befrilled rubber ring and slips it gently over my nylon-enveloped cock. She then attaches a short length of narrow silver chain to a tiny eye fitted to the centre of the ring and attaches the other end of the chain to a small hook attached to the edge of the dress at the waist area. This has the effect of holding my stiff deeply tormented sex firmly in place at a forty-five degree angle. My feet are then slipped into the gorgeous silk-lined court shoes and I am ready for the Ball.

I turn to face Pansy and find myself looking at a reflection in powder blue. She looks utterly stunning and her sex-tormented eyes betray the fact that I also look quite spectacular.

But before we are allowed to reveal our splendidly decorated sissy forms, there are two final touches: a pair of white glacé ball gloves that stretch longingly up to my upper arms and a white rubber ball gag with two thick white leather straps that are buckled tightly together at the back of my neck as I moan with a deeply masochistic pleasure, a pleasure inspired by the fact that my gag has been coated in the unmistakably tasty sex juices of Ms Blakemore.

As we moan our appreciation of this final kinky touch, Ms Blakemore takes a vibrator control box from a leather handbag on the table and turns its sinister dial towards the highest level of vibration. In seconds, the fat long vibrators permanently positioned in our sissy backsides are buzzing furiously, and so are we. Then we are led from the room in a state of helpless bliss, fighting back well gagged squeals of dark bottomless pleasure, our strange adventure about to take a new and exciting turn in an even more bizarre direction than even I can imagine.

We are led from the room and out into the main foyer area, a space now full of elegantly dressed, beautiful and very jovial women – over one hundred of them. And as Ms Blakemore, flanked by the lovely Mistress Donna, leads Pansy and me to the Ball's relaxed noisy reception area, heads begin to turn and the eyes begin to focus in on the spectacle of the two new sissies. As we totter forward, our breasts and sexes bouncing helplessly before us, we are aware of a wave of unnerving silence crashing over the crowd, a wave of calm fascination, a wave of helpless and careful curiosity.

We descend into a jungle of powerful sensual perfumes and exotic feminine plumage. I feel eyes burn into every inch of my sissified form, a dreadful group attention that is both highly disturbing and deeply erotic. I feel my body in a way I have never felt it: under these hungry eyes I am alive in a way I never felt possible. My sex twitches in its teasing nylon prison and I fight back more squeals of appallingly irresistible pleasure as the vibrator buzzes angrily inside my tenderised and expertly stretched arse. The rock-hard nipples of my impressive tormented tits brush against a wall of soft silk and I know this is my dreadful eternal sissy heaven.

We are led through a corridor of mature exquisitely cultivated beauty towards the main banquet room. I notice the catering staff walking amongst the women serving drinks from silver trays. One of the girls, a petite busty redhead, turns towards me and nearly drops the tray in astonishment. Then we are in the banquet room itself, which is gradually filling with guests.

The room has been set out as a series of large circular tables, with a long narrow table on a raised platform at the very front. It is here that the senior figures will sit, looking out over the assembled guests. We are led across the floor of the room, between and around the tables. As we totter along besides our mistresses, I notice that the housemaids are busy at work putting the final touches to the tables. Each is dressed in a beautiful and very short pink maid's dress supported by billowing lace-trimmed frou-frou petticoating. Over the dress is tied a white silk pinafore decorated with a large pink rose at the bulging chest section. Added to this are ultra-sheer white tights decorated with hundreds of tiny sparkling roses and pink patent leather ankle boots with pink silk ribbon lacing, six-inch stiletto heels and a silver rose positioned at the end of each sharply pointed toe.

Here they all are: Christina, Annette, Kathy and, of course, the gorgeous and so very troubling Myriam. And it is Myriam's eyes I meet first. I find myself beholding a look of pure guilt, a look that fills me with a deep dread about the hours ahead. She avoids my gaze and tries to continue with her duties, but her distraction and distress are made apparent when she accidentally knocks a slender wine glass off the table. As it smashes to pieces, Christina looks up angrily from her own efforts and then comes rushing forward. We totter past them and soon the large imposing room is echoing with poor Myriam's cries as she is soundly spanked by the fearsome ultra-sexy senior housemaid.

We are led up onto the stage and made to stand together by a microphone. Mistress Donna then ties our arms together behind our backs with rubber cording at the wrists and elbows, a painfully tight binding that forces our chests forward and inspires more moans of pain and pleasure, the two now utterly indistinguishable.

We stand side by side and stare out at the huge hall, a sea of oval tables serviced by busy aroused slaves. Then the main double doors to the hall are pushed open and Eleanor Groves enters, followed by Lady Emily Ashcroft and the other mistresses. I feel Pansy's beautiful form stiffen as she recognises the handsome fear-inspiring form of Taylor at Mistress

232

Eleanor's side. She is dressed in a red silk trouser suit with cruel seven-inch stiletto-heeled pumps; he is sheathed in leather – tight black leather trousers, black leather biker boots and even a black leather shirt. His arrogant countenance is unchanged and more paradoxical than ever amidst this gathering of female dominants.

The mistresses are followed into the room by the guests. The maids take up strategic positions once the mistresses have passed, so that they can show the guests, each of whom has a gold dining card, to their places at the tables.

As the mistresses file onto the stage, I find myself suddenly aware of my strange position of public display and a sense of acute embarrassment washes over me. Then I am aware that Ms Blakemore and Mistress Donna have disappeared to take up their places at the 'high table' and we two sissies are alone, facing the mass of guests whose eyes are, once again, drawn towards our tethered and displayed forms with a helpless fascination. Indeed, as they sit and the maids move from table to table serving the first course and the catering girls follow them with bottles of wine, a disturbing quiet falls over the hall, a quiet rooted in dark anticipation.

And once everyone is seated and their drinks topped up, it is Mistress Eleanor, the stunning startling Eleanor Groves, who rises from her seat and walks to the font of the stage. And as she approaches the microphone, the guests, impressed as ever by this powerful icon of the Bigger Picture, burst into spontaneous and loud applause.

She stands at the mic for a few seconds, a slightly embarrassed smile on her face, and then signals for the guests to be quiet. The applause dies down and her smile becomes more confident.

'Thank you,' she says, her voice calm, authoritative, the voice we have all come to associate with the most powerful woman on the planet Earth. 'I think it is fair to say we have come a very long way in a very short time.'

There is more spontaneous applause, which she indicates should pass as quickly as possible.

'Yes, it is impressive. We are all amazed by the speed of events. But perhaps we shouldn't be so surprised. Our message is one that all women will instinctively take to their hearts. Our message is one of hope for a peaceful future for the human race, a future freed from male violence, greed and blind ambition. A world of genuine democracy, or rather – Femocracy.'

There is yet more loud enthusiastic applause. I feel the vibrations in my arse suddenly quicken and know that Ms Blakemore is sitting behind me, tormenting me quite deliberately. I close my eyes and fight the mind-bending effect of this increased anal stimulation. I fight to listen to Eleanor Groves's admirable words. And as I listen, I remember the other words and the different vision; I remember the vision of the future encapsulated in Mistress Anne's elaborate video, a future based on a fascistic feminist elite and a dictatorship built on war and oppression. I remember Mistress Helen's elegantly neo-Nietszchian analysis of the female future and I remember the name of the island paradise that will house the global government of the Femocracy: Sados. I remember the discussions with Ms Blakemore, her ironic analysis of the extremism of Helen and Anne. Then there was the argument at the Steering Group, the disagreement on tactics. And finally, I remember the mysterious arrival of Aunt Jane and Justine and the bitterness of their analysis of the Bigger Picture. As Mistress

Eleanor elegantly spins the web of the female future for the patrons and would-be patrons of the Bigger Picture, I understand her role a little more. Whatever she might believe – and this remains disturbingly unclear – she remains a figurehead in this organisation, a mouthpiece for ideas that amuse her, but for which she seems to have limited sympathy. And if she is not the true leader she is presented as being, then who is the leader? Lady Ashcroft? No; despite her authority and control, despite the respect she is held in, I suspect that she too has only a nominal role in the true leadership. Ultimately, the leadership is unclear because no one faction has yet established a firm enough foothold to create a position of genuine dominance. But, despite this, it is now clear to me who the *factional* leaders are: Ms Blakemore for the moderates and Mistress Helen for the radicals. It is these two powerful determined personalities who will determine the ultimate nature of the Bigger Picture and its vision of the future.

Mistress Eleanor delivers a polished speech worthy of the former wife of the President of the United States. She presses all the right buttons and describes great plans and their ongoing implementation: the injection of Senso into the world's fashion markets, the emergence of the regional training centres, the nearing completion of the Sados facility, and the new technologies of sissification pioneered by Ms Blakemore. And then, as she describes the medical and technological systems used to create Pansy and myself, she finally introduces the two newest sissies to the enraptured audience.

At first, there is a strange contemplative silence as the audience takes in the visions of sissy perfection we have come to represent. Then there is a smattering of applause which slowly builds to a more enthusiastic response and, finally, to a standing ovation. Yes, the gathered mass of powerful women are impressed by the spectacle of Pansy and Shelly and by the vision of the future painted by Eleanor Groves. As we squirm with a furious embarrassment and the deepest darkest masochistic excitement, as our buxom figures vibrate and are tormented by the relentlessly exquisite kiss of Senso, we witness a turning point. We represent the reality of the Bigger Picture, the truth of the conviction and power of the feminisation process. We are the guarantee which will underpin any investment these women will make in the Femocracy.

Eventually, Mistress Eleanor manages to quieten the women and then talk further about the levels of additional funding required and the urgency of progressing key projects associated with the globalisation of the Bigger Picture. At the core of the developments will be the transformation of the Sissy Maids Company, or SMC Incorporated as it will become known, into a multi-national operation, a vast front for the activities of the Bigger Picture. Expansion will be swift and relentless, and will be led by a global President. Not, as I might have suspected, Mistress Eleanor herself, but Mistress Helen. The plump English beauty is then introduced to the crowd and I cannot help but look round at her. She is flanked by Mistress Celine and Mistress Anne, both of whom are smiling triumphantly. And it is at this point that I know the radical wing is in control, that this is the moment they have chosen to step forward and impose their will. My eyes meet Ms Blakemore's and I see a terrible, if still vaguely amused sadness. She smiles and shrugs and I sense an awful change is about to take place.

Eventually, once the clapping has subsided, we are led from the stage. As I pass the mistresses on the high table, I notice that Mistress Anne is speaking in a very animated manner to Mistress Helen. Their eyes fall on me and I see a sudden powerful hatred. Mistress Celine takes over from Mistress Eleanor and then we are guided through the crowd of women that has formed at the foot of the stage. Their hands fall upon our delightfully decorated sissy forms and our helpless horny moaning increases in volume. Eager fingers roll across my bottom, my silk-sheathed breasts and my nylon-wrapped cock. The hot alcohol-scented breath of a hundred women mingles with their expensive perfumes to create a sensual cloud of feminine hunger that envelops my tormented excited sissy form totally. I squeal with pleasure and beg for release, for a final heart-shattering orgasm that will free me once and for all from this constant craving.

Then, after some fifteen minutes of the women's eager attentions, we are led from the banqueting hall. And it is here that Christina and Annette, clad in their beautiful ultra-sexy pink maid's costumes, step forward. Annette grasps my tethered arms roughly and I look at her with anger and fear.

'Mistress Helen wants to see Shelly in her quarters immediately.'

Her words are delivered with a fierce frightening conviction, her tone making it very clear I am in serious trouble.

Annette leads me away from Pansy. We exchange frightened, yet also gentle looks of love. Suddenly I am aware that I may never see her again and tears begin to well up in my helplessly doe eyes.

I look at Annette as we climb the stairs to Mistress Helen's quarters and see a grim happiness in her delicate sissy totters. I remember the sadistic punishments she has inflicted on me and the obvious pleasure she has taken in my pain and humiliation. I also remember our time together in the Nursery and the terrible torments of the joint suspension before Mistress Anne's dark vision of the future. We have drunk deep of each other's most intimate liquids and suffered terribly for the amusement of our mistresses. Yet there is still no love lost between us. Annette remains very much Mistress Anne's creature and thus committed to the radical path, despite the terrible fate it promises her. Or perhaps she feels that, as Mistress Anne's pretty sissy poodle, she will, in some way, escape a full sex change?

As my eyes feast helplessly on her long white nylon-sheathed legs and helplessly wiggling and perfectly formed bottom, we arrive outside the door to Mistress Helen's quarters. Annette enters without knocking and I follow fearfully behind.

Surprisingly, the rooms that make up her luxurious chambers are deserted. I am made to wiggle-mince into the bedroom and sit on a single white wooden chair placed by the large double bed. To my surprise, there is a long coffin-like wooden box next to the chair and as I look down at it with genuine trepidation, a cruel smile crosses Annette's beautiful face.

'Don't worry, Shelly . . . that's not for you. Mistress Anne has something face more radical in mind for you.'

I am made to sit on the chair and Annette leaves the room.

I sit alone, my arms still secured tightly behind my back, my mouth filled with the ultra-effective white rubber ball gag, the vibrator still buzzing furiously in my arse, my sex pointing up at me like a finger of dark accusation.

My sissy heart pounds angrily and I consider why I have been brought here. Officially, I have now completed the second stage of my training and am due to begin the placements on Monday. Officially, I am to be presented with the list of my five special external tests at a brief ceremony tomorrow evening. Then, I am to spend the day with a specially selected mistress and the night with a specially selected sissy. But, as I sit frightened and alone, I very much fear I will never start, never mind complete, my placements.

Then there is a disturbance outside and, with a sudden burst of terrifying energy, the door to the main chamber flies open. I hear raised voices: Mistress Helen, Mistress Anne, Ms Blakemore. In the background there is a desperate high-pitched squealing. Then they are in the bedroom, rolling through the doorway from the main chamber like a sudden black storm cloud. There is an argument taking place, between Mistress Anne and Ms Blakemore.

'But I have the evidence. Once you've seen it, they'll be no question.'

Mistress Anne delivers these terrifying words and Ms Blakemore dismisses them with an angry wave of her hand.

'You've spent the last two years using video technology to tell stories, Anne. It's a con, a trick. You're trying to take advantage.'

'Of what? Of what?'

'The consolidation of Helen's position, of your position.'

'What utter paranoid rubbish! Can you believe this nonsense, Helen?'

Helen indicates that they should both be quiet and faces me. As she does so, Annette enters the room again, tugging violently on a leather leash. At the end of the leash is a squealing struggling Myriam. Dressed in a black latex rubber body suit that covers her buxom form like a coat of glistening black paint, her arms lashed behind her back with black rubber cording at the wrists and elbows, her mouth filled with a huge black rubber ball gag, tears of utter horror and despair flooding from her beautiful blue eyes, a thick leather collar fitted tightly around her neck, she is the perfect vision of the damsel in distress, and also a dreadful indication of why we have all gathered in Mistress Helen's bedroom.

Mistress Anne then hands Mistress Helen a silver DVD in a clear plastic case. Helen walks over to a home entertainment centre placed a few feet beyond the bed. As she inserts the DVD into a silver state of the art player, I look into Ms Blakemore's dark eyes and no longer find an ironic distance. Instead, I find myself confronting a real heart-stopping fear.

The large flat-screen TV is turned on and within a few seconds my fate is sealed. For here is the guest room, thirty hours previously, and here is Myriam and myself making violent helpless love. The whole thing had been filmed: an elaborate set-up. A trap I fell into with only a pathetic whimper of resistance.

And now there is silence, the silence of the undeniable truth. Even Myriam's desperate squeals of protest cease. I look at her and she returns my angry gaze with a look of weak protest. She has betrayed me, she has been the tool of my destruction. She has led me to a truly terrible and cruel fate. Yet her eyes say NO: I too am a victim. Her costume would seem to support her pleading eyes. But then I realise that she too has been used – used to betray me and then herself betrayed by Mistress Anne. I can find no sympathy for Myriam, although I cannot deny my continued painful desire for this beautiful French maiden.

After a few minutes, Mistress Helen switches the TV off and turns once again to face me.

'The evidence is overwhelming. Don't you agree, Amelia?'

Ms Blakemore's silence is the equivalent of a thunderous YES.

Mistress Anne's smile is large and brutal; the cruel smile of the arrogant victor. Annette looks at me with utter contempt. How much I want to hurt her!

'You will perform the full gender reassignment operation in the morning. Then she and Myriam will be sold.'

My eyes widen in utter horror: I am to be subject to a full sex change procedure and then sold into white slavery! I look to Ms Blakemore for assistance, but all I find is a harsh gaze of indifference.

'Make sure that she is suited and hooded,' Ms Blakemore says, her voice filled with a cold disappointment. 'I never want to see her face again. And make sure Myriam is hooded and crated up. We will ship her out in the morning, and then Shelly will be transported on Monday.'

Her words are directed to Annette, who has now been joined by Christina, whose own beautiful brown eyes are filled with sympathy and sadness.

Ms Blakemore then turns her back on me and leaves, followed closely by Mistress Helen and Mistress Anne. We are thus left in the dubious care of Christina and Annette.

'You deal with Myriam,' Christina says to Annette. 'I will prepare Shelly.'

Both Myriam and myself protest violently with a series of well gagged squeals and furious shakes of the head. Annette tugs violently on the leash to silence Myriam and Christina produces a nasty looking riding crop from beneath her pinafore.

'I don't want to use this, Shelly, but I will if you make me.'

I fall silent and look at her through tear-stained eyes. There is nothing I can do. I am doomed to the removal of my sex and a dreadful slavery.

I watch as Annette takes a black latex rubber eyeless and mouthless hood from the pocket in her pinafore and then stretches it with a cruel slowness over Myriam's beautiful head. The terror in her eyes is almost unbearable as they disappear beneath the layer of skin-tight rubber. Her squeals of fear and outrage quickly return, but by this time, she is totally helpless – bound, gagged, blind, deaf and dumb. She is hauled over to the crate and left to balance precariously as her determined she-male captor removes the lid to reveal a rubber-lined interior and much leather strapping.

I watch with a deep horror as Annette forces gorgeous helpless Myriam to step over the rim of the crate and then lie face down, so that her voluptuous body fills the length of the crate. The strapping, which is fixed to the sides of the crate, is then used to bind the poor maid in place at the neck, the middle back, the thighs and calves. Thus, she is totally immobilised and ready for shipment. And this, I know, is the fate that awaits me.

As Annette secures the lid to the crate, my eyes turn toward Christina. She has taken from the wall closet another black rubber body suit and matching hood. It seems I am to spend the night before the awful final operation trapped in the same rubber cocoon as my lovely Myriam.

Aided by Annette, Christina helps me to my feet and then the two stunning sissy maids begin to untie and undress me. The fat ball gag is left in position, but other than that I am soon completely naked. As I have not been restrained, the two she-males find themselves staring at my still rock-hard long cock with hungry eyes.

242

'Use the pin restrainer,' Christina whispers, her voice filled with sissy need.

Annette's smile widens and she heads off to the closet. I look at Christina with angry hurt eyes.

'I'm sorry,' she says. 'Mistress Anne has insisted that you spend your last night as a biological male wearing the pin restrainer.'

Tears of despair and terror pour from my eyes and in a few moments, Annette has returned with the wicked torture device.

Christina takes it from her silk-covered hands and then very slowly, even apprehensively, rolls it into a fearsome mouth before beginning to slip it with a paradoxical gentleness over the hard hot length of my cock. I squeal and wiggle. Annette grabs my shoulders and holds me still as the restrainer makes its terrible progress towards and then over my bulging testicles. It feels as if a thousand tiny very sharp teeth are nibbling at my sex flesh and my squeals of considerable discomfort increase substantially. My buttocks clench instinctively around the still-buzzing vibrator, and then, very suddenly, my cock and balls are tightly sealed in the awful rubber prison.

As I whimper with fear and discomfort, I am forced into the rubber body suit. There are no zips or buttons – just a single opening which I am made to step into. Christina then pulls the suit up my body and in a few minutes I am enveloped from toe to neck. I feel the rock-hard nipples of my substantial breasts push angrily against the second skin rubber and I know that every single contour of my buxom she-male form is outlined and accentuated by the rubber, a fact made very apparent by the looks of desire in the maids' wide doe eyes.

My rubber-sheathed arms are forced behind my back and bound with rubber cording at the wrists and elbows and so are my legs at the ankles, knees and thighs. Then I am made to hop back to the chair and forced to sit down upon it. I look up at Christina with pleading eyes and I see tears well up in her own gorgeous orbs.

'I'm sorry, Shelly. I really am. It was so good to have known you. So very good . . .'

And these are the last words I hear before the rubber hood is pulled down over my face and I am plunged into a terror-framed darkness and absolute silence.

Despite my blind terror, my fear-driven heart, my shaking body, I remain helplessly excited. The Senso rubber body suit, the furiously buzzing vibrator and my ultra-sensitive constantly aroused breasts make sure of that. And I remain in this deeply unnerving state for what seems like a dark terrible eternity, yet which, on reflection, is probably no more than an hour or so. Locked in a total silence, so very tightly tethered, in a deep blackness, I can only ponder the ease with which I have been manipulated by Mistress Anne and Myriam. And as I think of Myriam, I again see that she too has been a victim, that she had been betrayed equally by the wicked, beautiful and utterly remorseless Mistress Anne. Indeed, the two of us have been nothing but pawns in the battle for the Bigger Picture, expendable pawns who, having served their purpose, are now being clearly and cruelly disposed of.

A quiver of horror crashes over my rubberised tormented body as I imagine the coming hours. Soon, I will be taken to the operating theatre hidden deep in the bowels of the Ashcroft mansion house. There, still tightly hooded, I will be put to sleep and subjected to full sex change surgery using the revolutionary techniques developed by Ms Blakemore, techniques that will ensure a near perfect remoulding of my cock and balls into an ultra-sensitive and fully functional vagina. Then I will be crated and shipped abroad, eventually to be sold into sex slavery in the secret markets of a well known third world country. The agents of the Bigger Picture will ensure that both Myriam and myself fetch a high price, and thus that SMC will make a handsome profit.

Then I find myself thinking of Myriam again – beautiful wildly sexy Myriam, whose buxom perfect body is wrapped so tightly in second-skin Senso rubber and bound so very securely in the crate just a few inches from where my own tethered form is positioned. I remember our time together once more, the terrible glorious intimacies we have shared in the closet and then in the moments of sex madness so carefully planned by Mistress Anne, moments that led directly and deliberately to this terrible fate. There is no longer a lack of sympathy for Myriam, but there is a black hatred for Mistress Anne, a hatred that surprises me and which I saw, even after the truth had been revealed, in Ms Blakemore's beautiful eyes.

But then I sense movement. Somebody has entered the room. Then there are hands at my neck – the hood is being removed.

The hood is pulled off in one rough powerful tug and my eyes are suddenly blinded by a painfully powerful white light that gradually fades to reveal, standing directly before me, the striking fear-instilling figure of Master Taylor. I squeal with shock into the fat ball gag, a shock quickly increased when I behold the strange vision behind him. For here is Ms Blakemore with my Aunt and Justine. And Justine has a gun, a gleaming silver revolver. And standing before Justine is none other than Mistress Anne. But this is a very different Mistress Anne. For she has been stripped down to just bra, panties, suspender belt and black stockings. A thick strip of silver duct tape covers her mouth and her bulging crimson cheeks betray a fat panty gag. Her eyes are wild with anger and a very real fear. There is a large bruise on her left cheek, and her arms have been lashed tightly behind her back with rubber cording at the elbows and wrists. She moans furiously, but is clearly terrified of the gun that Justine presses against her ribs.

Then, to my even greater surprise, there is Annette. She is standing next to her gorgeous frightened mistress. But instead of the lovely pink maid's costume, she is now wearing the exact same Senso rubber body suit as myself. She too has been panty gagged and her lips taped shut with powerful silver duct tape. Her arms are secured in exactly the same way as Mistress Anne's. Also, a strip of duct tape has been spread cruelly over her eyes.

Ms Blakemore looks at me and smiles gently.

'Sorry about the little performance earlier,' she whispers, 'but we needed to subdue Helen before we made our move.'

Master Taylor helps me up off the chair and carries me over to my Aunt. He places me before her and I fall into her arms. She pulls me tight against her gorgeous plump body, burying my face in her large maternal bosom.

She then turns me around so I can witness the summary justice this gathering of 'moderate women' intend to apply to Mistress Anne and her treacherous sissy slave.

As Master Taylor drags a squealing sobbing blinded Annette to the chair, I begin to understand their plan.

'I deliberately instructed Annette to keep you hooded, my little pet,' Ms Blakemore explains. 'When we come to get the sissy my colleagues will think is you, it will be a relatively easy task to pass Annette off as Shelly and thus subject her to the sex change procedure. By the time "we" discover the truth, you will be long gone and Anne will be on her way to the slave markets.'

As Master Taylor forces poor Annette down onto the chair and takes up the hood that has, until a few seconds ago, covered my head, Mistress Anne squeals her terrible useless anger into her own panty gag, outraged by this strange and dreadful turn of events. And as soon as Annette has been secured, Master Taylor turns and walks towards the tall redheaded beauty, a look of hateful determination in his dark sensual eyes. Then all the fight goes out of her. Anger is replaced with an awful girlish fear, a fear made so much worse as Aunt Jane walks in front of her and holds up another black rubber body suit.

'Your travel wear, my dear.'

Then she is shaking her head furiously and tears of terror are pouring from her eyes. Justine steps forward and rips the lace bra from her body, revealing a pair of pert, beautifully shaped and delicately freckled breasts. Before she can even react to this latest outrage, Master Taylor has grabbed her and ripped away her panties and stockings in two or three powerful strokes that leave the gorgeous dominant naked and utterly helpless.

I watch with wide aroused eyes as Mistress Anne is forced into the rubber body suit. After a great deal of struggle – including a violent cropping administered with some enthusiasm by Ms Blakemore – Mistress Anne is sealed in the suit and her arms and feet are tightly bound. Then the lid of the crate is removed and poor Myriam is freed from her terrible premature burial. Mistress Anne watches this with horrified eyes, realising now that her fate is truly sealed: she is to be swapped for Myriam and, in a few hours, shipped to a foreign slave market.

'I'm sure they won't be disappointed when they find a slightly different model to the one advertised,' Aunt Jane teases.

Taylor pulls the hood from Myriam's head and, as the French beauty struggles to come to terms with the light and the bizarre spectacle of this erotic turn around, Taylor passes the hood to Aunt Jane and the beautiful cruel-eyed brunette then slowly pulls it down over Mistress Anne's head. And soon the redhead's angry, pathetic squeals fade and she is completely sealed in inescapable teasing Senso rubber. Aunt Jane and Taylor then lay the unfortunate Anne face down in the crate and strap her tightly in position. The lid is replaced and Ms Blakemore steps forward. She takes my head in her hands and guides my astonished eyes to hers.

'This is goodbye for quite a while, Shelly. There was no way I was going to allow them to ruin my greatest creation. By the time they understand what has happened, you will be safe. They will question me, but the blame will fall squarely on Anne and Justine. They will never know that Mistress Eleanor has supported us; that Taylor is our agent. That, ultimately, the moderate wing will triumph.'

She kisses me on the forehead and I whimper my helpless gratitude into the fat ball gag.

'The van is waiting at the rear entrance. The driver will take you to your own transport, at the edge of the wood. It will be 24 hours before the truth becomes apparent. I will make sure of that. By then, Annette will be the ideal plaything for Christina and Anne will be dancing for her new master.'

Aunt Jane and Ms Blakemore embrace and then exchange a long passionate kiss. Then Myriam and I, still tethered, gagged and sealed tightly in erotic Senso rubber (but with our ankles and knees freed), are led by Aunt Jane and Justine from the room. I take one last look at the wiggling figure of Annette and feel an awful sense of sadistic pleasure. How I wish I could see her face when she beholds her new body before the tall merciless mirror that dominates the room she shares with Christina.

We are led via the back stairs to the deserted kitchen and through a back door to a waiting people carrier. Myriam and I are put into the rear storage space, lying sideways face to face, our buxom forms pressed tightly together. A black silk sheet is pulled over our bodies and the rear door is slammed shut. I hear Aunt Jane and Justine exchange words with the driver and recognise the soft North American tones of Master Bentley. Then the van is moving, slowly, over the gravel of the large tree-surrounded forecourt of the mansion house.

I feel Myriam's body against mine and moan with relief and a dreadful aching pleasure. Her response is a gentle whimper of desire. As the van disappears into the woods, I wonder what the future holds. We will be on the run, pursued by the relentless radical forces of the Bigger Picture. They will wish us nothing but harm. The strange adventure that is tomorrow explodes before me in the intimate darkness. My rubber-sheathed nipples brush against Myriam's and we both moan with a cosmic desire. Then I know the future is nothing, just as the past is irrelevant. All that matters is the glorious immediacy of sexual desire and physical arousal, the sweet and endless torment of our beloved silken servitude.

To be continued.

nexus

The leading publisher of fetish and adult fiction

TELL US WHAT YOU THINK!

Readers' ideas and opinions matter to us. Take a few minutes to fill in the questionnaire below and you'll be entered into a prize draw to win a year's worth of Nexus books (36 titles)

Terms and conditions apply – see end of questionnaire.

1. Sex: Are you male ☐ female ☐ a couple ☐?

2. Age: Under 21 ☐ 21–30 ☐ 31–40 ☐ 41–50 ☐ 51–60 ☐ over 60 ☐

3. Where do you buy your Nexus books from?
☐ A chain book shop. If so, which one(s)?

_____

☐ An independent book shop. If so, which one(s)?

_____

☐ A used book shop/charity shop
☐ Online book store. If so, which one(s)?

_____

4. How did you find out about Nexus Books?
☐ Browsing in a book shop
☐ A review in a magazine
☐ Online
☐ Recommendation
☐ Other _____

5. In terms of settings which do you prefer? (Tick as many as you like)
☐ Down to earth and as realistic as possible
☐ Historical settings. If so, which period do you prefer?

_____

☐ Fantasy settings – barbarian worlds

- ☐ Completely escapist/surreal fantasy
- ☐ Institutional or secret academy
- ☐ Futuristic/sci fi
- ☐ Escapist but still believable
- ☐ Any settings you dislike?

_____

- ☐ Where would you like to see an adult novel set?

_____

6. In terms of storylines, would you prefer:

- ☐ Simple stories that concentrate on adult interests?
- ☐ More plot and character-driven stories with less explicit adult activity?
- ☐ We value your ideas, so give us your opinion of this book:

_____

_____

_____

7. In terms of your adult interests, what do you like to read about? (Tick as many as you like)

- ☐ Traditional corporal punishment (CP)
- ☐ Modern corporal punishment
- ☐ Spanking
- ☐ Restraint/bondage
- ☐ Rope bondage
- ☐ Latex/rubber
- ☐ Leather
- ☐ Female domination and male submission
- ☐ Female domination and female submission
- ☐ Male domination and female submission
- ☐ Willing captivity
- ☐ Uniforms
- ☐ Lingerie/underwear/hosiery/footwear (boots and high heels)
- ☐ Sex rituals
- ☐ Vanilla sex
- ☐ Swinging

☐ Cross-dressing/TV
☐ Enforced feminisation
☐ Others – tell us what you don't see enough of in adult fiction:

_____

_____

_____

8. Would you prefer books with a more specialised approach to your interests, i.e. a novel specifically about uniforms? If so, which subject(s) would you like to read a Nexus novel about?

_____

_____

_____

9. Would you like to read true stories in Nexus books? For instance, the true story of a submissive woman, or a male slave? Tell us which true revelations you would most like to read about:

_____

_____

_____

10. What do you like best about Nexus books?

_____

_____

11. What do you like least about Nexus books?

_____

_____

12. Which are your favourite titles?

_____

_____

13. Who are your favourite authors?

_____

_____

14. **Which covers do you prefer? Those featuring:**
    (tick as many as you like)

☐ Fetish outfits
☐ More nudity
☐ Two models
☐ Unusual models or settings
☐ Classic erotic photography
☐ More contemporary images and poses
☐ A blank/non-erotic cover
☐ What would your ideal cover look like?

_____

15. **Describe your ideal Nexus novel in the space provided:**

_____

_____

_____

_____

16. **Which celebrity would feature in one of your Nexus-style fantasies?**
    We'll post the best suggestions on our website – anonymously!

_____

THANKS FOR YOUR TIME

Now simply write the title of this book in the space below and cut out the
questionnaire pages. Post to: Nexus, Marketing Dept., Thames Wharf Studios,
Rainville Rd, London W6 9HA

Book title: _____

NEXUS NEW BOOKS

To be published in December 2005

THE OLD PERVERSITY SHOP
Aishling Morgan

In a foggy Victorian London, gambler Edward Trent is intent on making his grand-daughter Nell wealthy from his winnings but instead manages to lose all his worldly goods and the right to her virginity to the money leader Daniel Quilty. Charles Truscott rescues Nell from her fate but cannot resist taking advantage of both her innocence and her voluptuous body, as does just about everybody she meets as she flees London for Plymouth with Quilty in pursuit. But none of it comes close to what he intends to do when he catches her.

£6.99   ISBN 0-352-34007-X

NIGHTS IN WHITE COTTON
Penny Birch

Normally, if a beautiful young woman comes to Penny Birch and asks to be taught the joys of a well smacked bottom, she would be only too happy to oblige. This time it's a little difficult, as the status and connections of the beautiful young woman would make the tryst a scandal. But Pippa is not easily put off. To make matters worse, both Penny's girlfriends and sadistic diesel-dyke AJ, all want Pippa and aim to give her far more than a playful spanking.

£6.99   ISBN 0-352-34008-8

ANGEL
Lindsay Gordon

Newly selected by a corporation to work as a companion to high zone women, Angel must do whatever his clients demand of him. So when an executive demands to be handled by a stranger in uniform, and a Japanese business-woman wants to perfect her correctional skills, Angel is there. When a celebrity adores rope and wet underwear, it is Angel's duty to honour and serve her. But extreme games with dangerous lovers can lead to unpredictable ends, as Angel discovers when introduced to a powerful and insatiable female surgeon.

The wildly imaginative fourth novel by Lindsay Gordon, is back in print.

£6.99   ISBN 0-352-34009-6

If you would like more information about Nexus titles, please visit our website at www.nexus-books.co.uk, or send a stamped addressed envelope to:
Nexus, Thames Wharf Studios,
Rainville Road, London W6 9HA

NEXUS BACKLIST

This information is correct at time of printing. For up-to-date information, please visit our website at www.nexus-books.co.uk

All books are priced at £6.99 unless another price is given.

ABANDONED ALICE	Adriana Arden 0 352 33969 1	☐
ALICE IN CHAINS	Adriana Arden 0 352 33908 X	☐
AMAZON SLAVE	Lisette Ashton 0 352 33916 0	☐
THE ANIMAL HOUSE	Cat Scarlett 0 352 33877 6	☐
THE ART OF CORRECTION	Tara Black 0 352 33895 4	☐
AT THE END OF HER TETHER	G.C. Scott 0 352 33857 1	☐
BARE BEHIND	Penny Birch 0 352 33721 4	☐
BELINDA BARES UP	Yolanda Celbridge 0 352 33926 8	☐
BENCH MARKS	Tara Black 0 352 33797 4	☐
THE BLACK GARTER	Lisette Ashton 0 352 33919 5	☐
THE BLACK MASQUE	Lisette Ashton 0 352 33977 2	☐
THE BLACK ROOM	Lisette Ashton 0 352 33914 4	☐
THE BLACK WIDOW	Lisette Ashton 0 352 33973 X	☐
THE BOOK OF PUNISHMENT	Cat Scarlett 0 352 33975 6	☐
THE BOND	Lindsay Gordon 0 352 33996 9	☐

- - - - - - ✄ -

Please send me the books I have ticked above.

Name   ....

Address   ....

           ....

           ....

           .... Post code ....

Send to: **Virgin Books Cash Sales, Thames Wharf Studios, Rainville Road, London W6 9HA**

US customers: for prices and details of how to order books for delivery by mail, call 1-800-343-4499.

Please enclose a cheque or postal order, made payable to **Nexus Books Ltd**, to the value of the books you have ordered plus postage and packing costs as follows:

UK and BFPO – £1.00 for the first book, 50p for each subsequent book.

Overseas (including Republic of Ireland) – £2.00 for the first book, £1.00 for each subsequent book.

If you would prefer to pay by VISA, ACCESS/MASTERCARD, AMEX, DINERS CLUB or SWITCH, please write your card number and expiry date here:

....

Please allow up to 28 days for delivery.

Signature ....

Our privacy policy

We will not disclose information you supply us to any other parties. We will not disclose any information which identifies you personally to any person without your express consent.

From time to time we may send out information about Nexus books and special offers. Please tick here if you do *not* wish to receive Nexus information.   ☐

- - - - - - ✄ -